MASQUERADE

Stealing Napoleon's Treasures

MASQUERADE
Stealing Napoleon's Treasures

SHIRLEY BURTON

HIGH STREET PRESS

HIGH STREET PRESS
Niagara-on-the-Lake, Ontario, Canada
Calgary, Alberta, Canada
www.highstreetpress.com
First printing 2024

Printed in the United States of America, Canada, UK, Australia, and global distribution in Europe, Asia, and South America.
Available in paperback, hardcover, and eBook formats.
Cover photo licensed Shutterstock.com.
Design and edit: Bruce Burton

Library and Archives Canada Cataloguing in Publication.

Burton, Shirley, 1950-, author
        Masquerade: Stealing Napoleon's Treasures / Shirley Burton

ISBN 978-1-927839-36-2 (pbk.) —ISBN 978-1-927839-37-9 (bound)
ISBN 978-1-927839-38.6 (ebook)

Gala Costumes - Main Cast

Napoleon Bonaparte	Antoine Coulliere
Duke of Wellington	Jacques Guilliard
King Louis XVI	Hollande Bertolier
Count of Monte Cristo	Kace Chastain
Duchess de Parma	Maxine Campbell
Count von Nepperg	Alec Campbell
Musketeer Inigo Montoya	Dylan Moreland
Maiden of the King's Court	Solange Petite
Member of the Press	Gabriel Dupont
Bodyguard	Andre Poulin

ONE

Louvre Museum, Apollo Hall, Paris, 2017

Sirens blared. The gendarme officers charged along the Seine toward the Louvre. A breach in the construction scaffolds over the atrium left glass shards littered across the courtyard and a gaping hole near the pinnacle of the apex.

At Apollo Hall, the security alarms pierced the air over the Napoleon exhibit of painted masterpieces, gems, and magnificent swords, many encrusted with silver and rare diamonds. Uniformed personnel and guards ran into the chaos.

Several abandoned, overturned hoist baskets dangled from the scaffolds as the culprits scaled the walls, emboldened by the thrill of the getaway in broad daylight. Bystanders were shocked as the masked thieves fled in matching Peugeots.

Two getaway vehicles screamed along the Quai François Mitterrand beside the river racing toward the Pont Royal Bridge, with the law in hot pursuit.

A shabbily dressed woman in a tattered coat and jogging shoes waited with her cart in an alley, shielded by an empty dumpster beside a cargo van. Nervously, she looked at her watch and peered out at the traffic waiting for something.

The Peugeots barely came to a stop, and the exchange took

mere seconds before they veered back into the lane. The front driver glanced at the rear-view mirror at the bridge as sirens and flashing lights closed in.

In his hesitation, the collision happened. In an instant, the screeching brakes and the horrific crunching of mangled metal drew crowds of bystanders.

Hearing the crash, Rookie Officer Dylan Moreland, on duty nearby, hurried toward the melee. He noticed the vagrant woman on the same block looking guiltily into traffic. She waited for a cargo van, dropped something in the back, then sprinted in the opposite direction. Panic-stricken, she stopped twice to look back.

Rescue personnel and a troop of police gendarmes quickly converged on the accident vehicle. Leaning into the driver's seat, Moreland saw the bloodied face of a severely injured man—a moment he would never forget.

The other door was open, and although the passenger suffered injuries, he was alert. Moreland reached for an abandoned wallet with a driver's license lying on the floor beside the driver's seat.

The driver was agitated and struggled to say something. Moreland tried to calm him, and as a medic fitted him with an oxygen mask, the man's eyes rolled. The victim surrendered to unconsciousness.

Moreland stepped back to allow medical staff to work on the driver and radioed details to his police station.

"The driver's license says Coulliere."

Seven Years Later, April 2024, Paris

Andre Poulin, a veteran undercover unit leader out of Interpol, was lunching with an informant and, by chance, overheard the conversation of two men at a nearby table.

Andre's ears tuned to the discussion.

"The Louvre theft was genius," boasted a cocky, older refined man. "With the cooperation of a few inside pawns, we're free and clear."

The shorter obtuse man's voice rose from a whisper to become audible for nearby patrons. His hands were clasped, then rubbed together to gloat. "I know where it is and can get it whenever I like. The beauty is in the goldsmiths' vintage and quality, and its likeness to Jerome Bonaparte's coronation sword."

Andre perked up at the word 'goldsmith'. Discreetly, he made close evaluations—their appearances, voice inflections, and noted the steely nerves of the intimidating silver-gray man as he locked onto his companion's gaze. The conversation continued with the two men confessing to one another of their devious successes.

The second man had his back to Andre. "And consider the demand for Napoleonic artifacts worldwide. The regime boasts of the latest high-tech security, but I'm not a conventional thinker."

The old man's voice raised to a fever of irritation. "I can be an architect, plumber, or mason as I decide and in broad daylight when least expected. Don't underestimate me."

"The gold you produced is remarkable," the other man confirmed, "and the craftsmanship of the silversmith is astounding. I'm curious where you found this conspirator. From my museum work, I have rarely seen such a specimen as the Napoleon sword, that you claim to have been owned by Marshal Ney on Elba."

The aging gentleman enjoyed the praise until the nervous, round-headed one boasted and boldly queried him. "And the crusted scabbard diamonds—are you certain they are authentic?"

He looked over his shoulder and then leered at his

companion. "Don't dare challenge my skills, my network of expertise, or question my resources. Be grateful you are allowed this opportunity."

"Of course not! I'd never—"

"Have you forgotten my work passed the scrutiny of the best insurance investigators? The introduction of an authentic piece makes the gold and silver untraceable. Ney's diary and Ségur's accounts substantiate the trail of ownership. All you have to do, Antoine, is play the part of the curator. Your brother said I could count on you."

The stodgy man flinched at the mention of his brother.

Andre was stunned by the revelation. The details matched an old dossier that crossed his desk months before, piquing his curiosity more.

Releasing his glance at the connivers, Andre made excuses to his informant to conclude his meeting. The snitch confidante across from him, accustomed to such distractions, eased out of his chair and was gone. Andre paid the bill and followed him to the door, then returned having left his eyeglasses on the table as an excuse.

When the two cagey men that now held his full interest left, Andre sidled close enough to read their credit card receipt— Antoine Coulliere.

"Why tip so extravagantly?" Andre mused. "It only makes the waiter remember. But I know the Coulliere name!"

Rushing back to his office at Interpol, he picked up an open letter from an insurance company about suspicious movement at the military museum and a connection to the Louvre robbery seven years before. He pulled the file.

Despite many unanswered questions, the insurance company paid a substantial claim to the museum for the stolen Napoleon gold and silver, among other artifacts and military relics. Names in the investigation included Antoine Coulliere.

"Must be an old picture." Andre phoned Dylan Moreland at once with his national security concern, that a criminal web was threatening France's historic preservation.

"Dylan, we cannot rewrite history. I sent you a dossier minutes ago that gives me great concern; perhaps you have been able to peruse it. I'm copying the communication for you of the persons of interest."

"I'm reading it now."

"There's more about Coulliere! Coincidentally, he sent a plea letter to Interpol implying his family is in peril. The file was referred to this office and I have it here. I'm not clear on his motives. An investigator at the museum will expect to hear from you."

"Andre, I'll request the details of an accident report on the night of the Louvre robbery. I was a rookie then in the gendarmerie police and remember it well. I'm certain that one or more of the occupants in the vehicle were named Coulliere. After the accident, I visited a victim that left me with a cryptic message."

Poulin was surprised by Moreland's revelation. "Will you be recognized?"

"It's been seven years so I don't expect a problem. However, I have an idea. Two undercover decoys with police training and research expertise will visit me in the summer. Quite reliable, you'll see."

"You're sure we can count on them?"

"Yes, we're family. I can trust them for certain. I'll arrange their specs from New York so Interpol can vet them."

Les Invalides, Paris

Dylan was a stealthy, handsome, mysterious man, who could

become invisible in his Interpol undercover appearance and behavior. He disappeared into the subway toward Les Invalides near Rodin and the Military Museum. A woolen beret covered his curly dark hair, as he pulled his collar up under his chin to avoid identification.

He lived a quiet avenger's life, preferring to remain in the tourist nest of Paris. Having served nine years in the gendarmerie, he was recruited by an Interpol espionage unit dedicated to cold cases. He had an uncanny talent to infiltrate covert activity, and then slip into the underworld to expose criminals.

Distracted, he left his third-floor Montparnasse apartment in a hurry to walk to his office along the Seine. He didn't notice the bicycles, the water taxis, buses, and fast-moving cars that accounted for the morning rush hour. With his mind on the memories of the Napoleon heist, he realized he had overshot his morning coffee stop.

He pondered the case aloud. "A needle in a haystack! A little more background would be useful."

Turning into a café on his route, he ordered a hasty breakfast and tapped into the raft of internet history of Napoleon's era.

During a government transition at the palace decades ago, documents written in Napoleon Bonaparte's hand were found. A list of loyalist names plotting a royal revolt was sealed in a vault. An astute historian recognized surnames that had continued in service to France, and the revelation of the list would be disparaging. Only a few bound by an oath of secrecy knew the Napoleon vault's location under the stone floor.

The inherited cold case archives regarding the Louvre heist included a diary belonging to Marshal Ney, detailing his allegiance and battles at the right hand of the great emperor.

It described a revolutionary plot by a subversive sect loyal to the emperor, corroborated by General Philippe-Paul, Comte de Ségur. A code of coordinates was scribbled on parchment, suggesting the treasure would stabilize alliances and the war coffers.

Perusing the file, Dylan discovered the disfavor that befell the emperor and his subsequent exile before a triumphant return to Paris in 1815.

Sliding the microdisk into his computer, he examined the list of evidence:

Exhibit A: Excerpt from Marshal Michel Ney written during Napoleon's exile to Elba.

Exhibit B: A copied investigator's report depicting a museum robbery at the Louvre seven years before and a list of stolen items.

Exhibit C: Newspaper article detailing an automobile accident on the same date as the Louvre theft with grainy photos. The Coulliere name was among the victims.

"I've seen this. I have no doubts about this exhibit."

Exhibit D: Surveillance snapshots of a dozen men in various forms of disguise and shadows.

Exhibit E: Graphic detail of artifacts from the Napoleon era; cataloged, with locations. Several had reappeared in South America.

Exhibit F: An architect's blueprint specifying every nook of the palace, the gardens, and outbuildings.

Exhibit G: An original excerpt from the diary, almost indecipherable in fading ink, but signed by Comte de Ségur, purportedly authenticated.

Exhibit H: A photo of a residence in Le Marais.

Exhibit I: Blueprint of the emperor's palace at Tuileries, including hidden passages.

He picked up a text from Andre. "Antoine Collieure called here at Interpol. He wants to meet. Says it's urgent."

TWO

The Set-up, April 2024

Dylan Moreland turned onto rue de Grenelle in the 7th arrondissement. He stopped in the shade of the Dome des Invalides museum, an imposing horseshoe-shaped edifice filled with royal paraphernalia and the tomb of Napoleon under the golden cupola of Englise du Dome.

Slipping into a side alley, he headed toward the rear prohibited entrance. From Andre's briefing, he knew the security camera locations. He routed himself in the shadows, then tapped twice on the steel door.

The manager, a short, monotonous, middle-aged man, peered through the tight opening and asked for a code.

"Monsieur Bonaparte?"

"Oui, Monsieur Coulliere, Andre Poulin asked that I meet with you."

The small agitated man deactivated the alarm, and with clicks and slides of locks, the heavy door opened just enough to let Dylan in.

"Quickly, before you are seen."

Antoine Coulliere led him through a warehouse maze of stacked wooden crates and pallets, arriving at an office with security monitors and logbooks.

Coulliere was nervous and looked over his shoulder repeatedly, stopping to listen for the slightest sound, before he spoke.

"I only have fifteen minutes before my security supervisor, Norman, returns from his break. Go to the first monitor and turn up the volume; you will see a gentleman approaching me. He was unaware that I was wearing a microphone."

Dylan listened with headphones and watched the video as an unidentified man handed Coulliere an envelope before departing.

Dylan popped in a disk to download the scenario. "What date is this recording?"

"About a month ago. It's timestamped in the record."

Without explaining, Coulliere handed Dylan the package from the video. He tucked it into his breast pocket with the letter and invitation.

Coulliere pressed, "Do you guarantee me protection? The consequences have historical significance for France. And for the safety of my family."

Moreland feigned his lack of understanding. "Andre Poulin informed me of the threat to your family, and I understand that a Napoleonic artifact is at risk. The sword, that is. I presume it is here now on exhibit in the museum?"

"The sword has great value and *is* my family's heritage. It must remain in my possession. Emperor Napoleon bestowed his battle saber upon his commander, Marshal Ney, in return for securing the Russian gold when the Grande Armée fled into Italy and France."

"That's an impressive heritage, sir."

"It is indeed," Coulliere said, standing taller, reflecting his pride. "Napoleon had a sword fetish, and the family hired goldsmiths and silver craftsmen to commission battle scabbards from the Revolution until his final exile."

"Please elaborate," said Dylan as he continued to study the man. A flashback to the accident after the Louvre heist drew his attention to Coulliere's facial features, searching for scars or evidence of tragedy. Confident that Antoine had no recognition of him that night, he continued.

"Are you suggesting a connection between the Coulliere family and Marshal Ney?"

Coulliere nodded. "I have a vested interest in protecting my heritage. Pardon me but you must go now, monsieur. I hear the door at the end of the hall."

But Coulliere's attention was not in that direction. Dylan followed his eyes toward a closet door and a quiet shuffle of feet.

Dylan shrugged and left the room without acknowledgment, but Coulliere did not see him depart. In his exit, Moreland pocketed a security-coded badge lifted from Norman's desk.

Easing into the corridor, he tucked into an access space between pallets with a vantage of Coulliere's office door and waited.

"Someone else was in there. Coulliere isn't laying all the cards on the table, that's for sure."

Seconds later a tall, lanky man left. Standing outside the office door, he glanced both ways, pulled his windbreaker collar up, tightened his herringbone hat, and skulked toward the building's rear door. As he passed Dylan's waiting place, he stopped.

Moreland froze in silence to wait it out. Moments later, the man slowly moved away, his shoes barely clicking on the cement floor. Finally, he slipped out the back door.

Dylan tuned in to the listening device he planted and

ventured into the back passages with high artifact shelving. Squeezing past hand trucks, a pallet hoist, and an automated forklift truck, he entered a narrow, congested alley. Tapping on weakened joints between hollow wall sections, he noticed a slit of light coming from the other side. As he pressed gently on a panel, it swung open into the museum.

Minutes later, he stood before the gilded tomb of Emperor Napoleon Bonaparte. Intimidating, white-gloved guards stood on either side.

During the distraction of a school tour, Moreland slipped into the great hall behind the case of the touted Coulliere crested sword.

A brass plate etched the last date that the blade was used in a duel when Napoleon was in Elba.

Dylan scrutinized the relic for signs of wear and aging. In the privacy of the room, he opened the security manager's envelope from his pocket and unfolded a typewritten letter to Coulliere. He was convinced from the video that the contact was simply a hired delivery service.

Dylan read the threatening letter in a silent whisper.

"Monsieur Coulliere,

To protect your family, you must attend the public Masquerade Gala at the Royal Lodge in Paris on the 15th of August. A script will be provided, and you will play the part of Napoleon Bonaparte. That night, you will relinquish the crested sword that once belonged to Marshal Ney. I know how it came to be in your possession. This will right the debt.

Do not involve authorities, or the outcome will advance and bring grief. You and your family are being watched.

Failure to follow instructions will bear consequences.

"Protecting his family! Relinquishing a sword! Why deliver the communication to the museum? If the perpetrator is proficient in blackmail, surely, he could intercept Coulliere at any place or time in his daily routine. I'll need details about his family's schedules and obligations." Dylan made mental note.

When Dylan returned to his Montparnasse flat, the moonlight was shrouded by clouds, although the streets were still boisterous from the after-theater crowd.

The bachelor walk-up was simple yet provided a comfortable sleeping area, kitchenette, and a small library wedged into a corner. No pictures or personal items were on display. It was the way he lived his life.

"It's too late for a drink; I'll just prowl the internet and give my cousin a heads-up. Alec and Maxine should be arriving fairly soon."

Researching Coulliere's ancestry, he pulled an online image of their upper-class residence in Le Marais in the 4th arrondissement. Zooming in, he examined the private, historical home with its landscaped yards surrounded by a wrought iron security gate.

"It's accessible from the streets, near the river and Pont de Bir-Hakeim bridge, and within walking distance to the military museum. The two daughters attend private school, and his wife works in the souvenir shop at the Eiffel Tower. Every route will surely have security camera coverage."

In the morning, Dylan threw open the balcony doors to a heavy sky with the threat of drizzle. Focused on his mission, he dialed a direct line to Andre Poulin.

Hurrying to meet with him, he skirted the main route to his destination, a café near the Moulin Rouge. Rounding the corner onto Boulevard de Clichy, he spotted his colleague, a nondescript man at a bistro table on the patio.

Andre was lean, medium-height, nearing his fifties, yet his eyes betrayed a painful past. Since his wife died, he'd become accustomed to a solitary life dedicated to his career.

A leather portfolio lay on the table with a folded Le Monde newspaper on the top. Sipping a cappuccino, Andre barely looked up but shoved the portfolio across the table.

"Take a seat, Dylan."

"Now that I have reviewed the dossier, I must remind you I am the gendarme rookie officer that assisted at the collision scene of the escape vehicle driven by one of the Coulliere brothers."

"It's a long read, Dylan, but it explains why Coulliere was threatened. This article was published two years ago in Bordeaux in the Historical Digest, in writings about the Napoleonic Era. It discloses that the secret diaries were found at Napoleon's exile residence on the Italian island of Elba, Tyrrhenian Sea, and remained in a private collection for many years."

Excerpt from Historical Digest, Bordeaux, Napoleonic Era.

Michel Ney, Marshal of the Empire, served as a loyal aide-de-compte to military leader Bonaparte, introduced by Napoleon's first wife, Josephine, in 1802.

Renowned in battle, Ney was extolled as the bravest of the brave, and his battlefield exploits earned him the title Duke of Elchingen. He then led the Third Corps against Russia in 1812.

Napoleon was exiled to Elba in 1814 after defeat by the Austrian-Prussian-Russian coalition. His fragmented army remained loyal, and Ney smuggled a cache of treasure to Elba and ensured that part of it made its way back to Paris.

Soon after, Napoleon became disgruntled to hear that his second wife, Marie Louise, Duchess of Parma, had taken up with an Austrian nobleman while he was in exile.

At Elba, two royal ships ported in the bay of the Gulf of Portoferraio on the north side of Elba to verify that the defamed Napoleon was secured. The Irish Anglo Captain

Thomas Ussher, commander of the masted ship, led his party up the long, cobbled incline to the perch overlooking the azure sea.

He was startled to see the luxury at the Villa of San Mulini, the lush gardens, and the astounding sea view. Napoleon was hardly considered imprisoned as he delighted in parties and mademoiselles of his choosing.

Philippe-Paul, Comte de Ségur, watched from the hilltop, distinctive in his two-cornered, eagle-crested bicorne, the red and green gabardine, and black garters.

Napoleon Bonaparte stood erect in the courtyard.

"Bonjour, Captain Ussher," Napoleon snapped and saluted disparagingly. "Unfortunately, I'm on a break from my bonds; otherwise, you would find me tied to the flagpole prepared for lashings."

"Bonjour, my esteemed comrade."

The captain's eyes wandered to the luxurious mansion with French doors, balconies, and fine dormers. Finding it not lacking for gardeners or servants, Ussher smiled with amusement.

"I see that your accommodations are in order, Monsieur Bonaparte."

Napoleon bowed and gestured toward the terrace leading into the mansion.

"Come inside, and I will ask my cook to find some rations, and we will feast on the king's stores."

"It's gratifying that you still have your sense of humor, monsieur." Ussher sputtered.

Marshal Ney moved closer, respecting the importance of his conversation with Napoleon. He removed his hand from his belted sword, grasped his gloves in his left hand, and tossed them back and forth.

"I have not come to disparage you, my dear emperor; we have brought a chest of rewards."

Marshal Ney gestured to a pair of soldiers hauling a trunk. "It is not right for the treasure to be buried in the palace when the rightful leader is here in exile."

"Be careful of your compliments, my dear sir. They can have dire repercussions."

Napoleon paced on his balcony with his right arm behind his back as he pondered the situation.

"Marshal, we have served France with honor. But my close and loyal friends are few. My time on Elba is temporary, and I fully intend to return to Paris as emperor and to save France from tyranny."

The Comte de Ségur spewed his passionate loyalty. "My dear emperor, I am sworn to serve my country with nobility. But have no fear; we will be redeemed upon your return."

The audience hushed as Napoleon spoke.

"As a reward for your faithfulness, I entrust my father's sword to you, Marshal Ney. It is pure silver and of great sentiment worth an inheritance. It is now your loyal reward."

Napoleon turned to the Comte de Ségur and retrieved a gleaming, ornate sword from his cabinet. He reached it out to the aide, who had stepped forward.

"To you, my loyal friend, I give the Bennais saber of Bonaparte pride."

Seeing Ussher standing to the side, Napoleon gestured to step forward. "Captain Ussher, for your kindness and humility, accept this diamond-encrusted snuff box containing a miniature statue of my likeness. I will ask a favor of you."

The Comte de Ségur's sword then made its way to the French commune of Ajaccio in Corsica, hidden under the Bonaparte home's floorboards.

Dylan placed the papers on the table. "I presume one of the swords is the artifact for ransom."

Kace Chastain, Banks of the Seine

Kace Chastain hovered over his desk, littered with cold takeout coffee cups. His hair was shoulder-length, tied at the back. Over his bulky frame, he wore a loose, semi-tucked shirt and a silver, etched belt buckle. The room was shabby and under-furnished, but premium in its view overlooking the Seine River.

"Every detail has been planned, and contingencies accounted for," he muttered. "The Gala's costumes have been pulled from the costume boutique. Bertolier sent the VIP invitations, and they can be reissued."

He stomped to the window in anger.

"Coulliere was sufficiently warned to be silent and cooperate. I haven't been unreasonable. I deserve my reward for the risks I took with the old man at the Louvre. I am one of only two witnesses who knows the truth about Remy, so I shouldn't worry about keeping him under my thumb."

Once more, Kace calculated his plans for the August 15th Gala at Royal Lodge, not leaving anything to chance. He retraced the steps from his apartment, taking an exact count of every minute to l'avenue de la Bourdonnais. Using a false name and stolen credit card, he had pre-booked a seat on a tour group leaving Paris by a forty-five-minute luxury motorcoach traveling south to the palace on the night of the Gala.

A knock at the door annoyed him. "Go away, Monsieur Severini; I'm busy. I'll bring the rent before supper."

The landlord hollered back, "You said that yesterday, Monsieur Chastain. The building owner wants his money."

The tenant charged toward the door and jerked it ajar. "I said I was busy." Then, in a fury and without thinking, he yelled, "Here, take this belt until I pay you—it's solid silver and worth much more than your measly rent."

Perplexed by the offer, the landlord gingerly accepted the item thrust into his hands. The door slammed behind him.

The landlord's final words wafted through the door. "Pay me tonight, or I'll take this to the pawnbroker!"

Poring over his charts again, it struck Chastain that he'd accidentally parted with a clue that could reveal his identity, a relic that could be traced to the Napoleon treasure. Pulling at his hair in frustration, he plotted to retrieve the buckle.

"How could I make such a terrible mistake?"

Rage overtook his common sense, and in the following moments, Kace Chastain plotted a scheme to retrieve the belt buckle and eliminate any record of the exchange.

Two days later, the gendarmerie responded to a body floating in the Seine. The victim had been disfigured, and identification seemed unlikely.

The police department recorded the official report as a robbery and deadly assault, and the victim was buried unclaimed without a name in the pauper's cemetery.

Three weeks later, a concerned tenant in Chastain's building made a missing person's report of Monsieur Severini, the landlord.

Andre was across town in his office reviewing Interpol reports when he stopped and backed up several screens to re-examine the specifics.

"When a perpetrator goes to this much trouble defacing the victim, there is usually a reason. Someone didn't want this man identified or a search into the motive," he mused.

THREE

Alec and Maxine Arrive in Paris. July 2024

The color and scent of Paris presented the magnificence of springtime. Pink pastel cherry blossoms cascaded over the promenades by the canal, energizing the birth of the new season and invigorating the old world with its fragrance.

Montmartre's quaint, cobbled streets atop the hill were vibrant with energy. The romance of music wafted in the air, and artists' easels boasted the season's masterful wares.

Playfully dressed mimes, ventriloquists, and marionette players kept the tourists spellbound at the Place du Tertre under the cathedral's shadow. Buskers serenaded diners with violins and accordions while below the hill, life bustled, illuminated by the neon glow of Moulin Rouge.

A tourist couple walked from their Montmartre apartment rental in the 18th Arrondissement part of the Right Bank, toward the famed Basilique du Sacré-Coeur. Their eyes danced over the rooftops toward the distant Eiffel Tower and Notre Dame.

Strolling arm in arm toward the Trattoria, they planned to celebrate the beginning of their long-awaited vacation in Paris.

She stopped him under the cathedral's shadow and gasped at the view.

"I love these times together, Alec," Maxine pined. "It was good of Mother to look after the children for us. A romantic getaway has taken too long."

She pointed at a café and tugged his elbow. Six-foot-two and muscular, Alec leaned close, and she looked teasingly at the stout man beside her.

"It's only French to have our afternoon coffee," he said, "and there's time now. Tonight, we'll dine with my cousin Dylan. He'll have tales as a French detective, first with the gendarmerie and now with Interpol. The head office is in Lyon but they have a regional detachment here."

Halting, he swept a mahogany wisp from her brow and brushed her lips with his.

"I'm looking forward to meeting him," Maxine said. "The life of a detective in European espionage is a far stretch from the mundane of motherhood in New York. We could imagine that we're involved in a Parisian caper."

She laughed at herself, then slowed and pointed at the café. "Mmm…I can smell roasted coffee. Can we stop here?"

"But Max, I thought you'd want to hit some stores today," he teased.

"I have the rest of my life to shop, but espionage and intrigue in Paris is a once-in-a-lifetime opportunity."

"Dylan said every month in Paris has mysteries, but he teased in his text to be prepared for surprises on our vacation. He hinted he might need to use us as a decoy."

"Then let's make the best of this."

Maxine Campbell married in her early twenties. In university, she majored in European history research, a passion that grew into a hobby, before becoming a stay-at-home mom to two youngsters.

Max was a college beauty with golden auburn curls and blue

eyes. Alec was always attracted to her sense of humor and zest for getting into solving his cases. She was relentless when she smelled a puzzle or caper.

Having joined a knitting guild, book clubs, and local live theater, she occasionally filled in as a singer at an off-Broadway dinner club in New York. Her nature was inquisitive, to the point of embarrassment.

Alec Campbell graduated from the police academy a year after their marriage. His ambition was to become an undercover detective, bringing justice to forgotten cases and peace to families waiting for answers. With attrition in his NYPD precinct, an opportunity for advancement had opened up for him, that he would begin when they returned.

"I won't be James Bond, but I can at least pretend." He teased Maxine. "After all, Europe is a place we can live in our dreams."

Married ten years, it seemed this was their first chance to travel. Alec was strikingly handsome and trustworthy with twinkling brown eyes that Maxine was fascinated by. His mother suggested they visit some of the Moreland relatives in Paris, and the couple jumped at the chance.

With a deep breath, Maxine sighed at the whimsical tones of Montmartre. She closed her eyes as if to dream, with the background of a busker's whistle, birds chirping, and a dog's bark.

A strolling musician broke her trance.

"Listen to his words, Alec. 'I Love Paris in the Springtime.' It couldn't be more appropriate."

Outside the café, a waiter on the terrace caught their eye and waved them to the empty bistro table under a red canopy. Maxine sagged into the stylish rattan chair. An envelope was near the linen napkin at her place setting, and she assumed the server hadn't cleared it yet.

Her lips barely touched her café au lait, and she sighed at

the flavor, but the relief was not long-lived. She raised her hand urgently to Alec. Her posture stiffened, and she jumped to her feet.

She whispered, "A man is watching us. He just took our picture."

The man was talking into his cell phone, and when he saw Alec turn and stare, he backed into the street.

"He's just a people watcher. Don't pay him any heed."

"I suppose you're right. I'm used to keeping my eye out for the children. You know what I mean? Do you have a photo of your cousin?"

Alec touched her hand. "Relax, sweetheart; it's a vacation."

Maxine fingered the envelope as her curiosity yielded and finally picked it up. It was formal and embossed. Her eyes widened. The front said 'Campbell', and she pulled out the folded parchment.

"It's an invitation to a Masquerade Gala … a VIP night with dancing and orchestra."

"Where?"

"At the Paris Royal Lodge. It looks like a fancy palace."

"Must be for someone else."

"It has our name. But how would anyone know?" She stretched to look around for anyone suspicious.

"Cool," he said. "But a masquerade party?"

"It says a reenactment of a historic ball and stage event from the times of Louis, King of France. That's about two hundred years ago. I've heard those go on all night with dancing and music."

Alec examined the envelope and invitation. "The tickets are for August 15th." He looked at her eyes, still sparkling. A card fell to the table.

"The man watching us is gone," Alec said.

He dug into his wallet for Dylan's photo. It was faded and his face was among a group of relatives. "It's hard to make out details, but he could have been the man that took our picture."

Maxine gulped the Beaujolais. "This is awesome, Alec—a luxurious palace gala. Dylan is delightful. If this is his introduction, I can't wait to meet him."

Alec looked across at the vacated table beside them. The waiter had cleared the wine glass and ashtray.

"Excuse me, was something else left on that table?"

"Non, monsieur."

"I thought I saw a domino tile. I'm sure of it."

"I'm sorry, sir. Whatever was on the table has gone to the busser's tray or the dishwasher. We're busy, but I'll ask in the kitchen if anyone has seen such a thing."

The server waited with an open palm and an expression that could be guilt or expectation.

Alec removed his billfold and drew a convincing handful of euros to motivate the man to look.

"Max, I think we're being set up," Alec whispered, then laughed to see her transported into an imagined world of intrigue.

"How much do you know about Dylan and his family? Is he an undercover detective? Maybe he's deep in a case and we've come at a bad time."

"We'll know soon enough. He's meeting us near the Louvre tonight. When I was growing up, we had family trips to Europe, and I got to know him well, but it's been some time since the last visit. Max, he's lived in France his whole life."

Alec looked at his wife, eager for a dalliance with danger.

"I can't wait to meet Dylan. Hopefully, he can clue us in about the invitation." She pulled out her phone to search for events in Paris.

"Awesome, Alec. Event planners hold these VIP parties in old royal castles and country lodges. Ohhh . . . we'll need disguises and costumes!"

Her eyes darted back and forth. "Don't laugh Alec, this one

is authentic. A Count of Monte Cristo will be wearing a costume . . . wouldn't you like to arrive as the Count? Imagine walking into a ballroom of mystery!"

"And mayhem! Smiling, he rose and stood beside Maxine with his hand extended.

"It's time for my lady to retire to her quarters and dress for dinner. We'll be at our condo in twenty minutes, and it will be dark before we meet Dylan."

Dylan's Moreland's Interpol office was in a discreet building several blocks from the Louvre and a twenty-minute walk from the Butte-Montmartre condo, his cousin had booked. His shared undercover workspace on the second floor of the ancient building. While finishing a local homicide case file, the large station clock over the door caught his eye.

"I've got to go."

Dylan looked around to see who else was lingering and spotted his partner, Oliver, preparing to leave for the night.

"Ollie, I need a lift! I'm meeting my American cousins for dinner at the Louvre. I've gone out on a limb and left them an invitation for the Masquerade case we're assigned to."

"You've got work to do if you want to pull the wool over their eyes."

As Oliver dashed out, he called, "Out front in four minutes, Dylan."

Maxine flipped the invitation over and laid it on the bureau. The back had hand-written instructions on how to order costumes from La Boutique de Mascarade near Tuileries.

"Costumes, Alec! The tales of King Louis' mistresses already intrigue me, but now I have new curiosity about the Count of Monte Cristo. I already visualize parades of counts and dukes. Can you see them, strutting in brocade waistcoats and pantaloons across the ballroom floor, with powdered wigs and baroque-style high heels? I have a hundred questions for Dylan."

"Are costume parties traditional in history?" he said.

"I read that masquerade balls became fashionable in the 1700s. Louis XV used the ruse to woo Madame Pompadour under the nose of Marie Antoinette."

"Wow. Did Marie know?"

"Ironically, both Louis and Marie-Antoinette had a mistress and a lover respectively. They carried on affairs in public at these masquerades. Deception under the public's noses became a tradition. Parisians' love of dance and theater since welcomed the annual events known throughout Europe as the festival of festivals."

He placed her evening wrap over her shoulders, and she leaned in for a kiss. "We're running late, Max, so I ordered a taxi. It would take us too long to walk to the funicular and get to the restaurant in time."

Arriving at the Brasserie on Place Andre, Alec spotted his cousin near the outer patio. Barely out of the taxi, he called loud enough that other heads turned. "Hello, Dylan."

Dylan tentatively turned to see his cousin. "Bonjour, Alec. How did you know it was me?"

Dylan's gaze followed Maxine as she squeezed her arm into Alec's elbow for an introduction.

She was taken by Dylan's dark eyes and curly hair, with the effect of a mysterious rogue. It was immediately obvious to Alec that Dylan was enamored with Maxine's beauty and eagerness.

Maxine thought, "This must indeed be the Count of Monte Cristo."

She reached out her hand. "Dylan, I'm delighted. I've heard tales of your boyhood antics with my Alec and now I get to hear your side of the stories."

Dylan's eyes twinkled with tantalizing suspicion. "I hope you've kept your vacation calendar open for some mystery. I hope you got settled in alright. But for now, come inside, a table is waiting. The food here is superb, and we won't disappoint you. We have a lot to catch up on."

The maître d led them to a window table with terrace shutters open for a gentle breeze. The music of a wandering busker's violin filtered into the restaurant.

Across the way, the Louvre's atrium was filled with light as a silhouette against the sky and stars.

"Thank you for this extraordinary evening," Maxine gushed. "It's perfect."

"Max is right," said Alec. "We've looked forward to this trip for too long as it's been hard to get away, with career pressures. We left our two little ones with their grandparents. They are planning to take the kids to Disneyland so we won't need to worry about them not having fun."

"I understand. I almost married once but as my work often places me in dangerous situations, it wouldn't be fair for my wife to wonder every day if I'm coming home or not." Dylan came to a stop knowing he had said too much.

The waiter arrived with menus and specials to recite. Dylan motioned for the wine list. "Do you mind if I select a good wine for us? I suggest either a fine French Beaujolais or a fine Bordeaux."

"I'm so glad to have finally met you, Dylan. The temptation of a mystery is just what we need to escape our mundane life in the United States. Can't wait to hear the details." Maxine twittered.

FOUR

Dylan Moreland's Recruitment

Dinner conversation moved at a light pace reminiscing childhood memories and how experiences in life changed each of them making them stronger and better.

"It seems we have both ended up policing the justice system in one form or another," Alec said. "In cold cases, you must encounter elusive suspects, keeping you awake at night and listening to messages and clues left behind by the dead."

Dylan's face tightened with a glimpse of his serious side. "Did I say something to make you believe we are hunting an elusive suspect?"

Maxine leaned in to ease the conversation. "Certainly not, Dylan. You see, Alec has an opportunity to advance in the field of detective work and we are curious. Danger won't frighten us, it intrigues us, isn't that why you are recruiting us?"

Dylan had to let out a chuckle at Maxine's forthrightness.

"I'm more than curious," said Alec. "I truly want to know." He pulled out the Gala invitation and placed it on the table. "I believe that you left this for us earlier."

"I thought you might find it an exciting experience."

"Is there more than that?" said Max.

"This masquerade event involves a serious case, and I can use your detective instincts and training. You know the saying about getting a 'fresh eyes' perspective. That's just what we need.

"I know of your special training in cold cases, Alec, and yours in investigation and research, Maxine. I confess I did my detective work on both of your profiles. Interpol and the gendarmerie have pre-vetted and cleared you both for this assignment."

"Both of us?" Alec said. "Now, while we're in Paris?"

"Yes. NYPD has been helpful; if you're willing, we've scripted a role for each of you on this case and at the Gala."

Maxine and Alec were startled but gave each other a knowing glance.

"A script . . . like a drama?"

"In a way, it could help us capture a network of elusive criminals. My boss, Andre Poulin, wants to meet you tomorrow. If you agree, you'll become players once I confide in you. There's no turning back."

Alec winked at Max. "We'll be players, Dylan. If NYPD has given consent, I'm all in. We've been Jack and Jill in New York for ten years, time for a bigger challenge."

Dylan crossed his arms over his chest, and his mischievous smirk broke into a smile knowing he had a united team.

"We have intelligence to suggest a crime will happen at the Gala. I've been working on a case that took place seven years ago. Thieves from a daring Louvre robbery have resurfaced and they plan a sophisticated bait and switch of national artifacts at the Royal Lodge on August 15th. We will be prepared by setting up decoys, perhaps a Duke and Duchess."

Dylan lowered his voice and glanced over his shoulder. "A little research on Napoleon's exile will set your background.

When he returned from Elba, his vengeful plot to rule France was put into play again."

Alec was engrossed in the deception, while Maxine's eyes danced with anticipation. Dylan looked on trying to disguise his proud amusement with their enthusiasm.

"You'll be surprised," Max said with excitement, "that I adore history. In university, I studied Napoleon's aspirations and quest for treasure. There are theories of buried fortunes and maps throughout France. Even the fictional Count of Monte Cristo, Dantès, was supposedly the King's confidante and possessed a treasure map. Am I on the right track?"

Her outburst surprised the two men, and she lowered her eyes to search her cell for further details of Napoleon.

"Max, you've been holding out on me," said Alec. "I had no idea of your fascination with Napoleon."

She grinned at their reactions. "You didn't ask. Napoleon's Grande Armee's lost treasures are legendary from his Moscow retreat in 1812. The Armee, with Marshal Ney, packed whatever gold they could in wagon loads to get the loot out of Russia as they fled for their lives. It was purported that Napoleon managed to get some of the gold to his Elba exile. It seems unfathomable, but some swear it to be true."

"Where is it now?" Alec asked.

"Some say it was buried under the stone flooring of the presidential palace before Napoleon's demise. As you know, there are many royal palaces in Paris. It is believed that at one time it was under the Tuileries."

Maxine laid her fork across her plate. "Fascinating, really fascinating. My entrée was fabulous, but I couldn't eat another bite."

"I'll take your reactions as a yes then. You two are the perfect fit. I'll talk to my boss tomorrow and arrange for your meeting. I can't show my gratitude enough."

Dylan Moreland dug into his pocket and pulled out a lone

domino tile. "My papa played dominos nightly after supper, and the tile's touch brings back good memories." He turned the smooth tile over and placed it on the table.

"The double-six was always my favorite. Protect this, Alec; it holds valuable information. If you are sightseeing tomorrow, I suggest you visit Les Invalides Museum and see the Napoleon exhibit. It has King Louis XIV's infirmary for wounded soldiers with the military collection from the French Resistance."

Alec began caressing the tile in his fingers. "If I'm not mistaken, this has more weight than a regular tile."

Dylan gestured to the waiter for the bill. "I burn the midnight oil and must get back to my office. Shall we schedule an update for some time later tomorrow?"

Maxine looked up with disbelief. "You mean that we are on the case now?"

With a wink, Dylan bowed and left through the terrace.

Maxine and Alec were silent in thought as they walked along the Seine in the moonlight. At their condo, Alec showed her the domino in the light. "Feel it. I need to inspect it."

"We can take it apart. I'll get my nail file."

At the coffee table, Alec slid the tip of the file into a slit at the side.

"Voila, it's a microchip—it carries data."

Click, pop! "It's a list of some sort. And a crude map on the other side."

Alec awoke at sunrise to review the domino disk. Dylan had dangled enough mystery about the stolen Napoleon artifacts that sleep eluded him. He quickly saved the domino encryption onto his computer to inspect the files.

"My dear friend, Dylan, what have you gotten yourself into? You have an incredible life of intrigue. Among the pictures here, I assume that is Andre Poulin, and with him, not surprisingly, a disguised Moreland! Crime has no borders, nor does it have trackers."

It was six a.m., and his phone was filled with messages, mostly from Dylan. After a quick read, he roused his wife.

"Maxine, remember you volunteered for covert work with Dylan last night. We've got work to do. We'll meet him and his supervisor at Les Deux Magots Café in Saint Germaine. You were right; we are conducting a full-scale investigation to salvage Les Invalides artifacts. It seems an inside job may be in the works."

Max jumped from her bed and pulled on a silk blouse and designer pants. Dashing to the bathroom, she fluffed her hair and closed the door.

"I don't know how women can do that," Alec said to himself. Then rifling through a stack of computer files, he drew out a ragged, thick compilation.

"Ah, yes, the night of the Louvre robbery, a terrible car accident was not far away. Two brothers, with one on the brink of death. Yes, the name is Coulliere."

He wrote it down and ran the name through the computer.

Andre was at his desk at the crack of dawn at a secured office tower in the business section of Paris.

"Your cousins should be along at any moment."

"I didn't intend to bring them in so soon. However, Alec's training will be invaluable, and we can use his experience."

Dylan's eyes raised at the alluring woman approaching in knee-high boots, long auburn locks under a cloche hat, and a rust-colored, midi wool sweater. He then shifted to her gentleman companion, with golden curls, and a folded umbrella under his arm.

Poulin waved his arms then rose to extend his arm for a welcoming gesture. "Bonjour, mes amis, Alec et Maxine. Come and join us."

Maxine spoke softly and feigned a curtsy as she approached Dylan. She extended her hand.

"Do I have the pleasure of being introduced to the Count of Monte Cristo?"

Dylan rarely smiled, but he couldn't deny Maxine her amusement. "I'm afraid, madame, you have confused me. I am Inigo Montoya, the famed Musketeer."

"Ah, a musketeer, all the more mysterious!"

Andre pushed the portfolio in front of Alec and Maxine. "I hope this isn't too abrupt but we don't have time for pre-amble. Have a look at this tale about a historical silver sword. It seems that it has something to do with the upcoming gala at the Royal Lodge. The Coulliere family is being blackmailed for the legendary Ney sword."

"Intriguing," said Alec.

"I understand Dylan gave you a micro file," Andre said.

"Inside the disk, yes."

Dylan added, "I had a conversation with Antoine Coulliere. He was instructed to attend the August 15th gala wearing Bonaparte's costume. It has already been delivered to him. We need to enlist your help." He looked pleadingly at Alec and Maxine.

"The domino disk was puzzling, but it gave us an idea of what's ahead. Do we presume that Coulliere as Napoleon will carry the authentic sword on loan to the military museum?" Alec asked.

"About the domino and the disk, Dylan," Maxine said, squinting, "you could have just waited a few more minutes instead of playing these games."

"That wouldn't be sporting, Maxine. I work best in the shadows."

"The clues are falling into place," said Andre, ignoring the counterparts' banter. "We extracted security footage in the last two months near the Coulliere residence. See if anything is out of the ordinary. Maxine, women have a good eye for detail."

Maxine returned a wry smile. "I'll take that as a compliment rather than a suggestion."

"Most definitely. Take your time. But can we all meet near my office sometime tomorrow?"

"Andre, I am a first-rate cook, just ask Alec . . . and we are staying in a condo with a full kitchen," said Maxine. "Let's say we all rendezvous there tomorrow at seven. I'll text the info to Dylan, we have a lovely apartment rented in Butte-Montmartre near the bottom of the funicular."

Before Andre could speak, she focused again on his eyes. "I have a request, however. I watch spy movies that all have gadgets. Is there a tech gizmo that would help me in our investigation?"

Andre's face broke into a smile. "As you wish, madame. Something like this?" He quickly produced a lipstick tube from his desk that resembled a small pen.

"Simply click this directly at a security camera, and it will erase your image from their system. We often use this type of technology to cover our tracks. Is that what you had in mind?"

"Ah, yes!" With a broad smile, Max planted a grateful kiss on Andre's cheek.

FIVE

Dinner at Maxine's

The Butte-Montmartre apartment was a second-floor walk-up in an old renovated house with balconies and quaint dormers. Maxine had the doors open onto the street to take in the sounds of Paris.

She prepared a succulent meal of veal shanks and osso buco to entertain Andre and Dylan. She enjoyed poring over recipes to create this fine meal. But her mind was in a complicated dilemma.

"Alec, so who accompanied Napoleon to his Elba prison? I dug through the data chip about the emperor's loyalists. One thing is certain, that he would have had an entourage accompany him from France."

The doorbell rang downstairs as Alec viewed security tapes from Coulliere's residence. "I'll get it, Max. Maybe Dylan or Andre can enlighten us."

Alec went to the balcony and called down to the pair. "Door's open, come on up to the second floor."

Dylan was carrying a bottle of wine, and a few steps away,

Andre called out from the flower shop, panting, "Bonsoir, mes amis. I'm right behind. I decided to get some exercise and walked the staircase through Square Louise Michel and I am regretting that."

Maxine waited for them at the top. "Andre, you must be exhausted, that's was the funicular is for."

She turned to Dylan, I hope this will remind you of Aunt Jeanne's cooking.." She could see him taking in the aromas from the kitchen then reached her arms for a welcome hug.

"It sure does. Mom said that you should go to Aix-en-Provence for a visit before you return to America."

Alec joined in. "Does Aunt Jeanne still live in that villa above the village? I remember that wonderful summer, Dylan, when the two of us learned to drive the tractor. Uncle Luc took us to town with a wagon load of produce to protest!"

Dylan laughed. "Ironically, we had to dump all the produce just to make a political statement. Really, what did we achieve?"

"Well, we do have memories, don't we, Dylan."

"I'm sorry, Max, for heaving a case onto your plate amid your vacation," Dylan said. "However, this is the only place in the world where a commoner can attend a royal ball. I hope you will enjoy it, with good memories."

Alec watched the exchange and the prolonged hug. "Go ahead and open the wine, Dylan," he grunted, then continued his review of an incident on the tapes at La Marais.

He motioned to the others to watch as he rewound a section on the Coulliere residence, then the area around the barbershop.

"See here?" he said. "This was two weeks ago—see the fellow behaving like a wandering vagrant? It's the fourth time in a matter of days. He's paranoid and waiting for a bus but doesn't get on any of them.

"Keep watching. A woman comes out from behind the

Coulliere residence pushing a wheelchair, and they walk to the park. I can't be sure if she is from the house or was cutting through the laneway.

"Also, the vagrant packs up and enters the barbershop. Half an hour later, he emerges freshly shaven and boards the tram for the West Bank. I checked that bus routing and found that it passes the Pont de Bir-Hakeim bridge. Security tapes show him getting off, and we follow him to a tenement. At the front, he is accosted by an older gentleman. They argue."

"Zoom in on the door number," said Maxine. "We can find the boarding house and identify the tenants."

"I'll take that up if someone else can chat with the barber," Dylan said. "I have no plans on getting a haircut. It's shocking what secrets a coiffeur ekes out of his customers." Maxine gave Dylan a smirk but said nothing.

Andre unfolded a printout from his pocket. "I'm concerned that *this* might be connected. A man was pulled from the Seine in the same area as the boarding house. It wasn't an accidental drowning. Someone thoroughly bashed him beyond recognition."

"Any clues who he might be?" Alec queried. "The boarding house location, the drowning, and the passenger videoed from the bus. Is it more than a coincidence?"

"Yes. Sometimes you feel in your gut that you're missing something important."

During dinner, the discussion reverted to the public Masquerade Gala and Bonaparte.

After Alec toasted their new endeavor, he raised the obvious question. "So why did you leave us the invitation, Dylan?"

"Before you arrived, Andre was alerted to a blackmail scheme with the culmination to take place at the Royal Lodge that night. Monsieur Coulliere was in touch, and then I met him at the army museum.

"He fears for his family's safety as he is told to take the sword to the gala as a ransom for his daughters. It all sounds preposterous, but we can't risk public security."

Andre interrupted. "And I needed your help. The protocol encourages foreign governments to send a dossier on employees with visas into France, your names came up and Dylan's name was a contact. Due to Napoleon's historical significance, I urged Dylan to ask you both, as we needed trusted assistance.

"I'm plagued with a crossover to an old, renowned Louvre theft that may have intersecting implications. It was years before you arrived in Paris, but you may have read it in the news as it was blatantly daring."

Alec nodded. "The robbery link?"

"At the time of the Louvre robbery, an auto accident on the getaway route involved victims named Coulliere—perhaps that's too coincidental."

"The famous Louvre robbery?" said Maxine. "I read about that, but they didn't capture the perpetrators."

"No. Never caught!" Andre said and returned to the case. "I've arranged for security surveillance to follow Coulliere's daughters to school and both parents to their places of employment. We'll need a team at the event to cover the concourse with so many costumed guests. I brought a floor layout for you."

As Maxine unfolded the venue's floor plan, her eyebrows raised. "Oh, yes! The Royal Lodge. It sounds breathtaking, and I'm all the more curious now. I could make an advance trip to wander the Marble Hall. Without distractions, I can get us a lay of the land and visualize the crime scene."

"Is Coulliere's family aware of the danger they are facing? His daughters?" Alec asked. "The museum's website has inconsistent pictures of the period of Coulliere's management, as though there were two different people over the years."

Dylan glanced at Andre but didn't take up on the Coulliere management.

"I doubt that the family would be suspicious about the dangers of dealing with the black market of art and artifacts," said Dylan, "but the less they know, the better."

"That's noble of him. I'll be more at ease if I check on the girls' school and routing," Maxine said. "If you send the details, Dylan, I'll follow up on the car accident while digging into the Coullieres."

"You see, a woman's intuition is vital in a case like this," said Andre.

Maxine's face tightened and she wagged her finger. "Don't patronize me!"

"That is not my intention. Rather, I appreciate that the balance of this team is so effective, and everyone is on the same thinking plane."

The evening wore on into the early hours as they scrutinized the historical inference, the kidnapping risks, the surveillance tapes, key players, the Louvre heist, and the costumes at the gala. Divvying up assignments, they agreed to rendezvous the next night at the Moulin Rouge café for cocktails.

Andre stretched on his chair and rose with a deep breath. "I know I can count on this team. We'll get to the root of the matter and dispel this ransom ruse. Thank you, Maxine and Alec, for your help. Perhaps, Alec, when this is over and done, I can send an official recommendation back to New York with you."

"Let's get the job done first."

SIX

Scouting The Route

Before 8:00 a.m., Maxine was on the Paris Metro to the Champs-Élysées. Stopping at a roastery for coffee, she found a seat on a sidewalk bench to take in her surroundings.

"The Louvre, the Eiffel Tower, Montmartre, La Marais, the Museum all intertwined. The sounds, the smells, the flowers, the incredible beauty!," she mused.

After a sip of coffee, she pulled the gala invitation from her purse. "La Boutique des Mascarades for costumes—I'm sure the fabrics and crinolines are marvelous, all lace and satin just fit for a queen. Imagine another world and a luxurious life in the palaces of Paris."

She checked the Metro route to the boutique on her cell and texted her plans to Alec. "On the way to the costume store. I'll let you know what I find."

Riding the train, she visualized herself in that era, in Marie-Antoinette elegance, Wedgewood blue, with plenty of satin rosettes, lace, and ruffles.

The Champs-Élysées presented a new world of luxury

goods that she knew would be out of her budget. Suddenly, she halted at a display window.

"The card says to go to La Boutique des Mascarades; but look at this shop—the Pompadour Boudoir. But I'm sure the outfits will be registered with the event to keep a balance without duplications, like a potluck."

Nearby, the window at des Mascarades featured mannequins in full regalia in King Louis XVI's and Marie-Antoinette's likenesses. A menagerie of puffs and elegance under the spotlights brought the statues to life.

"She's wearing acres of crinolines. Oh, and a seductive bustier." Max allowed a giggle.

Studying the invitation before entering, she noticed two handwritten numbers on the corner. She snapped a photo.

A stern gentleman in an elegant, gray business suit greeted them inside the door.

"Bonjour, how can we be of service today?"

"We might be late making our requests, but we're invited to the Masquerade Gala at the Royal Lodge and will need a costume for my husband and me."

Maxine handed over the invitation.

"I see . . . please wait here; I need to consult with my manager, Monsieur Sloane."

The stevedore's demeanor changed instantly from formal pleasantry to concern. Without excuse, he disappeared into a back hallway.

Minutes later, a short, well-polished man in a crew cut emerged with a tailor's measuring tape around his neck. His eyes fell on the invitation, now in his hand.

"Madame Maxine Campbell, I presume."

She extended her hand politely. "And you are?"

"Excuse me, I forgot my manners. Monsieur Percival Sloane at your service, madame. Please come this way; we have already put aside the requested costumes."

"May I ask who requested them?"

Sloane ignored her query and gestured disapprovingly, nodding to an assistant waiting behind him to bring the ensembles.

"Do you always predetermine the choice of your patrons?" Maxine felt rebuffed.

"It is not at all up to me. You see, this number on the back of the invitation is precise. I have no decision in the matter. The costumes were preassigned to be historically correct."

Glass cases of marvelous ensembles lined the walls creating a fantasy of colors and fabrics. As Sloane clicked a remote control, a sliding door peeled back to reveal another bank of hanging costumes.

"My husband was interested in dressing as the Count of Monte Cristo. Is that possible?"

"Ah, he is a romantic then. But I'm sorry that is unavailable as it has already been taken. Madame, it has been requested that you play the part of Marie Louise, the Austrian Duchess of Parma. She was the wife of Napoleon but she did not accompany him into exile. She was a bit of a rascal, you see."

Sloane stopped to snicker at his humor and peered over his pince-nez for her reaction. "The ensemble is one of our more opulent in a variation of blue tones, lots of lace and bustle."

"Then will Monsieur Campbell accompany the Duchess? Surely, he would not dress as Emperor Bonaparte?" Max asked.

"Non, non. We made a special outfit. We'll explain when Monsieur Campbell comes for his fitting. Since this is a special VIP event, there is a unique script to play out. A drama. We don't see that very often."

Sloane became preoccupied with a copy of a map and the script for Duchess de Parma. "This is most peculiar, but surely it will unfold accordingly."

Alec sported a two-day beard growth when he entered the barbershop in the Marais district on the pretext of a shave.

"Bonjour, I've heard this is the best coiffeur in Le Marais. My friend lives not far from here and recommended that I ask for Marcel."

The young girl sweeping the floor gestured to an older man at the last chair. "Take a seat, monsieur; Marcel is finishing with a client—it will be worth your wait."

Marcel was curious about the recommendation and peered over his spectacles. "You say your friend recommended us. Who's that?"

"Antoine Coulliere—he lives a few blocks from here. Do I have the wrong place?"

"Non, indeed Antoine frequents us the first Monday of every month like clockwork."

"That's commendably regimented. He introduced me to an acquaintance a while back, and I've forgotten the fellow's name, but he too said that he comes to your shop."

Alec had cropped a photo from the security tapes to look like an online portrait.

"Here, this is the fellow. Have you seen him?"

Marcel studied it briefly. "Yes, he was here just like you talking about Antoine quite a while ago. He asked personal questions about monsieur--I thought it was offensive."

"What kind of questions?"

"Something about Antoine's ancestry and if I knew about his inheritance. Claimed to have a past association with the emperor." Marcel burst into a laugh. "I've heard everything in here."

"Not the usual chit-chat you'd expect?"

"Non, I finished him up pretty quick. I draw the line between being inquisitive and rudeness."

"Do you know how I can get in touch with him? I believe he lives in an apartment on the left bank; we had coffee a month ago, and I lost his business card. I understand he had an artifact for sale."

Marcel raised his eyes again over his glasses at the predicament of being directed for more information. He made a conscious decision to remember Alec's face.

"I can't say I recall his last name, but I know his first was Kace. I remember it only because it is peculiar. It reminded me of something fluffy like lace with a nice ring yet memorable."

"Yes, that's it; I should have remembered with a name like that. He wasn't much for talk but did mumble about his family being wronged by Napoleon. He might be a brick short of a load, but he wore a distinctive silver belt buckle that must have been worth something. That might be what he was trying to pawn."

"I don't think I noticed that, but it's been a while. I'll track him down."

Marcel finished cleaning up and patted Alec's face with a pert after-shave.

"Ah that feels much better, Marcel. Thanks for the shave and the assistance in finding my friend. You have been helpful, but I have one more question if you don't mind. Do you know of a fencing or dance studio anywhere nearby?"

The barber looked at Alec with an odd expression. "Like pretend sword fighting? I heard that an abandoned dance studio near the Eiffel Tower opened its doors to karate-type activity. You could ask there."

Alec smiled. "I can see why your shop is recommended."

Outside, he texted the information to Dylan, who was already on the prowl for tenement housing on the left bank. Then he hopped the Seine water taxi in the Eiffel Tower's direction to follow Marcel's suggestion.

A few inquiries about Kace at a local café and newsstand directed him to a side street with a row of decrepit tenement buildings. Nothing stood out, other than one. Its front door was open and a couple struggled to move furniture to a rusty pickup truck. The entry was wedged outward for access, and a sign on the lower window advertised for a building manager.

"Excuse me, how can I find the landlord?"

"There isn't one anymore . . . he up and disappeared weeks ago. The building owner's number is on the sign. Give that a try, but I'll tell you the only unit empty is on the third floor beside a real freak."

"What do you mean by that?"

"An angry fellow, very peculiar. We avoid him whenever we can. He had a row with the manager a few weeks ago, and I was scared for him. We haven't seen Mr. Severini since! "

"Thanks for the heads up," Dylan said. "Let me take one end of the dresser you're hauling. It's the least I can do for your sparing me grief."

True to his word Dylan pitched in taking the weight of the couch, and helped to pivot it onto the loading deck of the pickup.

Nursing several coffees at a café near the boarding house, Dylan kept Kace's old apartment in his sight.

A long-haired man strolled out the front two hours later, then looked nervously over his shoulder before darting into the alley. Dylan snapped a series of photos.

"Yes, he matches the pics on Andre's disk."

Deft in the shadows, Dylan followed the suspect from alley to alley until they reached a footbridge. Finally in the sunlight, he could observe the man's physical appearance.

A bottle picker was going through a bin along the railing. "Hey, Kace?"

"Not today, Rawley; I'm in a hurry."

Kace spun around abruptly, then ran and blended through a crowd. After a search, Dylan scoured the area near the riverbank for a sign of the bottle picker. "I'm sure I heard him call the fellow 'Rolly' or 'Rowley' perhaps."

Dylan found the lad sitting on a stoop, smoking a cigarette and counting a handful of loose coins.

"Hello!" Dylan called out. "I can pay you for some information if you're interested."

Rawley raised his head with mild interest. "It depends on the type of information you want. My friends around here are tight, and I wouldn't want to ruin my trusty reputation."

Dylan was prepared with a quick print business card that indicated he was a genealogist researcher.

"I understand. Here's a card with my number. If you change your mind or need an escape route, get in touch."

Rawley was puzzled by Dylan's comment but immediately realized he was being offered a wild card in the game of life.

Dylan returned to the tenement to scrutinize the getaway man's identity. A crude, handwritten tenant guide was inside the front door: Apartment 3C – Kace Chastain.

Leaving the building, Dylan heard a spit of rapid gunfire and took cover behind a dumpster. He scanned the surroundings to get a sight of the perpetrator, and then the shots repeated.

Pop! Pop! Pop! As the ground-floor apartment window shattered, a woman passing by ducked to the ground shrieking in fright.

Dylan searched the nearby streets in the direction the shots had come from, then the street, but didn't see the culprit. A pedestrian ran to the aid of the woman who had fallen on the sidewalk uninjured but frightened.

A remote camera over the lobby doors caught Dylan's eye, and he dialed Andre. "Looks like I've blown my cover. I need tracking when we find the source and a cleaning crew to recover storage data from a security camera."

"Be evasive, Dylan; the suspect can't be far. Alec is on his way to back you up. Don't confront the man; tail him. We can't risk exposing our unit."

"I'm on the go, Andre. I see him towards the bridge."

Alec overheard the call. "Wait Dylan, I'm coming. Kace is an erratic and dangerous man!"

SEVEN

Maxine Investigates

As Sloane's assistant left to retrieve the Duchess costume, Maxine noticed an open appointment book or ledger on the counter. Pretending confusion over the predetermined selections for the event's costumed characters, Maxine eased her way toward the manager's journal.

Her heart pounded and she knew it wouldn't be easy. Fumbling through masks on a shelf as a diversion, she positioned herself at a mirror that reflected her sightline to the logbook. She surveyed the store for security camera locations and removed Andre's lipstick wand from her pocket.

Maxine's view allowed a focus on the numerical listing; however, it was too small to distinguish every detail. Beside each name were notations that she assumed to be of discretion and restrictions. Her eyes ran down the list.

18433 - Queen Marie-Antoinette, Mme Nicolette Fauste;
18434 - Duchess Marie Louise de Parma, Maxine Campbell;
18435 - Austrian Count von Niepperg, Alec Campbell;

18436 - Duke of Wellington, Jacques Guilliard;
18437 - Napoleon Bonaparte, Antoine Coulliere;
18438 - Count of Monte Cristo, outside special reserve;
18439 - Captain Thomas Ussher, Raphael Laporte;
18440 - Musketeer Inigo Montoya, Dylan Moreland

Restraining a laugh at the final entry, Maxine smirked at her success until the assistant returned. Then, as if applying fresh lipstick, she clicked on the security cameras to delete her image.

"My apologies, madame. The de Parma ensemble is not available at this time. Can we schedule a return appointment? Then we'll have all the accouterments ready for your fitting."

"I suppose. Will my husband's costume be ready when we return?"

Sloane himself stepped forward and bowed to make amends displaying excessive comical grace. "I will see to it myself. I have a brochure and itinerary for every guest at the VIP event. Please go over the minutest detail for your character and be punctual."

He drew closer to her, irritated at a tiny piece of debris from the floor.

"Monsieur," Maxine said. "I loathe tardiness."

Sloane nodded, satisfied that he'd completed his assignment. But returning to his register, he observed that the book lay open on the counter. Looking up with chagrin at his laxness, he picked up his phone.

Outside, Maxine's cell lit up with messages from Alec, Dylan, and Andre.

Alec picked up her call immediately. "Hello, babe!"

"I got your text. I'm on edge. Tell me about the morning."

"The barber was helpful. The pictures I sent show the suspect we believe to be Kace Chastain. In several shots, he wears a unique silver buckle that stands out. It is similar to one of the robbery artifact photos on the disk."

"Where are you, Alec?"

"Outside the Coulliere residence, and I'll continue here."

"And Dylan?"

"He had a physical encounter outside Chastain's apartment near the Pont Neuf Bridge. Andre sent backup and sweepers because the culprit's video system recorded Dylan. I'm sure we'll retrieve the data. Chastain is paranoid about being followed, so stay out of sight he doesn't hesitate to shoot. He knows the location of every security camera, but won't deter me—no one is invisible."

"I'll carry on to the Royal Lodge to study the scenes the costume boutique gave me," Maxine said. "I can catch a sightseeing tour from Avenue de la Bourdonnais in an hour, and I'll be there the rest of the day."

"Text when you arrive," said Alec.

"Of course, you must keep me apprised as well."

On her way, Maxine ducked into a tourist office for a booklet on the residence of King Louis XVI and Marie Antoinette before the 1789 French Revolution.

"It all began as a rustic hunting lodge . . . incredible!"

Perusing the racks, she selected a guide, 'The Best of an Afternoon in French Palaces.'

A luxurious coach waited at the curb with the destination labeled 'Royal Lodge'. Maxine secured a seat near the front, expecting the guide to position himself near the driver for questions and information.

The bus filled quickly, and an older, silver-haired gentleman with a walking stick took the empty aisle seat beside Maxine. He tipped his herringbone flat cap in greeting, and she noticed his watery, gray eyes inspecting her and gave a half-smile.

"Bonjour, is this your first tour to the Royal Lodge?" he asked.

Maxine acquiesced to his monotonous queries about her

knowledge and reasons for being at the historic royal residence. The older man didn't introduce himself but rambled on as if they were long-time acquaintances. His opinions passionately covered the Parisian attitude, social status, and the sad state of the world's political affairs.

Max politely showed interest and redirected queries to the old gent for details. "Have you ever been to one of the public masquerade events heralding the monarchs of France?"

"Oh yes. I took my wife years ago before she passed away. It was her dream to wear one of those fancy gowns. It cost me a fortune, but it was what she wanted. I had to wear knee stockings and pantaloons, also one of those heavy horsehair wigs and girlie coats." He laughed at his recollection.

"I'm sorry about your wife; I'm sure it was a royal dream come true for her. The baroque dances and promenades would take some practice."

"Indeed, we took a few lessons at a dance studio near Le Marais, and every night I waltzed her through the dining room leading up to the event. I'll never forget those memories."

"Do you remember what characters you presumed as your masquerade?"

"Most definitely, my wife was the seductive schemer Madame de Pompadour, and I played the inconvenient Charles-Guillaume d'Étoilles, her first husband. Madame de Pompadour herself, the famed mistress of Louis XV, was no saint, and that's one of the reasons the masks were introduced . . . so they could deceive one another.

"Masks… deception." A fleeting thought crossed Maxine's mind but she dismissed the idea.

"I'd rather have been Louis XVI. My wife was fascinated by the romance and deception in the royal household. She was fixed on imagining the private apartments and the garden gazebo rendezvous where Marie-Antoinette hosted her secret lovers."

"How exciting. I want to hear more about your adventure. I'm particularly drawn to secret passages and the tales they reveal. Sounds titillating!" Maxine confessed using exuberance to intrigue the old gent.

"From the Queen's private salon at the Royal Lodge, you can see the structure from her balcony. She would watch for her lover to skulk through the gardens and disappear. Giggling with anticipation, she would stroll through the maze of gardens and meet up there. Under the tapestry flooring is a trap door with a staircase into a luxurious love nest.

"It is no longer open to the public, but my wife and I saw it." The old gent snickered at his past success. "Myra was undaunted and thrilled—she was quite a rascal . . . I'm so glad I encouraged her on her quest. She's been gone seven years, but I still come on our anniversary to remember that day. We thrived here in our adventures and imagination of the forgotten era that the palace revives."

"That's a beautiful story, and I see in your eye that she is still very much with you. Thanks for sharing this. I'll think of Myra when I'm in the palace gardens."

Quietly she reflected. "Seven years, same as the Louvre robbery. Coincidence?"

"It's a place to forget the world and step into the luxury of royalty. I suppose I should have been a historian in my past life." He stared over his glasses as he pondered the occupational thought. "Or even a detective." He watched for her reaction but saw none.

"Either would be satisfying, I'm certain."

"I appreciate your interest, as often folks don't take time with an older person. The younger generation doesn't realize we are history in the making with so much to tell. I have seen a surprising amount in my years, and you've been kind to let me rattle on."

The guide described the Royal Lodge's history with

instructions about tickets, tours, and bus departure locations. The view of the palace and gardens was breathtaking, and Maxine was eager to get to the private apartments and to stand in the Marble Hall, the primary venue for the gala.

With a farewell hug and good wishes, the older man and Maxine went their separate ways. She didn't see him look back to snap a photo and sneer with self-congratulations.

Purchasing an audio cassette for a self-guided tour, she bypassed the tourist line and proceeded into the palace with rented headphones and her foot map. Using the costume couturier's material, she followed the mapped route for the ballroom and the congressional halls.

"Now, if I were in costume as Napoleon Bonaparte, I would be escorted to the Marble Hall by an entourage from the royal court. However, if I were the blackmailer, I would remain in the rafters out of sight until I sprung my attack."

She grinned at the comedic re-enactment.

"Alec or Dylan will know if Coulliere has been to the palace before. Andre could arrange for those security tapes, I'm sure. It would be helpful to know the suspect's route when he first plotted the meeting."

Standing in the middle of the Marble Hall, Maxine was in awe at its glistening polished floors and vaulted ceiling.

"I can imagine the Louis holding courts right here."

In her mind, the tourists disappeared into visions of the past, and the room filled with elegantly embellished brocades, silk, colorful feathers, satin gowns, and dignified uniforms. Dramatic, energetic Baroque music would emanate from the orchestra as processions of couples twirled and glided across the ballroom.

She closed her eyes, visualizing history. Every whimsical guest would be adorned with period wigs and gilded hand-painted masks, each more elaborate than the last, concealing their identities.

Through the crowd, Maxine saw the roguish character wearing the mysterious Count of Monte Cristo's disguise. His eyes were intent across the room to the envious Napoleon Bonaparte, who stood alone and defiant with a sword at his side.

Suddenly Maxine felt a tap on her shoulder and spun around from her fanciful vision, feeling goosebumps. It was the old gentleman from the bus, and he was pleased about the encounter.

"Sorry to have startled you, Maxine; I noticed you standing here and thought I'd see if you need any guidance."

"My mind was back hundreds of years ago here in this magnificent palace. I thought I was amid great ghosts and fantasy of grandeur."

"I do believe the royal family haunts this palace. Come with me; I'll show you the private entrance to the royal suites. You would regret not seeing them." His satisfaction for enticing Maxine made him deviously giddy, but she didn't notice it.

Stooped over, he pressed a button at the back of a carved sideboard, then led her with surprising agility, jerking his folding, silver-tipped walking stick into a short baton. The remaining tourist queue congregated across the hall behind the guide, and Maxine assumed that she and the man were unnoticed.

With a subtle pop of a latch, the pair eased through an opening into a darkened passage, and the door closed silently behind them. With a prickly sensation, a chill of a bygone era overwhelmed Maxine.

Dim wall sconces created shadows as they walked the length of the hall, and at the end, a turned set of stairs led to another landing, then to the outside.

"How did you say you first located this entrance, monsieur . . ." It suddenly occurred to Maxine that she didn't know his real name.

"I told you, I'm the Duke of Wellington." His gaze lingered suspiciously, and he winked with a smirk.

Maxine's memory flashed to the costume manager's logbook that showed the Duke of Wellington as Jacques Guilliard.

"Well, I assume I'll see you again at the public VIP gala here in a few weeks."

He was taken off guard momentarily that she would know of his costume ruse.

With a bow and a salute, he was gone. For a moment, Maxine wondered if he had been a figment of her imagination. She remained, looking around the room and a chill of haunted ghosts sent shivers up her spine.

EIGHT

Coulliere Pressured for Answers

Pacing the Marais route to the Coulliere home, Alec calculated Antoine's likely daily walking direction to work along the park and boardwalk of the Seine. On occasion, Coulliere used a hired car but his preference was on foot keeping an athletic pace.

Following the route, Alec stopped at the corner, watching for a vantage point Chastain might have used to observe the comings and goings at the house and the occupants as they departed.

A school crossing and transit stop drew his interest. He prodded the ground with his shoe at a worn patch near a bench fifteen feet from the school bus sign. Something hard and sharp was under the soil pressed into the gravel.

On one knee, he scratched out a key under the surface and wrapped it in paper debris from under the bench.

"Maybe it's nothing, but Andre can check it for fingerprints or find the locksmith."

Panning the street, he focused on an alley beside the

Carrefour groceteria. The upper apartment was vacant with boarded windows.

Alec scrutinized every feature. "It's not all sealed up; one window has the sash broken out, a perfect vantage location. It looks easy enough to break in."

Scaling the fire escape from the lane, he ascended to the abandoned unit and climbed through a window. A soda can, burger wrapper, and water bottle indicated someone had watched from here. He made the mistake of leaning on broken glass and gave himself a small gash. Finding a paper towel, he concocted a bandage.

He set his sights back on the bus stop, and moments later, a yellow school bus approached. Instinctively, he checked his phone for pictures of the Coulliere daughters.

"Claudette and Celeste must certainly look like their mother, lanky with identical chestnut bobs," Alec guessed, zooming his camera's telephoto lens.

Four children departed the bus first, and he studied each face. Then two thin girls tripped down the steps, chattering and oblivious to others.

"Clearly, they have not been instructed to be cautious about strangers. Claudette is taller and older; therefore, the target would likely be Celeste, the follower. She'd be easier for a kidnapper to intimidate."

Alec waited until the girls strolled out of sight, then followed from a distance.

They continued down the sidewalk through a gated fence toward the two-story Marais home of Antoine Coulliere, entering through an unlocked side door. Observing the house, Alec watched the shadow of a man move the curtains aside at an upstairs window.

"Strange that another man is in the house when Coulliere is at his office." His cell suddenly buzzed with an incoming call from Dylan.

"Meet me outside the Military Museum, Alec. I have more questions for Coulliere. I'll find you in half an hour. If I'm not wearing my cap, you'll know I'm being followed, and you should pick up the tail. I had a close encounter with Kace Chastain at his building, and he'll be looking for me. The man has eyes in the back of his head like a chameleon.

"If he had camera surveillance over his apartment, perhaps he also had it at the museum or Coulliere's residence to monitor activity without being on the scene.

"I'm staking out the residence," said Alec. "Only one security camera is on the front porch, fixed on the park across the road. No other precautions are in play. Not even a guard dog."

"Andre didn't pick up on anything regarding Chastain, but it's worth rechecking. Possibly he set a bug in an obscure location but managed to retrieve it before we were onto him. He has an uncanny ability to observe others while shielding himself."

"Watch your back, Dylan."

Dylan was evasive entering the subway and never followed the same queue for more than a few seconds.

He disembarked at La Tour-Maubourg depot rather than the popular Esplanade des Invalides and calculated it would be an eight-minute walk to the museum. He set his watch and kept a speedy jaunt in his steps.

Ducking into the crowd, he skirted a fellow in a loose, untucked shirt and a black bandana tied at the back. By the man's distinctive lope, he knew it was Kace Chastain.

Kace stopped, with his inherent antenna on alert. He darted a look back to search the crowd.

For an instant, Dylan thought they locked eyes, and he shot off a text.

"Alec, he's headed your way onto the esplanade. I've been made."

"I've got him in my sights," Alec assured Dylan.

Stuffing his jacket into his rucksack, Alec donned a plaid shirt that was out of character but enough of a disguise to lose a tail. He kept close to some stragglers who were mounting the exit stairs.

Chastain hung back behind a concrete column waiting for passengers to clear the platform, and then he burst into action, scaling the stairs like a cat before blending onto the boulevard.

Alec watched him reach for something from his back pocket and saw the glint of a switchblade.

In a flash, he changed again into a beige cable knit sweater and a sports cap. Kace was still in his sights as they neared the museum, but then he was gone.

"Alec dialed Dylan, watching from the promenade outside the museum. "Do you see him? He's acting paranoid."

"I got him headed into the rear alley. Go inside and pay through the tourist line. I'll call Coulliere and get in past the back security. Wait in the outer hall by the Napoleon exhibit. Be wary of any cameras. I hope you have one of Andre's security eraser wands!"

Kace darted toward the rear door in the museum's alley. Twenty feet from the door, he scaled a water pipe from the upper eaves into a sewer drain. The rain had left a puddle at the bottom, but Chastain swung over it with startling agility.

He removed an item from the drain pipe, pocketed it, and in a leap, he landed on the ground and darted back toward the esplanade.

"The rat has had a visual on the back door," Dylan mused. "It must be how he recognized me at his apartment. When I first met with Antoine, I would have been on the tape again. He's covered all the bases."

Antoine Coulliere was sweating, edgy now, and concerned that Dylan hadn't arrived to meet in the armory, as agreed. At last, he appeared.

"Monsieur, we are running out of time. Have you arrested the blackmailer?"

Dylan looked at the little man with surprise.

"Please, Antoine, we are dealing with a man who is erratic and angry. We haven't identified the culprits for certainty. He's set on revenge; patience is the only advantage we have. Use it!"

"You can't let this happen, Agent Moreland. Monsieur Poulin from Interpol assured me that my family would be protected. I thought once you were involved, the threats would stop."

Dylan was alarmed. "Are you suggesting that the blackmailer has been in touch again?"

Coulliere thrust a folded paper toward Dylan.

"He won't take money. He insists on public humiliation and proposes a duel witnessed by the audience at the Royal Lodge event. He's been following my daughters and said he would hold one of them hostage unless I cooperate. Don't let him near my family, I beg."

Dylan held the paper with a tissue, and with care, he placed it in an envelope in his backpack.

"Don't overreact, Monsieur Coulliere. It is a complication intended to keep you nervous. I doubt that your family is in danger. It's an empty threat. Remember, monsieur, you have involved Interpol, you are no longer in charge. We will make the decisions and keep you informed."

Alec arrived at rue de Grenelle at the Musee de l'Armee, a magnificent cathedral-style ancient building. Bounding up the front steps, he sidled into the authorized entrance and blended into a tour group about to enter the Hall of Napoleon. Loitering in the main lobby, he showed pretended interest in the wall of photos of past and present museum directors.

Above him was the photograph of Antoine Coulliere, inscribed on a metal plate as the managing director for the past ten years. The image was younger and thinner but similar to one of the photos on Dylan's domino disk.

Alec eased toward Dylan and Coulliere, who were walking ahead near the weapons display. They stopped in front of the stanchions.

"This sword is impressive, Antoine," Dylan declared. "How did it come into your possession? We need honest believable answers. Clearly, you are involved with other conspirators you are trying to protect."

Antoine paled at Dylan's accusation appearing stunned at the turn of the investigator's demeanor.

"I recall as a child; it was in my father's curio cabinet with an ancient book of letters and diaries that once belonged to Marshal Michel Ney, aide de compte to the emperor. Stories were passed down about the 1815 escape from Elba to usurp power in Paris. Raphael Coulliere, my great-great-uncle, served at Ney's side until he died.

"The Marshal instructed Raphael to take the sword for safekeeping to Ajaccio on Corsica, where the Bonaparte's lived, to a secured vault under the floor by the hearth. Ney knew he'd be unable to retrieve it, so he bequeathed the sword to Raphael. After Napoleon died in 1821, Raphael returned to Ajaccio to recover his inheritance.

"Once the sword was passed to me, I was concerned about the attention it would bring and the responsibility to guard its value. The story circulated in museum circles, and I was pressured to donate the item because of its historical significance, despite challenges to my right of ownership."

Coulliere's voice grew more animated. "I was reluctant to part with it entirely but the reality was that it was touted on the black market. I compromised by placing the sword on loan where it would be under guard. It is solid silver and worth a fortune, possibly up to ten million euros to a collector. Months ago, I received a letter from a potential buyer from South America, but it was a ruse only to see it and know the sword's location. I sensed it was a con in the making."

"Can you provide a list of anyone you talked to about it or who had seen the sword before it came to the military museum? There is something you aren't admitting to or you wouldn't feel so threatened."

"It would take time, and I will consult with my attorney, but I'll do my best. From time to time there have been antiquities dealers and fortune seekers."

"Tomorrow then!"

From a distance, Alec listened as Antoine scanned the placards in the imposing glass cabinets. At a display of battle artifacts, he paused to read of the victory of the ruthless British commander, Arthur Wellesley, the 1st Duke of Wellington, at the Battle of Waterloo in 1815.

Moreland and Coulliere were in intense conversation when Alec neared from behind and deftly slipped a tracker into Antoine's suit coat. Nodding his success to Dylan, he moved on to an exhibit detailing Napoleon's time on Elba.

A cluster of onlookers eased toward the mezzanine where Alec was loitering. He managed to dodge the group as they moved toward the next exhibit.

Coulliere didn't heed the intrusion as he was so absorbed in deep conversation defending himself.

Alec texted Dylan. "Who told Coulliere he was to be Napoleon Bonaparte? The blackmailer or the costume couturier? Ask if he had a fitting and how he'll retrieve the ensemble."

Dylan read the text as he continued his interrogation, directing Coulliere away from prying ears.

Alec sent one more. "How will Antoine know who the blackmailer is at the ball, if they haven't met?"

Most of Coulliere's answers were vague. "I couldn't believe my ears when he told me he was the Count of Monte Cristo representing justice. It's preposterous; my children watched that film years ago but what stood out to me was the spiteful man with six fingers. I've never even seen the blackmailer to know what to look for, but I'd recognize his voice."

"I'll bring a list of guests that will be wearing historic costumes related to Napoleon. You will be able to avoid those that could be threatening and possibly dangerous." Dylan offered..

NINE

Unraveling the Guest List

Maxine limped home on tired feet from her Royal Lodge tour, eager to impart her findings to Alec. Dusk had fallen, when they almost collided outside their Butte-Montmartre loft, she sagged into a welcome embrace.

"We must talk over dinner, Alec."

"Chinese, then. It can be here fast, and there's a chance Dylan may pop by."

"I'm starving. We had a tasty take-out dinner last week at the bottom of the hill, its not far from the metro at St. Pierre. Ask them to double that order and rush it!"

Still in the cobbled courtyard, Alec called it in.

"Tell him to rush it!" She waited with her arms around him and straightened up when she noticed a familiar shape loping up the hill.

"Dylan, we were hoping you'd come."

"It's always a pleasure, Max. I brought us a Beaujolais. Andre, however, has bowed out."

"A problem?"

"He says this case has swamped him. The bloke found in the river appears to have been Chastain's landlord. Interpol watched the whole debacle on the tenement camera's footage."

"Kace killed him?"

"Afraid so, with rage and no mercy. It culminated over the silver buckle stolen in the Louvre heist seven years ago. The unfortunate landlord ended up being bashed and dragged through the alleys in the early morning hours—it was too dark to pick up much on video by the time he dumped him in the river."

"Then it's doubtful that Chastain will return to his apartment," Alec said. He stepped to the curb to scan the street. "I'll return to the tenement and find the fellow Kace talked with. Andre got some footage."

"I talked to the witness and his name was Rawley something. I gave him my card as a lifeline." Dylan said.

"Let's get upstairs to the apartment first," Maxine said. "We shouldn't stand out here exposed telling our secrets."

Dylan helped himself to glasses and poured one for Maxine. "So, what's your news from the costume shop, Max?"

"My visit was enlightening. I found that I will attend as Napoleon's second wife, who remained in Paris while he was in exile. All the ensembles were incredible, and I would have been happy with any of them."

"That doesn't sound romantic at all," said Alec, overhearing it. "Second wife stuck in Paris!"

"Well, it's not that painful. An Austrian, Duke von Niepperg courted her, and his persona is assigned to *you*, Alec." Her boast came with a flirtatious smile.

"At least I'll have reason to stay close to you during the gala," he teased. "But Dylan, how did you get the role of the Musketeer, Montoya?"

I had no choice. The invitation assigned it to me; it was

predetermined. Dylan's mischief showed in a glint in his eye. "Chastain's planning is meticulous, and he wormed his way into Wellesley's favor. The man wields influence with the gala's event organizers. The same goes for Coulliere, as Napoleon."

"I'm convinced the costume shop manager knows more than he's willing to reveal," said Maxine. "But at next week's measurements, we'll see what else unfolds."

"I have yet to darken the place," said Dylan. "I gave my sizes by phone, and they'll courier the costume to me, thanks to Andre. But I need your help on a matter."

"With the costume?" asked Alec.

"No. A new suspicious man has tailed me the last few weeks."

"Chastain?"

"I'm not certain."

The doorbell rang, and Alec skipped down to the street level. "Take-out's here," he called back.

He expected the regular delivery fellow, but a thinner, younger man stood holding the order.

"Is the regular delivery man off tonight?" Alec asked.

"Dunno, there was a help wanted sign in the window, and I need the work. The owner said it was a wild night and gave me a tryout."

Dubiously, Alec paid him and watched as he departed.

"Hmm. He has no bicycle, motorcycle, or car. Where did he go?"

Alec shouted up the stairs. "Dylan! Come down! We have trouble."

Leaving the food bag on the landing, the two set out onto the dark streets to track the delivery man.

"I'll take the route to the Abbesses Metro station if you use the back alleys to the Chinese restaurant at the bottom on the hill," said Dylan.

Alec was the first to spot the imposter jogging uphill toward the Basilica. Clouds dimmed the moonlight, and the tall man avoided the lampposts and lights until he came out and loitered at rue Albert in the heart of Montmartre.

Alec surmised that the stranger was staking out his surroundings. He whistled as if he were calling a dog and texted Dylan his location. From an alley, he waited and watched.

Within minutes, an older gentleman with a walking stick emerged from a treed section near a townhouse row. The man edged close to chat and slipped something into the delivery lad's pocket. As the elder strolled away, the young man patted his pocket and headed in the opposite direction.

Dylan arrived slightly out of breath and crept up behind Alec. "Who was the contact? I didn't expect anything like this. Are we being challenged to Cat and Mouse?"

"A tall, distinguished man with a cane met him, then disappeared up the hill. I'd say one of us has been either bugged or tailed."

Dylan stared into the darkness in thought. "Something is familiar about a tall fellow. I'll go first thing in the morning to find Kace's pal. It may be the same person."

Maxine had set the table and warmed the food before Alec and Dylan returned to the apartment.

"Somber faces," she noted. "What happened?"

"Gather everything you wore today or picked up," Alec said. "Someone tracked one of us."

Maxine dumped her handbag on the sideboard and sorted items, then retrieved her shoes, sweater, and the book she'd purchased. Alec and Dylan emptied their backpacks on the table, and nothing was detectable. Dylan scanned every item with a tracker, and they all turned at the shrill sound.

Beep, beep, beep.

"It's stuck on the bottom of your bag, Maxine," Dylan

declared.

"It can't be. I wasn't near anyone that would have tailed me or would know who I was."

"Retrace the afternoon," Alec said. "Did you speak to anyone?"

Only one person stood out, and she gasped. "Except—surely it wasn't the Duke of Wellington!"

"Someone must have followed you from the costume shop," Alec said.

Dylan's charisma changed to an intensity they hadn't seen. "Elaborate on the Duke of Wellington."

"The costume store manager must have set me up. I walked directly from his store to the bus departure point for the palace tour. I bought a booklet at the tourist office."

"About the Duke?" Alec repeated.

"He's the least likely person you'd suspect, a kindly, older gentleman, a widower, who sat beside me. We had a pleasant chat on the way as he'd been to a similar event before with his wife."

"Is that it?" said Dylan. "Did you see him again during the tour?"

"We had a coincidental second meeting in the Royal Lodge, and he led me into a hidden passage to the royal apartments."

She swung around with a gasp. "I don't remember introducing myself . . . but he called me Maxine. It was in the Marble Hall ballroom. You know how you get to chatting, but then introductions are awkwardly too late? It was like that."

"Is there any way he would have seen your name? Did you remove your wallet?" Dylan prodded.

"No, the tickets didn't need a name, and I paid cash."

"Describe him again."

"He's an older fellow with a walking stick, a gray windbreaker, and one of those English herringbone hats." Maxine looked sickened by the realization that she'd been duped.

Dylan persisted, thinking back to the man who exited Coulliere's office. "Other than the man, was there an opportunity to pick up a bug in the costume shop?"

"My handbag wasn't out of my hand or sight. What if I'm not the only client that the store might have tracked? The manager hasn't met you yet, Alec. You should go for your measurements soon."

The three picked through the take-out containers while rehashing the day's events, and Alec told of his Marais route and the clues from Marcel, the barber.

"The blackmailer might have practiced at a fencing venue. Marcel said one is at an old dance studio."

Maxine dropped her chopsticks. "The studio in Le Marais! That's it! The Duke of Wellington referred to a spot where he took dance lessons with his wife years ago!"

She brought up a photo she shot of the store's logbook. "At the costume shop, the Duke's character is assigned to the name Jacques Guilliard. I'll search his profile."

"The overlap here is becoming ludicrous," said Dylan.

"Maybe it's a bigger scam than blackmailing Coulliere," said Alec.

"Discretion in our movements is paramount now. Let's meet at Les Deux Magots café tomorrow at noon. I'll talk to Andre."

"It's peculiar that Antoine hasn't taken precautions to secure his daughters' safety to and from school," said Alec. "If I had children, I wouldn't let them out of my sight without a relay plan. And he's never even mentioned his wife. Are you convinced he is innocent?"

"What other reason is there?" Maxine asked.

"When a valuable artifact is the focus of theft or deception, the insurance policy is the first place to look for validation," said Dylan. "I'll have Andre re-examine the Louvre claim for possible fraud."

"I did see the sword at the museum," said Alec.

"It's in their custody, so it is safe," Dylan said. "But I'll ask Coulliere for the insurance contact and authentication. We're not going to take his word that it is the genuine piece."

Alec pondered the ramifications. "Dylan, how did this blackmail situation end up in your lap? This can't be the typical case of national threat that goes with the job."

"A tip came to Interpol from a credible source, identifying a crime in play involving kidnapping and possibly murder. Andre recruited me to check it out. I was granted Interpol security clearance to do the legwork and identify the players. My first contact was a phone call with Antoine Coulliere. The original file shows a prior history involving him from some years back."

Maxine winced. "The list of players is growing. We're spreading ourselves thin, Dylan."

TEN

The Plot Thickens

Alec pored over the suspect data and downloaded the previous day's photo imaging. The tally was lengthy.

"Too many players, it's getting complicated."

Kace Chastain - suspected blackmailer;
Marcel (Le Marais barber);
Manager Sloane, Costume shop manager;
Duke of Wellington, possibly Jacques Guilliard, the elderly gentlemen
from the tour;
Delivery imposter sent from Marvin's, Montmartre;
Antoine Coulliere, museum curator and invitee;
Antoine's unknown brother;
Claudette and Celeste Coulliere, daughters;
Rawley, bottle picker acquaintance of Chastain;
Interpol agent first contact;
Security taff at the museum;
Masquerade organizer setting the guest list;
The prospective buyer of the sword is unknown;

and others known to any of the above.

"Dead men can't talk," Maxine groaned. "The only person we can rule out is the tenement landlord. I'd like to know why he ran afoul of Chastain."

"No matter, Chastain is guilty of Severini's murder. To begin with, the timing of his demise is not a coincidence. The video evidence convicts him."

"I'm intrigued about the level of animosity," said Maxine. "I'll delve into the historical aspect to find the rightful owner of the Napoleon sword."

"And the motivation," said Alec.

"Perhaps the entire case hinges on the tale of this sword."

"I'm not sure I buy the story in Andre's dossier, and my gut says that the seven-year-old Louvre robbery is the key. It could all unfold on the night at the Royal Lodge, with limitless characters there under suspicion."

"Napoleon generously gifted his supporters for bravery," said Maxine. "His swords from 1780 to 1800 at Solingen were initialed JSB under the sheath, for Johann Schimmelbush. Napoleon's brother, Jerome, owned other silver swords made by a goldsmith, Bennais, later stolen from the Louvre. The Bonapartes coveted ceremony and had many other swords and heirlooms."

"And all of value too. The museum's archive, will identify if the sword was in other exhibitions or previously stolen," said Alec.

"The Bonaparte descendants could also be motivated to retrieve Coulliere's sword as it was an unintended gift. The family home in Adjacio has become a museum open to the public so the hiding place has been long gone."

"Does the key lie with Kace Chastain?"

"I haven't found much on Kace," said Maxine. "Coulliere says the diaries were passed down into his father's possession.

But oddly, the Elba article was in a historical review just two years ago."

"Why was that item written so recently and nothing about it before? Alec pondered. "It has the makings of an orchestrated cover-up so it could be associated with the robbery."

"I agree, anyone can tell a story if it suits his purpose. I'm not satisfied the Coullieres are entitled to the sword and who owns the decision."

"Be persistent, Maxine; Andre has faith in your attentiveness."

It was past midnight when Dylan returned to his room in Montparnasse. Detouring by the Pont Neuf Bridge, he retrieved a garment bag from a bus depot locker.

He laughed with anticipation at his stage role. "I loved the Musketeers as a kid . . . this could be fantastic!"

Unzipping the garment bag at his apartment, he drew out a silk blouse, a worn leather vest, pantaloons, stockings, a privateer's belt, a side sword, and tall, turned boots. A sealed, sanitized bag held a wig and musketeer's headband. A separate padded parcel contained an elaborate mask.

Donning the costume, Dylan sparred with the sword in front of the bathroom mirror. His voice deepened.

"En garde . . . I am Inigo Montoya. You stole my great-grandfather's sword; prepare to die."

He dramatically thrust the lance toward an imaginary Napoleon. Grinning at the ruse, Dylan reviewed the venue's escape options, if the sword were relinquished.

"There's the secret passage Maxine talked about. It couldn't be a coincidence that she encountered the older man. He must have a cache of secrets.

"With all the guests unidentifiable in the ballroom, it's ideal for someone to blend in and disappear. Guests will be fully enamored with the costumes and characters and be oblivious to their movements. I'll watch for the arrival of the Count of Monte Cristo and the Duke of Wellington too."

⁓

Working into the night, Andre Poulin returned to Interpol's headquarters in the early hours. He slumped behind his desk, and the sound of his phone jerked him into reality. He swiped his finger across the phone.

"Hello, Alec."

"Did I wake you, Andre?"

"No, I work day and night. Something on your mind?"

"Yes, I couldn't sleep, sensing something out of order. Can I come by and meet you for coffee?"

"We've scheduled a lunch rendezvous in Saint Germaine. Is it more urgent than that?"

"I'm going out now to do some legwork, and I'd like your advice."

"Okay, I'll be here."

Maxine was now awake, and Alec whispered, "Sleep more. It's early, but I'm going to see Andre. I'll also go to the dance studio and try to sort out Chastain and the old gent."

"Then I'll catch up with you at noon," she said. "I'm going to the 7th arrondissement to chat with an old friend of Andre's, Gabriel Dupont. He's a retired long-time agent and Andre suggested he like to help on difficult cases and might enlighten us."

"When did you meet with Andre?"

Maxine stiffened. "Yesterday. A woman has to follow her instincts; you know that. I find Andre's charm and wit invigorating. He understands motivation, I trust his instincts."

"And so do I, my love! So do I."

Near the Quai des Tuileries, an older man twirling a walking
stick sauntered toward the Pont Royal Bridge. His sights were
on the Louvre ahead. The gardens were robust with foliage
and flowers that draped from lamppost planters. He stopped
to appreciate the fragrance and listen to nature's sounds.

Breathing in the freshness of the morning air, the Duke
seated himself on a park bench to watch the Parisian pace.
With a tiny sketchbook, he made a graphite drawing of the
Louvre ahead and the Arc de Triomphe in the opposite
direction. Then, from memory, he drew the portrait of a
beautiful young woman.

An anxious, squatty man approached and settled at the end
of the bench, barely glancing until the older one spoke.

"You're late, Monsieur Coulliere!"

"I had to make sure I wasn't followed. The gendarmerie
has brought in others to investigate."

"Sloane tipped me that the woman was at the costume
shop with a coded invitation that she'll be the Duchess Marie
Louise. He observed her snooping at his notes, but I doubt
she found anything conclusive. I discreetly joined her on a
tourist bus to the palaces. Using my favorite ruse as the Duke
of Wellington, I enticed her with tidbits of secret passages,
enough to pique some wayward sleuthing. It will be her first
resource of escape. I'll be able to handle this."

The nervous man's anxiety showed in his jittery legs. "I say
let her be preoccupied with history and royal balls while we go
about our plan.

"Why are you nervous?" asked the Duke.

"It's the Moreland agent; he has an American detective on
the case. I thought this was going to be simple."

"I'm beginning to wonder how many cracks are showing,
Antoine. Kace has a tape from outside the museum showing

the gendarme agent entering *your* back route to the shipping dock a few days ago."

"Kace doesn't even realize he's a pawn," the short man spat with malice.

"Careful, he is capable of murder," said the Duke. "Don't underestimate a career criminal and the value he places on his freedom. Kace has no attachments, having lived in foster homes, and then put on the streets without a soul caring. I'm getting too old and have lived a full life of adventure and thrills. I still recall holding King Charles' sword in my hands the night at the Louvre. That itself was worth it."

"We agreed not to mention past escapades, especially the Louvre. It is dangerous." Coulliere's face paled in a pained expression. "If I could turn the clock back, everything would be different."

"No need to cry over spilled milk—you and your brother survived. But Kace still has the silver belt. One day he will be exposed, and then we're all vulnerable. Besides exposing us to the Louvre, he has the treasure map."

Antoine heard the reassurance but held back any reaction as he knew another truth. "Then perhaps that is a loose end to be eliminated."

"I'm not a murderer," the Duke sneered. "Besides he is useful to play his part at the Gala. This has been in the planning for months; it's too late to panic."

"The Moreland agent was at the museum today," Coulliere said. "He was asking questions and wanting certificates of proof that the sword belongs to my family and its value. Are you certain the Ney notes will stand up?"

"Maintain your cool. Don't be too forthcoming; you'll trip yourself up," the older man warned. "My inside voice assures me there are no holes in the insurance authentication."

By late morning, Andre had left his office, and Alec was en route on the Marais Metro by water taxi.

Dylan reviewed videotapes in his Montparnasse apartment before heading toward the team rendezvous.

Andre was the first to find a patio table and had his newspaper Le Monde folded in view, the signature cue that the site was audio-secured by a nearby surveillance unit. The famed historical café was a collage of umbrellas and clusters of patio tables, so public that anonimity is guaranteed.

"Bonjour, Andre, we missed you last night," Maxine said warmly.

"This case is time-consuming. I'm afraid we stepped into a hornet's nest. It's hard to get out of the office and do fieldwork."

Moments later, Alec jaunted across the boulevard to Les Deux Magots to join the pair. His eyes were on his cell as he slid into the vacant chair.

"Bonjour, mes amis! I put a tracker on Antoine at the museum. There's movement near the Louvre, and he's been stationary for half an hour at a park bench."

"Is he alone?" Andre asked.

"It seems he had a meeting—the tracker sound is barely audible, but I'll slow it down and recreate it at home. I'll text the coordinates. A street video might show who he met."

"I'm short-staffed and reviewing surveillance tapes. If one of you can spare some hours, we'll get further ahead."

Andre avoided a glancing hint at Maxine, but she got the point and patted his hand. "I'll partner with you on it. I could also use some computer hours for research."

"Alec, I didn't introduce you to Antoine Coulliere at the museum, just in case we need to tail him," said Dylan. "Something isn't sitting right. A spy cam recorded me at the back of the museum. Too bad I didn't have Maxine's image wand. Kace saw me and took some shots. He wouldn't know who I was or that I was looking for him, but he's paranoid. In the meantime, we'll see if Coulliere provides the history and insurance records as requested."

Dylan's statement triggered new thoughts for Andre.

"Insurance? That brings back another scenario of the Louvre robbery. Thugs used the window cleaner's scaffolding. It was clever and quick. They were after Napoleon's swords and also took the coronation sword of King Charles."

"That had to be worth a fortune," said Alec.

"A snap and grab job," Andre said. "A few items were found subsequently in South America, but others of Napoleon's were never recovered."

"Other museums with Bonaparte artifacts are also targeted for theft that feeds the black market," said Maxine. "An international database of stolen works has a long list of outstanding Napoleon items."

"Then we must learn more of the history of the Coulliere sword and the diaries," Alec said. "The historical data you provided is mentioned only once on the internet and with a limited reference to Raphael Coulliere, the supposed ancestor. Captain Thomas Ussher was an honorable member of the Royal Army, but neither Ségur nor Ney is prominently mentioned."

"I'll gladly take Maxine's help," Andre said. "We'll search historical accuracy while you and Dylan pursue the culprits. Did you uncover anything at the dance studio?"

"I did," said Alec. "It was once a ballroom dancing franchise that produced robust competitors during that era. As we didn't know the man's identity on the bus with Maxine, I looked for the name Myra who he said was his wife. I found a dancing couple—Lawrence and Myra Wellesley. The address now belongs to a dressmaker.

"When ballroom dancing waned, the studio closed and was taken over for karate. Two years ago, a fencing group leased it. The building manager didn't have complete records, but I found names of interest."

Dylan cursed under his breath. "This sounds entirely like a ruse, and we're the pawns. I'll not be an errand boy for Antoine to defraud the museum."

ELEVEN

Breaking the Ring

Kace Chastain huddled inside a dilapidated boarding house in a seedy area of the 9th arrondissement within view of Pont Neuf bridge. He had an uncanny ability to blend into the streets and avoid security cameras.

Chastain developed a lone wolf complex seeing himself as a worthy opponent of Wellesley and Coulliere rather than a complicit comrade. More and more, he found that he was being dispatched as an errand boy and removed from overall decisions. His new landlady ignored him, and for that she was safe.

Sitting at his rickety desk and computer, he enlarged pictures from the museum's surveillance. Zoning in on Dylan's face, he ranted from the Mary Howett poem with a grin and a sarcastic lilt.

"Will you walk into my palace?" said the Spider to the Fly.
Tis the prettiest little palace that ever you did spy.

The way into my palace is up a winding stair.
And I've many curious things to shew when you are there."
"Oh no, no," said the little Fly,
"To ask me is in vain,
For who goes up your winding stair can ne'er come down
again."

The door opened, and a pair of disheveled lads poured in carrying plastic bags they'd filled with retrieved trash and bottles.

"Ahoy, Kace, we lifted a few extra wallets today, and we've enough for a bottle of brandy. Join us for an indulgence?"

"Be off with you, Rawley. You smell like you've already been into the liquor."

"Well, that's thanks to you. My tip for delivering Chinese food in Montmartre was my week's paycheck. I might decide to go back to the Basilica and ply my trade. But you don't need to worry, Kace, I'll avoid your detective friends."

That was something that hadn't occurred to Chastain. He spun his chair around to face Rawley and leered skeptically at his counterpart.

"You said it was too dark for him to get a look at you."

"He stared at me and asked where the regular delivery guy was. I did exactly what you said and high-tailed it to the Basilica for the payoff."

"Yes, you did." Kace began to seethe.

Loose ends—can't have loose ends.

Rawley transformed instantly, showing a degree of sobered intelligence.

"I see the look in your eye, Kace," he spewed. "Don't you dare try to off me! I've taken precautions if I should disappear like your landlord."

"I don't know what you're talking about."

"Sure, you do. I see quite well in the dark."

"Are you threatening me, Rawley?"

"No indeed. But if I'm gone, they will come looking for you." Rawley saw an opportunity to barter without assessing his chance of success. "However, if you would place that silver buckle on deposit with me, it could seal my lips.".

Chastain took two steps forward. "You idiot, you have no idea what the value of this buckle is and how it came into my possession. If you did, you wouldn't dare suggest it leave me."

Kace turned away while caressing his beloved silver buckle, the bane of his dilemma. He heard Rawley's confession and knew his plan was in jeopardy.

Rawley gloated with defiance. "I know exactly how you got it, Kace. You have a fetish—you must keep something from every scheme, and I predict that will be your downfall. Yes, I know plenty, but as I said, I've taken precautions."

Chastain was unnerved by the threat.

It must look accidental, so there isn't an investigation.

Rawley saluted and slammed the door. Running down the stairs, he was overcome with fear, wishing he could take back his words.

"I'm a dead man."

Shaking, he found sanctuary on a rock precipice under a bridge and pondered his next steps. Searching for a source of refuge, he recalled the night that the dark-haired sleuth was pursuing Chastain in Montmartre.

"Once he'd lost Kace, he came back and questioned me. I wasn't going to snitch on my friend, but now I'm in imminent danger. He gave me a contact card for a detective."

Rawley rifled through his pockets and was about to give up when he found a folded paper in the back of his jeans.

Dylan had left his friends at the café when his cell beeped with a call.

"Hello, monsieur detective, my name's Rawley, you know from the bridge a while ago. You left me your number if I had any information regarding Kace Chastain."

Dylan could hear the fear in his voice. "I remember, it was you the other night on the hill."

"It's urgent now!"

"Yes, Rawley. What do you have?"

"I'd prefer to meet somewhere obscure. I'm being followed and fear that Kace will kill me; he's done it before."

"Stay in public space. I'll find you outside the Louvre. How soon can you get there?"

"Twenty minutes. Monsieur, if I don't make it, I am putting a letter in the mailbox to the gendarme captain."

"I'll wait for you at the Louvre."

"Oui, I'll tell you more when we meet."

The call ended abruptly, and in a quick message to the unit, Dylan asked that Alec back him up. Andre agreed and activated surveillance at the Louvre for Rawley.

Alec watched from the street as Dylan paced the courtyard. A flood of tourists lined up for admittance into the art gallery. It was nearing the end of the school season, and busloads of students queued up the outer stair landing.

"He's late; I'm guessing something has gone wrong, Alec."

"Stay here in case he shows. I'll watch from the bridge, as he'll come from the opposite bank. There's a clear vantage from this side."

Halfway across the Pont des Arts pedestrian bridge over the Seine was a stopping place with an emergency call box. Rawley surveyed his route and had a visual on the glass dome over the Louvre.

Two joggers raced past, then he heard a bicycle screech behind him, followed by a sense of dread. A glance over his shoulder was too late.

Chastain poked the tip of a knife into his back. "This can be painful, Rawley, or you can just jump, and it will simply look like a suicide—it's your choice."

"You have the advantage, Kace. I'm terrified, but you're too late. I told you I took precautions, and it's in the post."

Looking frantically for help, Rawley realized the futility of his circumstances. He could see the devil in Chastain's eyes.

"Please Kace, don't do this," he rambled in desperation. "I'll get the envelope back, and we can return to how we used to be."

Kace glowered with his fists clenched. It was too late, and he knew he couldn't stop this festering rage. "You know well enough, Rawley, that you only get one chance with me."

Alec recognized Rawley from Dylan's photo of the bottle picker near the tenement.

"Rawley is one of the men in conversation on the bridge," Alec said into the earpiece. "I have him in my sights, but he is under duress. The other is Kace, forcing him to climb the railing. Any suggestions?"

Andre said, "Alec, I'm activating special Interpol clearance for you to take the shot if the snitch's life is at stake."

"I see him too," Dylan said. "Alec, I'm behind you."

Alec charged at full speed in Rawley's direction. Knowing the distance was too great, he stepped in front of a cab and commandeered the driver, flashing a badge of sorts.

"Interpol! Get out of your car!" The puzzled driver acquiesced, waving his hands while backing toward the curb.

Alec roared on toward Rawley and screeched to a halt distracting Chastain. The split-second opportunity was enough for Rawley to brace himself, white-knuckling the hand railing.

Like a crazed animal, the attacker lunged at Rawley with his knife, piercing him through the back. Alec tackled Kace but was unable to free the knife from his grip. In the counter-attack, Kace thrust the blade into Alec's thigh, then turned and ran, cursing at Rawley.

Dylan aimed, but the bullets pinged off the railing to avoid hitting Alec.

"Medics, Dylan! Rawley is in a bad way. Mine is a flesh wound."

Maxine was with Andre when the words came across the earpiece. The color drained from her face as panic overcame her.

"Alec, are you alright?" she yelled.

Dylan replied while holding pressure on the wound. "He's okay, Maxine. A few stitches, and he'll be back on the trail."

"I'll meet you at the hospital."

"Not necessary, Max. The paramedics will stitch me up," said Alec. "I'll accompany Rawley; he'll need emergency surgery. Dylan's gone now after Chastain."

Kace, bloodied from the attack, made his way to the Wellesley townhouse near the Champs-Élysées. Pounding on the door, he demanded that Lawrence show himself. "Open up!"

The Duke pulled the curtains back enough to see who was at the door, then guardedly eased it open. Chastain boldly pushed through, his eyes darting about madly for Coulliere.

Dylan moved closer to the townhome and pulled a remote microphone from his pocket. Crouching through the hedge, he attached it to the front bay window and returned to a bus shelter across the street to listen.

The Duke showed genuine concern. "Good gracious boy, are you hurt?"

"Non, it's not mine. Turn on your news and see if there is a report about an incident on the Pont des Arts bridge."

"What have you done, Kace?"

"I had to take care of business. It has long been ingrained in me to deal with loose ends. There's a rat among my friends."

"What loose end?" Lawrence pried.

"A witness that threatened to snitch. He knew about the

Louvre and bragged about having evidence. We can't take that sort of chance."

"That's years ago . . . what has that to do with anything now? You're paranoid."

"Don't worry yourself, Duke. I'm pretty sure I eliminated the problem." Kace hesitated, deciding to withhold details of Rawley's threat of evidence.

"Look here, Kace, we need to talk with Coulliere."

"He's not taking the risk; it's us. All he needs to do is turn up wearing a feathery masque and dressed like the emperor with his sword."

"Calm down, man! It's all under control."

Kace continued his arrogance, self-congratulatory about his part in the ruse and being the focus at the Gala.

"I'm the one that will be center stage that night, crawling with Interpol officers. Aren't you worried about how you'll get the silver out, and to the buyer? Coulliere is simply an instrument to receive the payout."

Wellesley snapped back, as the volley for authority continued. "Don't forget Hollande Bertolier, the palace event contact. He's pivotal in organizing the characters and the Masquerade. While he doesn't truly understand the objective, he's been invaluable and the lifeline to the press and government officials. As for the buyer, I have that in hand."

"Bertolier will be paid handsomely for his deception. Otherwise, I care nothing about him," Kace said.

"I'm an old man," Lawrence surmised. "It's all in the thrill of adventure for me now."

He turned to the TV news channel. "It's just the regular feed except a notice running across the bottom of the screen of a pedestrian accident on the bridge this afternoon."

"Call the hospital and check Rawley's condition," Chastain demanded. "If need be, I'll go and finish the job."

Listening in, Dylan pondered Lawrence Wellesley's true

identity. "Why would he refer to himself as the Duke of Wellington, who wasn't even a Frenchman?"

He then called Alec. "So, the three of them are in cahoots with Bertolier! "It's part of a con to get the insurance payout for the Masquerade scheme. I want Coulliere's insurance certificate. If he thinks he can use me to pad his pockets, he has no idea who I am."

TWELVE

Divide and Conquer

Maxine was alone in their B&B and deep in research to unravel the claim to the Napoleon silver sword. She had discovered an article about Elba published in recent years, but its timing and content needled at her. She jotted the publisher's info.

"Historians recorded the event when a sympathetic Captain Thomas Ussher arrived on Elba with Napoleon, but they mention Ney and Ségur's presence only once. Curiously, how would such a significant event in French history be ignored."

Motivated by the suspicions from her findings, she scrolled on into pages of historical records.

"The London Museum verifies Ussher's tale of the diamond-encrusted snuff box as it was briefly displayed there. The box's lineage was tracked and verified before falling into the hands of a private collector."

Maxine's mind was still focused on the mysterious Elba

article, that hadn't appeared in prior records. She gathered her info about the publisher of the historical review and the freelancer who had submitted the byline.

She dialed and waited on hold. Finally, her call rang through. At first, the editor was reluctant to answer Maxine's questions, but she persisted, unwilling to let this contact disappear.

"S'il vous plait, monsieur, it is very important."

The editor huffed as politely as possible. "I see. What is it you'd like to know?"

"How did you corroborate your sources and footnotes? The validation is significant, relating to the French Revolution era, and is not to be taken as conjecture. I've been thorough in my research of Napoleon's exile. I'm curious about your article regarding Philippe-Paul, Comte de Ségur, the aide de compte to the emperor's visit to the island. Surely there are documented interviews with specifics."

Maxine paused to hear the editor's reaction, but he remained silent.

"I'll be specific, sir," she said. "I cannot validate the story of Ségur's presence on Elba. It is Ségur's name that comes up repeatedly who helped smuggle the Russian gold back to France. However, it strikes me as being odd that I have not been able to uncover other accounts of these meetings."

"I assure you, madame, our articles are credible."

Maxine demanded a better response from the editor, "Have you ever heard of Raphael Coulliere? If the story is factual, his name would have come up as being present at Elba."

"I'm at a loss when giving you answers, as the article you mentioned was a few years ago. I'll need to talk directly with the contributor who is presently unavailable. We pride ourselves on authenticity and have a reputable record."

Maxine's voice softened to remain diplomatic. "Monsieur,

this is a matter of paramount importance to France's government. The historical ramifications are in question. Surely you wouldn't want to become front and center in a national dispute. We're interested in tracking Marshal Ney's sword and when it came into his possession. Your article indicates that the exchange happened at Elba in the early 1800s."

"I do understand, and I'll get back to you. The same author also wrote an article about the attack on the Louvre. As I recall, the insurers and local investigators can substantiate those. If the insurance company paid the claim, then be assured it was thoroughly investigated."

"Thank you, Monsieur Ratcliffe. I'd appreciate information on the direct sources for those articles. One more question, did you review the actual diaries of Napoleon or Marshal Ney regarding this juggernaut period."

"I don't recall," said Ratcliffe. But he sounded nervous and agitated, anxious to complete the phone interrogation.

"I'll review your other articles, and I may have more questions. I look forward to hearing from you tomorrow."

Mulling over the outcome, Maxine recalled that Dylan said the diaries of Raphael Coulliere were part of the Napoleon exhibit at the museum.

Confused by the inaccuracies, she delved further into Napoleon's exile and opened documents from Captain Thomas Ussher, who had in-depth accounts of Napoleon's visits. At no time did his notes indicate the presence of Raphael Coulliere or a gifted sword.

"I can't see where the family name entered in the sword's lineage. I'll arrange with Alec to obtain a scanned image. Where was the article sourced?"

An idea suddenly popped into her head. "As in every case, the wife can be a source of information no matter how hard she tries to protect her husband. Dylan said Odilette Coulliere works at the Eiffel Tower souvenir shop."

Andre joined Alec to interrogate the bridge attack victim at the hospital, leaving Maxine to follow up at the Eiffel shop.

Nearing the Champs de Mars, she stopped momentarily in awe as the tower designed by the famed Gustave Eiffel rose across the city.

"Every time I lay my eyes on this Iron Lady, I am amazed by the imagination of its inventive structure. I loved spending a university summer here studying the history and culture of the French. Although I've been near her, I've never been inside the souvenir shop."

She strolled and observed on arrival, waiting for the clerks to converse. Two women were there, one with dark hair cut short over her ears with windswept bangs. The second was some years older, and Maxine eliminated her as unlikely to be Odilette.

The younger one was restocking the postcard rack, and Maxine inched into her space.

"Bonjour, you are so lucky to work in the framework of history," Maxine said. "I'm envious. I study every piece I can find of your country's history, particularly from the French Revolution. Do you have literature from the era of Napoleon?"

"Oui, but have you been in the museum to see the iconic pictorial display of the battlefields?" Odilette asked. "The most popular one is the Battle of Waterloo with the Duke of Wellington, which changed the course of our history."

She moved over to a shelf laden with books. "Here . . . this has a sequential review of each battle leading up to Napoleon's final exile to Saint Helena off the coast of Africa."

"It's exhilarating," Maxine said. "Being in the presence of artifacts that were part of Napoleon. I plan to see the swords at the military museum. I heard that the old diaries tell of the victories and defeats in battle. It's close to history, yet we must view it through a glass case."

Odilette stepped back to absorb Maxine's interest in the military museum. She eyed her with intrigue.

"I understand what you are saying, madame. My husband's family claims to have been close to some of those Napoleonic relics." Odilette paused, wanting to say more but rebuked herself.

"That would be an incredible honor to be tied in any way to actual history," said Maxine.

"Few people know that my husband has a connection, and I shouldn't have said that. He met an acquaintance, a young man, obsessed with one of the swords. He said it was a family heirloom intended for him—a long, complicated tale. It's a reminder that there are fortune hunters around every corner without moral scruples. Every Frenchman seeks a reason to have a patriotic heritage. It gives one status don't you think?"

It was apparent that Odilette was uncomfortable, and Maxine waited for her to continue.

"Unfortunately, my husband can no longer provide information. It's his condition."

"Is he ill?"

Odilette shook her head. "I'm sorry. I can't talk about it."

"I apologize, I didn't mean to intrude on personal matters. It's a shame to harbor a wealth of information concerning Napoleon. I have goosebumps thinking about it. It's like standing in the shadows of history."

Odilette brightened up. "It is refreshing to talk to someone with an appreciation for Bonaparte. He was a great emperor and should never have been disrespected and sent into exile. On Bastille Day in July, everyone dresses in period attire. We used to go every year; that is, before the accident."

"That will be amazing. In the meantime, I plan to get to the

Masquerade Gala at the Royal Lodge. It's difficult to get tickets unless you know someone."

Odilette's face tightened. "Once, someone from the Gala event organizers came to our house. His name was Hollande, and reminded me of Amsterdam. He had inside influence and gave us tickets to a VIP event. Perhaps you could call and ask him."

"Many thanks for the suggestion."

Odilette turned away as a group of tourists surged into the shop. "Our chat was enjoyable, but now I must help my clerk."

Maxine selected a Battle of Waterloo book and waited at the till. Odilette was already assisting others, but Maxine knew the woman was scrutinizing her nonetheless.

In a last glance back, Maxine saw Odilette step from the store to the museum lobby with her cell phone.

She could only decipher her first few words. "Antoine, are you okay?"

Connecting on the detective's earpiece to the others, Maxine detailed her visit to the Eiffel Tower with Collette and identified Hollande as a possible contact for the Royal Lodge gala.

"I know that name, the event man," said Dylan. "I overheard it in Chastain's conversation at Wellesley's residence."

Andre jotted down her findings and raised an eyebrow about Odilette's call to Antoine. He urgently delegated his concerns. "I'm curious about the brothers—which is the real Antoine and which is Remy? Dylan, are you still on Kace's tail?"

"I'll wait here for him to leave. If I get close enough, I'll plant a tracker, but that's doubtful as he's a got eyes in the back of his head."

"The investigation is expanding quickly," said Andre. "Maxine, did you recognize the older gentleman's voice on Alec's transmission of Coulliere this afternoon? I'm viewing the surveillance tape … and sending you his picture now."

She replied instantly. "Got it. Yes, it's the Duke of Wellington from the palace tour. I'll be at the apartment in Butte-Montmartre in an hour, and we can meet there if necessary. I'll be up late, going over videos."

"Maxine, I'm still at the American Hospital," Alec said. "I'm waiting for Rawley to come out of surgery. It isn't looking good for him. But if it helps, he said, 'It's in the mail, don't let him get away.'"

"Stay close to him in recovery," said Andre. "Chastain might be back to finish him off. There's something he didn't want Rawley to tell us that's worth murdering for."

"I'll hang out here to keep watch."

With doctors and nurses in and out of Rawley's room, Alec was sent to the waiting room at the end of the hall. He no longer had a direct view of the recovery room.

Seeing a shift change at the hospital, Alec loitered in an alcove in the hallway, watching for any movement toward Rawley's bed. Visiting hours had long passed and the halls darkened when he spied the shape of someone slinking, then freezing near the closets.

Alec's heart pounded, and he waited, but the shadow didn't reappear. After midnight the nursing shift changed again, and the lurker retreated to the stairwell door. Alec's wound was stiffening, and the aching was more intense. At two fifteen, as nothing more had happened, Alec took the elevator to the lobby.

There was no moonlight and the hotel parking lot was black. Alec walked cautiously without seeing anyone but sensed he was being followed. With his mobility challenged, he paused and waited again.

Tapping behind him somewhere in the darkness was the walking stick.

Walking stick. Max said the Duke carried one during the palace tour!

Ducking into the shadows between two parked vehicles, he watched for what seemed to be an eternity. Nothing.

Chastain slipped out of the townhouse's front door into the darkness.

Dylan was skilled in night detection and blended in behind in the shadows. But in a critical error, he didn't notice a second person leave the house minutes later, staying half a block behind Dylan, watching and waiting for an opportunity.

Chastain continued toward Avenue George V in the direction of the American Hospital in the 8th arrondissement. The Paris Metro transit service had ended an hour before, and they were on foot for three kilometers under dimly lit lampposts.

Dylan heard the click of a walking stick on the sidewalk but was sickened at his timing error as reality faded from his consciousness. The last of his senses were the sound of a snap of the cane receding and a foggy vision of a tall sneering man walking away at a good gait.

Just past five in the morning, Maxine woke at the creak of footsteps on the stairs. Reaching across the bed, she knew Alec hadn't come home.

She called out, "Alec!"

"It's me, babe. Sorry, I tried to be quiet."

Getting up, she needed his embrace.

"Alec, you're a mess. Your jeans are all bloodied."

"I got stabbed on the bridge, and I don't travel with a change of clothes." He tried to laugh but cringed from the pain.

"Lie down and let me look at the damage."

He sagged onto the bed and let her peel away the torn clothing. She leaned over and kissed him.

"My goodness, you have lots of stitches. And look at the bruising. You need an ice pack."

Returning, she found Alec already asleep. She curled up beside him with her head on his shoulder.

"Alec Campbell, I love you more every day. You are my strength and my shelter. Please do not take risks with your life, I couldn't bear it. You're my inspiration and forever my most faithful." Holding him tightly, she listened to their hearts beating together in rhythm.

The early incoming messages on her cell woke her in the darkness. Tiptoeing to the kitchen, she made a pot of coffee and read through her texts.

Andre's update was concerning. "Rawley didn't make it. Also, I can't reach Dylan. His microphone went dead about two o'clock."

She roused Alec from his sleep and brought him up to speed. The stiffness of his injuries prevented his urge to jump up and go to the Wellesley residence.

"You're in no shape to be chasing after Dylan. I can do it."

"Not a chance, Max, not alone. Give me a minute to loosen up. I'll take a pain pill, and we'll go together. Tell Andre we'll reschedule our lunch conference."

She gave him a stern look.

"There's no point in arguing," he said.

"Then let me help you. We'll take the car, and I'll bring your old cane from the closet."

"That's my girl."

Alec braced his arm around her shoulder and hobbled

toward the door. "The last signal was near the Arc de Triomphe," he said. "We can park there near the hospital. I'll keep trying to raise Dylan on the earpiece and his cell."

Taking the most direct route between the Champs-Élysées and the American Hospital, Maxine watched the ground for Dylan's phone or any signs of a struggle.

"Surely Dylan would leave us a clue of some sort."

Three blocks from the hospital, Alec shouted, "I see it! Pull over! That's his cell phone, but it's smashed like someone stomped on it."

Maxine knelt with a flashlight and patted the ground for footprints or signs of a struggle.

"An altercation was right here. There are scraping marks that left scratches on the sidewalk. Someone was dragged or crawled from here."

Alec called Andre with their discovery and continued scouring the surroundings for clues.

THIRTEEN

Confessions

Dylan had a swooning headache from the chloroform but slowly regained cognition. He was confused, bound, and in a dark, damp place.

The surface beneath him was hard and cold, and he recognized traffic sounds nearby. "It smells like a basement or a dumpster."

It slowly dawned on him how he came to be in this predicament.

"The sot, Wellesley, is relentless. How could I have let my guard down?"

He wriggled his hands, searching for a sharp object; then, his fingers fumbled over a broken beer bottle. With a piece of glass shard, he sawed at the knotted twine that bound his wrists.

A soft buzzing in his ear caught his attention. "Thank goodness. The earpiece."

He listened to a faint static until Alec turned up the volume frequency at the other end, hoping for a connection. Dylan tried to respond but his voice was too weak from the drugging to call out.

"Dylan! Dylan!"

There was no response.

"If someone took him down here, his weight would be difficult to drag very far," said Maxine. "There's a maintenance hole here by the curb. Think there's a chance?"

Alec stuck his penknife into a lift pin, then yanked until he felt leverage. He shifted the lid and leaned with all his weight to hold it open.

His voice echoed into the underground chamber. "Dylan, are you there?"

"Ahoy! Is that you, Alec?" Dylan groaned as he struggled to free his bonds. "I'm tied up."

"By golly, man, how'd you get into a pickle like this, didn't your Mom teach you better? Are you mobile?" Alec tested his cousin's sense of humor to establish his cognitive condition."

"I can't move."

"There's a ladder here. Hang in. I'm coming for you."

Alec looked at Maxine for help. "What's in your bag? You're always prepared for the unexpected. Tools? Anything."

"Let me rifle in here . . . a flashlight, a nail file, compact mirror, kitchen twine, lighter, granola bar, Tylenol, and a hairband. Oh, this will be good—hand soap. Dylan could slip out of his knots with that."

"I heard," Dylan called. "Send it down with the lighter and the twine."

"The sun will be up soon," said Maxine. "It's a multi-lane boulevard, and we'll have to deal with commuter traffic before long."

Minutes later, Alec emerged, holding his partner over his shoulder. Dylan's feet staggered, and then Alec deposited him on the grass boulevard. Dylan massaged his wrists to conceal the cuts from Maxine.

Although he was disheveled, wet, and bruised, Maxine admired his roguish appearance and the similarities between the cousins. She inched toward him for a close look.

"Let me see your cuts? Who did this to you?"

"It was the old man . . . the Duke. It was my mistake. I followed Chastain and didn't wait for anyone else. I'm sure he was en route to the hospital to finish Rawley."

"Sorry, Dylan, but Rawley died during the night. I'm sure someone was staking out the hospital while I was there, but he slipped through my fingers. We were going to the hospital just now when Andre called and asked us to track you down."

He rubbed the back of his head. "Maxine, I'll take that Tylenol."

At the American Hospital, the trio read Rawley's report. He had been recovering from surgery when he took a suspicious turn for the worse in the early morning.

Dylan rifled for his Interpol ID and insisted on examining the death certificate from the attending physician. Flustered, the head nurse paged the doctor on call for assistance.

A few minutes later a haggard young physician approached them in the waiting room. The nurse stayed at his side while he informed the trio.

"Are you friends or family of the deceased?"

"Interpol. I was at the scene of the accident on the bridge when the victim was stabbed."

"I see. But the patient didn't die from stab wounds. His intravenous was injected with a fentanyl overdose. The matter is in the hands of our security team and the local gendarmerie."

"Was anyone seen entering his room?" Alec asked. Surely someone monitored him after surgery?"

The nurse was concerned but rattled, and eager to hand it off.

"I shouldn't say anymore, Monsieur, but the individual was

disguised as a hospital worker and bypassed the line of command. An officer is making a report; perhaps you should direct your concerns to him."

"One more thing," said Alec. "Was a man here with a walking stick late into the night?"

She looked startled. "That's odd. I heard an annoying tapping on the floor. I thought it was my imagination."

"We're going to Montmartre. Can we give you a lift, Dylan?" Maxine offered.

"I'd prefer to track down the Duke. He won't be expecting to see me again so soon. I'll meet up with you at noon."

"Yes, the Les Deux Magots."

Parking his rental in the back alley, Alec limped to the apartment. In his efforts to access Dylan, he'd popped a few stitches, and blood seeped through his jeans. He did his best to conceal his wincing from the others.

Coming in, while Maxine was collecting the mail in the downstairs lobby, she encountered another tenant walking a pair of labrador retrievers.

"Bonjour! Are your dogs friendly?"

"Oui, to most people, however, someone was loitering near here the other night they took exception to. He took off toward the cathedral."

On the stairs, Maxine examined a thick manila envelope from the mailbox with a scratchy scrawl on the front: To the Detectives, Butte-Montmartre, tourist rental.

Bounding upstairs, she found Alec flaked on the sofa with an ice pack on his leg.

"Alec, Rawley's letter. It's here!"

"Read it to me."

Inside the envelope was a letter and a wool hat sealed in a plastic bag. Another piece of evidence fell onto the couch.

Maxine bent down to retrieve it.

To the gendarmerie detectives, Montmartre;

My name is Rawley Baker. I witnessed Kace Chastain dumping his landlord's body in the Seine on the night of June 2nd. Kace fought with Monsieur Severini and bashed him repeatedly until his face was gone. It was over the silver belt buckle that he stole at Apollo Hall in the Louvre seven years ago. He pretended to be a window washer at the Louvre that day.

After the burglary, I recovered one of the masks they used. These days DNA testing might confirm the person who wore it.

Kace and I were not friends, but I overheard him meeting with a short fellow, Tony, who works at the museum. He bragged they deceived the insurance company and could do it again with other Napoleon artifacts at the military museum. If you find the belt, its silver belt buckle has a hidden compartment with a folded map.

Another thing. There's something odd about the car accident on the Louvre night. There were two of them— twins—they made a switch.

I told Kace I'd taken precautions, and he still threatened to kill me. The next day he met with the same man on the bridge and waved a copy of an old diary in his face.

Whatever they are up to will come about at the Royal Lodge night, when Tony dresses as Napoleon.

Kace thinks I'm a fool and unaware, but I have a university degree and know what I saw. Check at the Saint Germaine bus depot, Locker 24. Don't let him get away with thieving and murder.

Rawley

"Andre can get a warrant for the locker, and we'll go there after Les Deux Magots," said Alec.

He radioed the others. Maxine replied, relaying her conversation with the Napoleon editor and her suspicion of a phony sword story.

"Excellent, Maxine," said Andre. "We'll do a background search on this Ratcliffe fellow."

"I visited Odilette at the Eiffel Tower shop," she said. "Our conversation mentioned twins, and that tweaks an idea raised in Rawley's confession that there were identical twins in the car accident. Why would Odilette call Remy, addressing him as Antoine, and question his health with such concern?"

"That puzzles me too," said Andre.

"This has become a masquerade of deception," said Alec. "On the museum's wall of employees, Antoine's photo is similar to the man we know. But it's an old picture, and with twins, it would be impossible to tell differences if they are identical."

"Good theory!" said Andre. "Maxine, let me know what you uncover. I'll have the department pull up old signatures for matches."

Dylan was determined to even the score with Wellesley and Chastain. He plotted revenge as he watched the townhouse near the Arc de Triomphe from across the street. The curtains were drawn on the main floor, but the outline of movement could be seen through the sheer panels.

A late-model black sedan was parked at the curb with a prominent crest imprinted on the front door, representing an institution of sorts.

Dylan saw that the audio bug he'd placed was still at the townhouse window. Staying low, he crept up beside the vehicle -- it was empty.

He slipped a tracking device under the driver's front tire rim and sent the coordinates to Andre. Settling back, he listened on his earpiece to the men in the townhouse. Adjusting the audio levels, he could discern Wellesley and Coulliere talking.

"Are you certain he didn't see your face, Lawrence?"

"He didn't have a clue until the last second, snapped Wellesley. "I used a chloroform rag, but if I'd had my stiletto with me, he'd be a goner. I bound his hands and feet and tossed him into the manhole where it's unlikely he could get out in his condition."

"Can we still rely on Kace to play his part at the gala?" Antoine asked. "He's erratic and unpredictable. I don't even want to know if he had anything to do with the fellow on the bridge. He was ranting and gloating, for my reaction. Besides the fellow is dead now. But the gendarmerie is not easily fooled."

"We can outsmart them!"

"They're pressing for certificates to authenticate the sword and the diaries," Antoine said. "They're asking too many questions. Can you arrange for some forgeries?"

"Antoine, do you doubt my expertise?"

"A magazine editor called me about the Elba story and the Marshal Ney dueling sword. He's insistent that I give sources."

Lawrence pushed more. "Why now. That article was years ago? Who is asking about that?"

"Someone made a freedom of information inquiry, and the professor has to reply. Will he cover for us?"

"I have old contacts through the universities; I'll produce something to satisfy him. The Ney letter is solid; the precedent is the insurance company's validation. They won't challenge that. Ratcliffe has to use his backbone at the university and play his part."

Antoine continued to persist to the annoyance of his counterpart. "And the insurance certificate for the Louvre theft, what did you use? Is Rodriguez still in your pocket?"

Wellesley huffed with bored irritation at Coulliere's fretting. "Relax, I'll take care of it. Just tend to your responsibilities and leave mine to me. I'll protect my sources for everyone's benefit."

Antoine's right eye showed a nervous twitch. "I can't afford to be blindsided at the museum. It wasn't easy getting Interpol to put an agent onside, and convincing them I was under imminent threat. I have video logs of every meeting."

"Are you sure he's working alone and will perform as anticipated? We need him to defend Napoleon in front of the public and press at the Royal Lodge. The failure to retrieve the artifact will fall squarely on Interpol, and the insurance company won't challenge that. I wouldn't tolerate this slip if I didn't feel indebted to Odilette.

"Lawrence, you mucked that up when you whacked the Moreland agent. Where is he now?"

"I assure you, Antoine, he didn't see me . . . but he needed a warning to back off. He'll survive with a miserable headache."

The squatty man mustered a pretense of authority. "I'm the point man in this scheme, so next time check with me before you go off rash and impulsive again."

At that, the Duke leered with disdain. Then almost in silence, he said, "Remember who *you* are, *Antoine*! It would be easy enough to remove your existence and reveal the switch. You'd lose everything."

Dylan seethed as he listened and sent the feed to Andre at headquarters. "We need to talk. I'm ready to expose the rat and end this caper."

"I understand how you feel, Dylan. A significant amount of money is at stake in the big picture, even considering past thefts from other museums. We'll bring the perpetrators to justice with a trap for the kingpin and his puppets."

"Do we know more yet about Rawley's death?"

"Alec will visit the morgue today for cause of death. Someone was determined to ensure Rawley wouldn't talk. The letter he sent to the Campbells confirms that. We all agree that guilt is directed toward Kace Chastain."

"There's activity here now; the men are leaving the townhouse," Dylan whispered. "Wait! Chastain is on the street, watching the townhouse too. I'll be a few minutes late at Les Deux Marots restaurant."

As Kace moseyed along the promenade from down the block, his eyes set on the familiar black sedan parked curbside. Dylan rolled down behind a nearby boxwood hedge to conceal himself.

Wellesley and Coulliere got in the car, and as Antoine turned over the engine, Kace quickened to a run, intending to intercept the pair.

Dylan snapped a photo of the license plate while maintaining his cover. Aware that Chastain had spotted him, he looped Maxine's twine to the townhouse downspout and scaled to the upper sills out of sight on the roofline.

With the car in the distance, Kace paced erratically, befuddled about Dylan's sudden disappearance. Angered by the escape, his voice echoed into the alley.

"Don't think I won't level the score with you. I know you're the Interpol agent. There isn't a rock anywhere to hide under." His unpredictable rage spewed, forgetting that he was standing exposed on the street and drawing onlookers.

With a search warrant, Alec and Maxine accessed Locker 24, but security had emptied it as locker fees hadn't been paid. In return for the overdue fines, they received a large brown envelope tagged as abandoned.

Maxine slit the end. "A cellophane bag with a balaclava! It must be the mask that Rawley took after the Louvre robbery. I wonder who the DNA will implicate."

Alec studied the contents and called Andre.

FOURTEEN

Exposed Conspirators

After their morning discoveries, the foursome left their city quadrants to meet at Les Deux Magots.

Arriving first, Andre settled at an outdoor bistro table under an umbrella with the Le Monde newspaper in his hand. Seeing the others coming, he folded the paper and held it in the air.

Alec and Maxine saw the warning from the boulevard. "Wait," she said. "What does that mean? Someone followed him."

"The only one who knows of Andre's connection is Coulliere because of his original plea. But he has nothing to gain by tailing Interpol. He needs them to substantiate his ruse," said Alec.

Maxine wrapped her arms around her husband to display the pretense of a halted romantic walk and whispered in his ear.

"Dylan is almost here. I can see him, but something is very wrong."

Andre didn't look toward his agents but slipped away from the patio table, tossing the newspaper into a trash bin, and exited by the sidewalk. Without a glance at the others, he was gone.

Seconds later a man in janitor's overalls retrieved the bin's contents, including Le Monde. He dumped it into a garbage van, and it was quickly gone.

"It's too late, Maxine. There'd be a message for us in that newspaper."

"I feel like I've been left standing on center stage with the curtain up. What's going on, Alec?"

Andre's static message crackled through the ear monitors from the corner as he hailed a taxi. "An older gentleman in a herringbone cap is across the street. Maxine, do you recognize him?"

Dylan said, "I see him, yes. But also, someone else is watching that same man from the other corner. He is from the Arc de Triomphe townhouse and could be the one who clocked me last night."

Maxine squinted, still tight in Alec's embrace. "The tall one is the man from the Royal Lodge palace. Yes, that is the Duke."

Dylan winced at the dignified description. "He's not a Duke, Maxine. He's Lawrence Wellesley, one of Coulliere's accomplices."

"But that isn't all. The second man is familiar as well."

She studied the shorter one, astounded that it was the costume shop's rotund manager. Although he behaved nervously, Maxine was sure he hadn't seen or recognized her.

"That's Percival Sloane . . . so he did put a tracker on me to the palace tour. What could he expect to find by doing that?"

Andre said, "Alec, as you haven't been exposed to the plotters, can you pick up the tail? Dylan, you and Maxine need to become incognito fast. Could we all meet at your loft tonight as this effort has been blown?"

"Eight o'clock," said Maxine. "If there are problems, go from the fire escape to the second floor. I'll leave the emergency exit unlocked."

Before releasing their embrace, Alec kissed Maxine. She closed her eyes to enjoy the moment. Behind a crowd of pedestrians, they slinked toward the boulevard.

Watching from the door of a coffee roastery, Alec focused his sound recruiter on Wellesley and Sloane as they commiserated.

Sloane's scowl couldn't be mistaken. "Why did you need to see me? We agreed our contact would be minimal and discreet!"

The older man dismissed Sloan's concerns with a huff and began firing questions. "Did the detective woman return for her costume fitting?"

"Not yet, and no, I haven't talked to or met the other one."

"Sloane, you are in this deep enough. It's your responsibility to ensure the costumes are distributed and identified according to our agreement. You must be on top of this without my asking."

"I listened to you as a favor to Hollande. My costume business depends on being in the good grace of the event coordinator. I have no interest in your elaborate Napoleon ruse at the Royal Lodge."

Wellesley, jaw angrily clenched, peered deviously over his monocle. "Look here, Sloane, no one backs out of a pact with the Vendemiaire. Be assured I have a long and vengeful memory."

"You're a fool to think this is politics. It's pure greed, and as you've gotten old, my friend, you can only look forward to the thrill of danger. The Vendemiaire were heroes and patriots, not thieves; how dare you lop yourself among them?"

Wellesley's face flushed with rage. "Of course, Sloane, you realize you're disposable, merely a cog in the wheel that can be replaced."

The stubby man recoiled at the threat and regretted his verbal attack. He felt small and insignificant as he looked up at the man's threatening eyes.

Scorn was on Wellesley's lips. His eyes bulged as his face reddened, but with a deep sigh, he composed himself.

"Do you honestly believe your costume shop exists because you are a promising entrepreneur? You naïve little man. You have no choice in this matter?"

The impact of Wellesley's words sent Sloane reeling in fear. Aware of his vulnerability, his eyes darted to his surroundings, looking for a way to escape.

Alec waited for the right moment to intercede. As he had never previously confronted Wellesley or Sloane, he assumed an innocent façade and barged along the sidewalk toward the two men.

Looking down on the pretense of an incoming text, he tripped within a few feet of Sloane, staggering into their path.

"Excuse me; I'm so sorry."

Alec reached toward the stocky man for support to prevent a fall and dropped a burner phone into his pocket. He whispered in Sloane's ear. "Pocket rescue." Alec winked to indicate he had arrived as a reinforcement, not a threat.

The startling affront puzzled Sloane but eased him into an instant realization of assistance. "By all means, monsieur, I shouldn't have blocked the sidewalk. I trust you did not twist your ankle."

"I'm quite alright," Alec said as he continued down the sidewalk.

Sloane turned back to Wellesley, realizing he was now facing a dreadful predicament. "I have a new understanding of my situation, Lawrence. I'll do my best to righten my perspective. I apologize for creating undue concern."

"Hmph . . . get your ducks in a row, Sloane. I'll find you tomorrow at high noon."

Wellesley sped away in a rusty, pale blue Citroen, leaving Sloane aghast on the boulevard.

Alec paid for a newspaper at the smoke shop on the corner, then returned to Les Deux Magots, laying the Le Monde folded on the patio table.

Sloane looked for any sign of Alec, then felt for the new weight in his pocket. As he retrieved the phone, Alec rang.

"Monsieur Sloane, I'm an Interpol agent, and you are in danger. If you cooperate, we are willing to arrange protection. I doubt you're aware there have been two murders in recent weeks tied to your accomplice Lawrence Wellesley. Your defiance of him today puts you next on the list."

Sloane was sweating with fear. "How do you know? What do I need to do?"

"Take extra measures that you're not followed and make your way to the Montpellier Tower in the 8th arrondissement. I'm texting a picture of a card. Give it to Monsieur Langdon, the head concierge, and he will take you to someone who will help you."

"I'm in a trap," said Sloane. "I don't see my way out."

"You only have two choices, Monsieur Sloane—take a chance on me or fall prey to Wellesley. Frankly, it comes down to a matter of life and death."

Kace let himself in through the rear security door using his private key, startling Coulliere in the back hall. Cocky and arrogant, he enjoyed taking liberties in the museum.

At Andre's request, Dylan arrived simultaneously. Casing the back alley, he watched Kace turn the corner and enter the museum.

"What are you doing here?" Antoine gasped. "Kace, you can't come and go as you please. You're putting us both in jeopardy."

"We need to chat."

The unexpected intrusion flustered Coulliere. He had become calculating, always anticipating who he'd meet and what outcome he expected.

"I hadn't planned to have a meeting with you, Kace. I hold a position of responsibility here at the museum, and we function at a level of security. I can't have you popping in at will. It would be disastrous if my peers drew speculation toward the clients I entertain.

Kace was put off by the admonishment but remained cheeky. "Since I am taking the bigger risk, I assumed we were equal partners. Would you prefer that I wear a suit?"

Coulliere led Kace to his office and opened a computer monitor where outside cameras recorded on split screens. He cut the feed to prohibit Chastain from seeing it.

"Why were you at Wellesley's today?" Kace raised a fist to demand an answer. "I saw you drive away."

"If you must know, I've been pressured to provide insurance certificates and authenticity for the sword. You know that Wellesley is the expert in that field. His manipulation is pivotal to our success. This whole fiasco is bringing unwanted attention."

Kace sagged into a chair opposite Antoine. He put his feet up on his desk.

Coulliere glared at the dirty boots propped against his workspace. "I see you don't have any boundaries of respect for another's place of business," he snapped.

"What has made you so edgy, Tony?"

Coulliere's phone lit up with an incoming call. Seeing the caller ID, he raised his hand to caution Kace into silence then pointed to a closet door.

"Hello, Monsieur Moreland. I didn't expect to hear from you again so soon. Has there been a development?"

"I've been following up on the history of the silver sword, and I have some queries. I'm near Les Invalides and wondered if I might have a few minutes of your time," said Dylan, knowing Chastain was there.

"I'd be happy to accommodate you; however, I'm on the brink of a meeting. Can we schedule for tomorrow?"

"When do you open in the morning?"

"Come at nine. I look forward to meeting with you then.

Across town, Wellesley parked outside a dilapidated office building with a walk-up to a third-floor office. Alec watched from a taxi behind as he changed clothes from his plaid subway shirt and dirty flat cap.

He loitered with a group on the sidewalk, then followed Wellesley into the stairwell, easing back in the landing when the Duke arrived on the third level.

"He doesn't need the walking stick for any support; he is sprinting along quite well," Alec noted to himself.

'Security Investigations' was imprinted on the door. Wellesley entered without knocking and scrunched his nose at the worn carpet and grime of the décor. Alec listened from the hallway.

A puzzled gumshoe looked up from his desk, with a cigarette dangling from his mouth. "Larry, what brings you to this part of town?"

"Good gracious, Brooks, don't you ever take a shower and air out your office?"

The investigator laughed, taking no offense to the remarks of his hygiene.

"I wasn't expecting a client of your caliber to walk through my door. We don't get many paying customers willing to climb the staircase."

Wellesley dropped an envelope on the investigator's desk. Brooks thumbed through the cash and assessed it as substantial enough for his attention.

"Is this to appease the editor, or do you need something else?"

"My friend at the military museum is being pressured to authenticate the Napoleon sword. Do your forgery magic and make it good!"

"That'll be no problem!"

The surly man rifled through a half-opened filing cabinet and brought out a sealed envelope. "It's odd that you've come this morning as I had a call from Bordeaux asking for the same thing."

Wellesley's brow raised in surprise. "What did you tell him?"

"He thought I was the investigating agent for the archives, and I convinced him that we had solid verification. I used insurance talk jargon and had him in circles." Brooks laughed at himself. "I searched a Sotheby's auction listing recently, and the price for Napoleonic artifacts has risen substantially. Let's hope the insurance fellow you use doesn't surface again."

"Did that appease his curiosity?" said Wellesley.

"I'm on my way out of town to take care of that. Funny you should ask that, but I don't think so. He sounded nervous and edgy. You might consider sending someone to Bordeaux to chat with the editor."

Wellesley left the detective's office with a weight on his shoulders. In the hall, he paused and glared both ways as if something wasn't right.

Alec slipped out through the fire exit to the alley. He waited to watch Wellesley get into a taxi.

FIFTEEN

The Real Antoine

Late in the afternoon, Maxine scurried up the cobbled streets from the metro to the Montmartre market for the evening meal's ingredients.

"With at least three men, it has to be hearty," she reminded herself. On her phone, she read the list for cheesy potato tartiflette: lardon, cured meats, and cheese for a charcuterie board. She added gherkins, pickled onions, and sweet mustard at the deli. Then she dialed Alec.

"If you're on schedule, can you pick up baguettes?"

"I'm on time. How about some wine and flowers too?"

"It's casual, but both if you can."

With the tureen in the oven, she set the plank dining table and plopped onto the couch to thumb through the literature of King Louis' palaces. She closed her eyes and imagined the gala night's events, intrigued about the persona she'd portray, and envisioned her costume.

The shop's brochure and walking map described the event's timing, from the palace arrival to the dining halls and the masquerade in the Marble Hall.

"Transportation is available from key points. I'll talk to Andre about it, but I'd rather be in control to avoid sabotage. I assume he will attend in a professional capacity along with Interpol security.

"And what about Odilette? If Antoine Coulliere represents Napoleon, shouldn't she have a role? From talking with her, I don't believe she is blind to what is happening. However, she doesn't appear interested in Antoine's museum position."

She sat up, hearing the door at the bottom of the stairs. "Come in. I'm upstairs."

There was no voice or footsteps, and she froze. She counted one, two, three, four seconds of silence. "Someone is waiting!"

She reached for the fireplace poker and peered over the staircase wall, then sighed at the tweed fedora of the Interpol director.

"Andre, you can come on up!"

"I'm sorry I let myself in, Maxine. I didn't mean to be presumptuous."

"I'll confess you gave me a moment of concern. I expected Alec would be here by now."

"I brought us a bottle of wine. Dinner smells terrific!"

"I appreciate a compliment, Andre. Please pour us a glass while we wait for the others."

Minutes later, Alec and Dylan arrived, comparing notes of the day. Alec embraced Maxine and took time for a passionate kiss. Dylan directed a smile to her and laid the baguettes on the kitchen counter.

"Bonsoir, sorry we have been delayed."

Andre's eyes wandered to the large opened envelope on the counter. "Locker 24, it says. Is that Rawley's evidence?"

"Yes, it's wrapped in cello, so it hasn't been contaminated."

Andre examined it through the plastic. "I'll send it to

forensics in the morning. I suspect it contains damaging evidence on Chastain or Wellesley. They're a cocky bunch, climbing up the Louvre scaffolding, boldly breaking the windows, and conking the guards."

"And the Coullieres," Alec added.

"If the Coulliere twins were both at the robbery, one would have been the inside man with the plans and security access to make a quick exit."

Maxine removed the oven's bubbling casserole. "Alec, can you lay the trivets? The rest can take a seat as the food is ready."

Over dinner, Dylan recounted the townhouse conversation between Wellesley and Coulliere and their incriminating scheme to defraud the museum.

"Kace has eyes in the back of his head, and he's paranoid about being tailed. I scaled myself out of the alley, but he was on to me. But I followed him to the museum where he met with Antoine."

"How did you listen in?" asked Andre.

"Coulliere was wearing the jacket where Alec placed the bug, so I heard it all."

"Here's to our success, folks," said Alec, with his glass in the air for a toast.

"Not yet," said Andre. "We'll celebrate when we've caught them."

"Are we going to let this all play out?" asked Alec. "Will we wait for the Gala, or do we pick them off now?"

"This isn't up for a vote," said Andre. "Interpol wants to bring the network down for its past crimes as much as this one. The thefts have been worldwide, and we don't know how extensive their cons or robberies are."

"DNA results should lead to the old crimes, too," said Alec. "Surely evidence remains on file from seven years ago."

"Here's a theory," said Max. "Is it safe to rule out that

Coulliere's daughters are not truly at risk of being kidnapped?"

"I agree it's possible; the family doesn't behave like they're in danger," said Alec.

"That's bothered me," Max said. "When I met Odilette, she didn't seem unduly cautious."

"I am inclined to think she is not involved," Andre said, "but that's only a hunch. So, where do we stand?"

"I'll visit Sloane tomorrow," Alec said. "I'll recruit his confidence. He's scared silly of Wellesley and can identify all those involved in the VIP Gala ruse. I'll then put pressure on Hollande Bertolier. He has a long-standing relationship with the military museum and its board of directors."

Dylan took the last helping of the tartiflette and sopped the remains with a baguette. Swallowing, he looked at Maxine sheepishly, for helping himself to the rest. "My morning appointment is with Coulliere to retrieve the validation documents. We'll see what Wellesley has provided. I might need a warrant, Andre, to get the diaries."

"You've got it, Dylan."

"The shoddy private detective that Wellesley visited today talked about an insurance scam," said Alec. "Perhaps it's someone on the Duke's payroll."

"Try to get more from the guy, if you can," said Andre.

"I'll visit, on the pretense of the article, that I'm rechecking my sources," Alec said. "I should be inconspicuous as Wellesley said he was heading out of town."

"Be careful of a walking stick on your trail," said Andre, rising with his plate. "Now, Maxine, I insist on clearing the table."

"Thank you; I won't object. I'll put together some Chantilly strawberry crêpes. They're Alec's favorites, with crème fraîche."

Andre was exhausted from a night of research and unsettled emotions. On his third morning coffee, he found a missing person's report of foul play in Bordeaux.

The distinguished journalism professor and editor of the long-established Historical Review, Monsieur Roland Ratcliffe, was struck and killed in a hit-and-run accident on the Boulevard Joliot Curie bridge over the Garonne in Bordeaux.

Witnesses claim that a black sedan chased him down, and he flew through the air with little chance of survival.

Professor Ratcliffe was known for his passion of Napoleonic history. He widely contributed to articles covering the French Revolution, the House of Bourbon's demise, and King Louis XVI's death.

He dialed quickly.

"I'm an agent, Andre Poulin, representing Interpol's Paris office. I wish to speak with your Bordeaux investigating agent for details of the automobile involved in the vehicular homicide of Professor Ratcliffe."

Andre waited for several minutes for an officer to come on the line. "I'm sorry, my friend. As the accident was after dusk, no one could decipher the license plate. It was a late-model, black sedan with a crest on the driver's front door. In our thorough investigation, we'll consider if there is any reason he may have been a target," the agent advised. "May I ask why your Paris bureau is interested in this case?"

Andre hesitated. "A friend of mine mentioned an article by Roland Ratcliffe, and the name twigged my attention. Please let me know if you receive further clues regarding the driver."

"Certainly, Monsieur Poulin. If you have any other reason to be concerned, I'd appreciate your sharing it."

After the call, Andre thumbed through the events of the evening before. There amongst Dylan's feed, was the photo of the crested sedan sitting in front of the townhouse at the Arc de Triomphe. He dispatched a copy to the investigating officer and hoped for a reply. He then called Max.

"Maxine, I'm afraid our editor source, Roland Ratcliffe, has been murdered. We'll back off on your follow-up, it's too dangerous with this development."

Andre elaborated on the hit and run, and although Wellesley's name wasn't raised, he and Maxine were of the same thought.

"I won't let this Ratcliffe matter go, Andre," she said. "I'm at the Montmartre loft, leaving now to follow Odilette today and see who she encounters. You know I can be resourceful."

"Indeed, you are."

"His article doesn't sit right with historical facts. History books have sundry accounts of Napoleon's battles and exile. Ratcliffe's was the *only* mention of the Ney sword."

"You have my blessing, but please be careful."

"As this is the second auto tragedy tied to Coulliere, I'll check every angle."

"Maxine, you know these people won't hesitate to eliminate any threat . . . including yourself."

"I can handle myself, Andre. As a detective's wife, I've been evasive for seven years, and today won't change that."

"I don't underestimate you, Max."

"I'll stay in contact with the earpiece, and behave like a tourist taking in the sights."

Dylan arrived early at Les Invalides for his nine o'clock meeting with Coulliere. He used his credentials to pass by the front entrance security unannounced.

Antoine appeared haggard and jittery when Dylan opened his office door. He jumped to his feet, startled.

"Hello, Antoine! You seem surprised. Did you forget I was

coming?"

Coulliere quickly shuffled some papers and stuffed a file into his top drawer. He gestured to an armchair.

"Of course not, Monsieur Moreland. Please take a seat. I'm sorry, but I have an urgent call."

He grabbed his phone and punched in a number, anxious for his party to pick it up.

"I need those documents, we discussed, emailed immediately. You assured me they would be here this morning. It's simple to ask your insurance company for the certificates."

An angry exchange of profanity spilled out from the other end. Hearing it from where he sat, Dylan knew which party was in control.

Coulliere's face was red with embarrassment. He turned away from Dylan to continue. "Yes, for the Napoleon sword given to Marshal Ney. The one here on exhibit."

He slammed the phone back onto his desk with exasperation, and Dylan rose.

"It seems, Monsieur Coulliere, that you're not fully in charge. Is there someone else I should see?"

Coulliere stammered, but Dylan hit him with a more challenging question before he could get out a word.

"Why did you contact Interpol to be a party to your insurance ruse?"

The man lowered himself back into his chair, sweating, and loosened his tie. "Please sit down, Monsieur Moreland."

"Let me caution you, Coulliere, you've asked for help from Interpol; we're not clock-in detectives. We have access to more intelligence than you and your cronies can imagine. Don't say something you'll regret. The contrived scheme you are in the midst of is beginning to fall apart."

Antoine couldn't control his chronic habit under pressure. In his angst, he clicked repeatedly on a ballpoint pen and rifled blindly through a clutter of papers on his desk.

Dylan watched and waited in silence for Coulliere to break. After a few minutes, he paced the office and stopped at the diplomas and photographs on the wall and the credenza.

Picking up a framed photo from the back, Dylan examined a group posing together at a museum exhibit. Two men in the foreground held an impressive sword, but it was the tall man watching in the background that drew his scrutiny.

"Who are these people, and when was this taken?" Dylan demanded.

Antoine put his elbows on his desk and leaned forward, letting his head collapse into his hands.

"You don't understand the power that man wields."

"It's best you tell us now, Antoine. If we need to take you in for questioning, you will bring undue notice of your bending loyalty. You might as well know that Interpol is listening in on our conversation."

"I don't care anymore about what happens to me, but please see that my family is spared," Antoine pleaded. "A man approached me many years ago with a proposition to get rich. He was cordial and persuasive, and it sounded harmless enough. Then, as I learned more, it was too late."

"Is that man in this photo?"

"Yes, the one in the back. He calls himself the Duke, but truthfully, he is Jacques Guilliard. He brought me Marshal Ney's diary and convinced me of its authenticity. I knew plenty about Napoleon's exile, and the details seemed factual, so I went along. He arranged for the fabrication of historical details. He boasted of having connections in the right places. I was under great pressure and confided in my brother."

Maxine checked the opening hours for the Eiffel souvenir shop and deduced that Odilette Coulliere would not depart her residence before her daughters left for school.

Instead, she took up a position in a park across the road to observe the Marais residence through a telephoto lens. She was in plenty of time as the school bus wouldn't arrive for another forty-five minutes.

Maxine noted that a ramp ran up the house's side, connected to a veranda. An employee dressed as a nurse or a maid opened the side door. At first, Maxine thought she was pushing a pram, but it was a wheelchair.

Seconds later, Odilette followed and took charge of the wheelchair. The occupant seemed frail. Odilette took great care to tuck a throw over the victim's lap, then patiently stroked the person's head before securing a beret. She seemed a bit on edge and took a careful glance at her surroundings.

Snapping a series of photos, Maxine was intrigued. "I wonder if it's a young child, an aging parent, or perhaps an invalid. I didn't see any clues in Andre's background file."

Odilette gingerly eased the wheelchair along the boulevard sidewalk and crossed at the corner to a manicured park that meandered along an artificial creek. It appeared to be a popular walk for mothers or nannies pushing prams, with public benches and gliding swings.

Maxine pulled a gray cloche over her ears and wrapped a plaid scarf under her chin. Catching up to a short distance from Odilette, she pretended to be photographing birds as she neared the wheelchair.

Timing her approach, Maxine waited for a pair of prams to pass, allowing her to get close to peer at the wheelchair's occupant.

Trying not to reveal her shock, Maxine looked into the frail, wan face of the real Antoine Coulliere. His eyes were gray and vacant, and he appeared to mumble incoherently the moment he spied her.

Keeping her pace, Maxine heard Odilette as she bent over

the patient.

"Are you alright, dearest? Remy promised to come tonight just like he always does. It's a lovely day for a walk, isn't it?"

A broken voice stuttered over scant words, "Yes, he must be with Napoleon today." It followed with the slightest of laughs.

Within a few minutes, the wheelchair returned to the veranda, and the two daughters bounded out to kiss the occupant before boarding their bus.

"Goodbye, Papa!"

Dylan was still at the military museum when Maxine revealed her discovery on the earpiece.

"Big development," she said. "I suspect Coulliere at the museum is the twin brother, Remy. The feeble one at the house is Antoine. I heard Odilette telling him about Remy."

"This matches Rawley's letter that there was an identity switch between the twins during the accident after the Louvre burglary?"

"Certainly looks like that."

"Dylan is with Couliere right now, Maxine. At the police department near Les Invalides, we've requested the original auto report and medicals from their archives. Seven years ago, the night of the heist."

Maxine hopped onto the metro line toward the Louvre and entered the gendarmerie station. She stood in the main entry observing, then decided on the most pleasant-looking clerk behind the desk, but her request was met with disgruntled resistance.

"I'm sorry, madame, but the investigating officer is unavailable, and the detective assigned retired a few years ago. Do you realize the case is seven years old? It's in closed storage, and we usually require advance notice to bring up those files."

Maxine quickly produced her detective's authorization credentials that Andre had provided and demanded the file based on the Public Records Freedom of Information Act. Seeing another hesitation, she said, "Perhaps you would like to call Interpol to verify our position?"

In resignation, but tweaked interest, the clerk said, "Wait here; I'll have to get authorization."

Maxine waited an hour on a long, hard bench in the outer hall until a flat-footed officer approached with a tied file under his arm. He surveyed the room and decided on Maxine as she was the only one left.

"Madame Campbell, please come with me. You may view the file in an interview room. I'm Detective Dubois. I was a rookie on the case at the time of the accident along with Detective Moreland."

Maxine controlled her gasp at the introduction. She sighed at the encouraging sign of cooperation and feigned some helplessness. "Thank you, Detective; I hope you can help me."

Dubois sat across the table as Maxine examined the initial on-scene report and the photos of a mangled wreck.

"Two different victims had the surname Coulliere," he said.

Maxine looked up. "The report says the driver was extracted in an unconscious condition. Who identified the driver?"

"You are exactly correct to ask that, Madame Campbell. My thinking was along that line as well. But my superiors discouraged me from pursuing DNA testing."

He lowered his head in his nervousness, and his voice softened. "You see, that was the same night as the extraordinary heist at the Louvre. It usurped the attention of the gendarmerie, and they paid little attention to the car accident. My instincts, however, told me that there was a connection."

"I'm aware that the Coulliere brothers are identical twins. How did you deduce that Remy Coulliere was the driver and Antoine, the passenger?"

Dubois raised his brow and shook his head. "I was a rookie, and my hands were tied. Be assured the conversation that we are having is not possible. My partner said he looked into the passenger's eyes. He was in a state of fear and told my soul the truth. I cannot say more without putting my career in jeopardy. Sometimes justice is not rewarded by evidence."

Maxine snapped photos of the documents and witness statements as Dubois waited patiently.

"I'm grateful for your openness, Detective. You see, I met one of the victims this morning, which left me with an unexplained curiosity about who he truly was. I'll not mention our discussion. However, I agree with your implication that there is a cover-up here."

"Be careful, madame."

"I will, Detective. I hope you won't mind if I call again if I uncover further information. Perhaps, the old rookie might soon resolve an old cold case. That would be a feather in your cap, wouldn't it, Detective Dubois."

The reality of the conversation found its place, and he nodded.

"Detective Moreland can be found on assignment with an Interpol unit nearby. He will be able to provide further insight."

"Thank you, I'll follow up with that."

SIXTEEN

Discovery

Alec sat in an interview office of the gendarmerie's homicide unit near the American Hospital. His inquiries brought him under suspicion and led to him giving a detailed witness and background statement about the bridge incident.

"I'm familiar with the covert discipline and identify with imminent danger. When the victim, Rawley Baker, contacted us for assistance, we were in the area waiting for the meeting. He feared for his life. Using binoculars, I observed him being accosted on the bridge and went to help."

The Inspector asked, "Did you recognize the attacker?"

"No, but I could see that Baker was violently stabbed and in distress as he tried to get away."

Alec was reluctant to give the name of Kace Chastain without Interpol's approval. "It's my understanding that Rawley didn't die of the stab wounds but was murdered at the hospital by outside intervention. Since his death was by fentanyl overdose, no doubt security footage may also indicate there was a break-in to a medicine cabinet nearby."

Looking at Alec with doubt, the gendarmerie Inspector jotted some notes, then laid several photographs on the desk before him.

"That does appear to be the case. Do you recognize any of these men?"

Alec was surprised to see a black and white surveillance photo of Dylan Moreland chasing Chastain near the tenement several days prior.

"The scruffy fellow there." Alec pointed to Kace. "I believe he's the same one from the bridge. After I was treated for my wounds, I waited at the hospital as a precaution to ensure there was no outside intervention with the victim. It must have happened after I left. The hospital identified this man as a medical imposter in their video It's possible it was the same man exiting the medical supply room before he entered the victim's room. Soon after his vitals monitor alarm went off."

"That is so, Monsieur Campbell. We have an alert out for the arrest of the suspect using the name of Kace. The other man, have you seen him before? It will be necessary for you to come in to view the lineup when charges are laid. Otherwise, you are free to go."

Alec shook his head negatively regarding the second man he knew was Dylan.

He was near the door when he turned tentatively. "Inspector, may I suggest you contact my superior at Interpol."

"Interpol! This is a local matter."

Andre heard the plea on the earpiece, and within seconds the phone rang on the Inspector's desk.

A terse conversation ensued between Poulin and the gendarme officer while Alec waited. At the conclusion, the Inspector appeared frazzled but conciliatory.

"For now, I'll let your investigation proceed without interference. But I'd appreciate a follow-up within twenty-four hours, Monsieur."

Driving to the 8th arrondissement to see Percival Sloane, Alec dialed Andre.

"I'll meet Sloane, the costume boutique manager, at the Montpellier Tower. I've called ahead to arrange to use an office, quoting your authority. When Sloane leaves, he will need protection, until we're convinced he's not in danger."

"I anticipated that, Alec. We're tight for surveillance for this case, but we'll manage. The more I uncover about Wellesley, the more dangerous this becomes. He's capable of murder, and I expect we'll uncover other past crimes."

"Has Sloane's name come up in any investigations?" Alec paused in thought. "How do you want me to play this out?"

"I'll rely on your instincts. I wasn't aware of his involvement with the Royal Lodge Gala until Maxine exposed him. Sloane is the pathway to the entire ring whether he realizes it or not.

"First, we'll follow the crumbs to the Palace and break down their network and bribes. Sloane will be our guide."

"He's frightened of Wellesley right now and will be cooperative."

A short time later, from outside a coffee bar, Alec watched Sloane approach the office tower and ascend the metro stairs. He was nervous and kept glancing back over his shoulder. Alec called with a heads-up to Andre's agent who was ready and versed to conduct the interview.

The agent had built a good rapport with Andre's Interpol team and was agreeable to oblige with another investigation.

"Thanks for the cover. We don't want this witness to know too much about what we've discovered, but we need him as an informant."

"No problem, Alec; we'll keep it formal. Give my regards to Dylan."

Sloane anxiously entered the foyer and presented himself

to the concierge using the pre-assigned code 'Langdon.' He fidgeted nervously, waiting for an agent to stroll out of the elevator and greet him. Sloane hesitated when he first met the agent, but he soon relaxed once they exchanged handshakes.

Sloane was deposited in a windowless interview room, and deliberately left in isolation for twenty minutes. The room was austere other than an emergency list for fire evacuation. Sloane took one of the two chairs but soon began to pace.

Alec waited outside for the Interpol shadow to arrive. True to plan, he waved a folded Le Monde as he approached. Inside the fold was a disk with photos of the museum plot conspirators.

By the time Alec opened the door to the interview room, the costume manager was hyperventilating.

"Hello, Percival," he said. "I waited downstairs to be sure no one followed you here. Be assured, there wasn't any sign of a tail."

"Where exactly am I?"

"You're in a safe office. You can't be coerced to divulge information if you know fewer facts. Understand?"

Sloane nodded but persisted. "How do you know about me and my involvement? All I do is fill the costume requests from Hollande, and ensure the client is outfitted according to specifics. I give them a personalized itinerary that the Gala organizer coordinates."

Alec stared at him with no response then tossed a collage of photos on the table.

"How many of these people do you recognize?"

It was apparent he knew several, but he paused. "I presume you already know which ones I'm familiar with, including this one." Sloane pointed at Wellesley.

"You placed a bug in the handbag of the Duchess de Parma a few days ago. Who gave you that instruction?"

"He refers to himself as the Duke. He's been coming to my

shop for years. At first, he seemed harmless. But then he kept pressuring me to obtain information from clients that didn't seem right. His persona was intimidating and I complied."

"Why does your patron's list for August 15th show the Duke of Wellington's costume assigned to Jacques Guilliard?"

"I made a mistake; it should have been Arthur or Lawrence Wellesley."

Knowing Sloane was deceptive, Alec stopped and waited for Percival to relent with the truth.

"So, you know that Arthur Wellesley is a facetious name," said Sloane. "I used to be enthralled with the characters and knew each player's historical reference. The historic Duke of Wellington's original name was Arthur Wellesley, and Guilliard adopted that for theatrical purposes. He's adept at assuming other personalities."

Sloane looked away to avoid eye contact. "I met him seven years ago when an old acquaintance, Remy Coulliere, brought him into my shop with Monsieur Bertolier, the event man. Remy introduced the Duke as Jacques Guilliard on the first occasion."

"Is Remy Coulliere among the photos here?"

Sloane peered closely, hovering over Antoine.

"It was a few years ago, but this one could be Remy. He had a brother who was slighter and less confident whom I met once. It was sad when he was maimed so badly in the tragedy."

Sloane pointed, then threw his hands up in confusion.

"Percival, understand this. You'll carry a tracker at all times, and you will be followed. We'll contact you with sensitive assignments when you must assist us, for example, setting up surveillance. Otherwise, go about your life as usual. If you come across information we should know, sit at a patio table outside Les Deux Magots. It's near the location where I met you yesterday."

"I know the place."

"If you recall, the Duchess de Parma's ensemble was ordered from your store. She will return to collect the Duchess' costume and the uniform for Duke von Neipperg. Do *not* inform anyone of her visit, and remove any security footage."

Sloane nodded his understanding.

"The burner phone I gave you will be your only point of contact. When needed, we will find you."

Alec dismissed the informant but called him before he reached the door. "I see you wear a straw summer fedora when you are out. Here is a blue feather. If you are in danger or need to contact us, place the feather in the hatband, and we'll intercept."

Sloane was smug with renewed confidence that he had been deputized to a higher calling.

Andre and Dylan were privy to Alec and Sloane's interview and were not shocked to hear the confirmation about Remy Coulliere.

Dylan stepped into the hallway to call Andre. "I'm near Les Invalides and haven't concluded my meeting here. Antoine is getting ready to break--I've left him to contemplate his next move."

Hearing a background noise, he swung around to face Couliere inside.

"Was that your voice?" Dylan asked. "Were you talking to someone? You have a secret access door to this office, don't you?"

Couliere didn't answer but looked toward a closet.

Dylan pressed and challenged. "Is someone listening and waiting? I saw your eyes go to that door!"

"No one has used it for years. It's more than a closet; a trap door on the floor inside leads into a passageway."

"What's the reason for it?"

"It was installed fifty years ago by a security firm to escape if a robbery became a siege. We knew of a case in South America once, with the staff murdered. Such a door sould have spared them."

"Yes, in Sao Paulo decades ago. Who knows this passage is here?"

"Just me and my brother." Couliere paled, realizing he had spoken of the mysterious twin.

Dylan knelt in the closet and examined the unopened trap door. Muddy footprints suggested it had been used recently.

"Could your brother have told the Duke about this? I'm referring to the real Antoine Coulliere, Remy!"

"Mon Dieu! How did you know?"

"It was you, Remy, who was behind the wheel during the escape from the Louvre. When Antoine was thrown from the vehicle with devastating injuries, you seized the opportunity to assume his life. It must have been difficult to persuade Odilette to go along."

Coulliere's head hung in shame.

"You're a foolish man. Why did you risk your brother's reputation at the museum?"

"No one was supposed to get hurt. It's merely a public switch to claim the insurance."

"What did you expect to gain, permitting the Duke to orchestrate your future? You don't understand the network of thieves and conspirators walking daily in and out of your life."

"What better con than having Interpol as a participant?" Coulliere said. "It was foolproof."

"That is the scenario Wellesley portrayed for you. Are you aware that your acquaintance Rawley Baker has been murdered? And the professor from Bordeaux who wrote the Ney article? Dead too."

Remy's face couldn't cover up his lie. "I've never heard of

those names."

Dylan didn't intend to play all his cards. He stare at Coulliere long and intensely to make his squirm.

"I could lose everything," Coulliere moaned. "My job, my family, my brother, my reputation."

"Haven't you risked that already when you participated in the Louvre heist seven years ago!"

"What do you want from me?"

"The truth."

"Mon Dieu! I'm trapped in a vicious web. I don't see how you can help me get out of this. It's like a runaway train."

"See that your office door is locked and lead me into the passage," said Dylan.

The real Remy eased the trap door open and pulled a cord, lighting a bulb that swung overhead. The dungeon below smelled musty and ancient and was stacked with boxes and artifacts.

A metal spiral ladder led to a room with a desk, an army cot with a rotting mattress, and a wall of shelves with wooden boxes, books, and cobwebs. Over the desk was a bulletin board with an assortment of newspaper clippings.

"Who put these here?" Dylan asked.

Remy peered at the clippings while mustering a fabrication. "They are from the Louvre robbery. It was before I assumed my brother's position here."

Dylan picked some up. "Oh, I see. Several prolific crime stories are here, featuring escapes from La Santé Prison in Paris. I'll read from one. 'This man is a glorified version of a master of disguise who inhabited the prison and orchestrated crimes from inside. Eight years ago, he walked out into the night in janitorial overalls and into a maintenance truck. Despite months of searching, he was never located. He used a variety of aliases, but among them was Jacques Guilliard!"

"I don't recall that name," Remy objected.

"Of course you do, Remy. Inmates revealed him to be 'the Duke'!"

"My brother, Antoine, was always intimidated by him, but I don't know how or where they met. I had nothing to do with the Louvre until the night of the heist when I was ordered to be an escape driver. Have you ever looked him directly in the eye with contradiction? Wellesley threatened to kill us if I didn't comply."

"After the accident, Wellesley came to the hospital. Antoine was in bad shape, and he convinced me to claim to be my brother so I could assume his place at the museum. He was adamant and conniving--not ready to cut off his inside access. That's when I assumed the identity of Antoine."

"I'll seal this as evidence, and you'll need to come into Interpol and give your statement."

Remy's eyes were wild. "But Wellesley will know I am cooperating with you, and the finale is in jeopardy."

SEVENTEEN

The Plan

Hollande Bertolier watched from his office window for his appointment to arrive. Relishing this lofty feeling near the royal palace, he looked down upon employees as they bustled about the grounds.

His pious demeanor and slick, pomade gray hair presented an air of superiority, seasoned with a luxurious lifestyle. He was a heavy man with squared shoulders, accustomed to delegating instructions. Bloated by living in excess of fine food and wines at his leisure, his chest puffed out with conceit of his accomplishments.

The event was weeks away, but he thoroughly enjoyed the meticulous details and the pressure it created. Each day it became more apparent that Bertolier was the man of the hour. Newly hired staff treated him like King Louis, standing aside while he walked down the halls during inspections with his hand tucked into the royal sash as if he were Emperor.

The upcoming press release was on his mind, knowing it would attract the public's interest, mentioning the Napoleon sword from the military museum. Negotiations had been laborious, requiring security and armed guards' agreements to accompany Coulliere to the Royal Lodge.

Across the room in the corner of his office was a glassed, walled closet protecting a fully dressed mannequin of King Louis XVI in full regalia, the ultimate costume for the master of the Gala. It sparkled with esteem and exuded power rightful of the personage.

Hollande gloated and paraded before the royal portrait, puffing out his chest and holding a sideways stance to admire his physique.

"King of the Gala once again. This year will be even more fantastic, Louis! Let us reign over this palace forever."

Across the commons toward the palace entrance, lines of tourists queued for admission to tour the exotic gardens and the mystique of the wonders inside, some on foot from Gare Montparnasse, others from buses. His eyes settled on the distant horizon of the Eiffel Tower rising in magnificence.

The tall man in the herringbone cap was strolling at the end of a group of passengers disembarking from the exclusive VIP motorcoach. With a glint in his eye and a gait in his step, he twirled his light walking stick, letting it click rhythmically along the walkway. His arrogance and air of superiority caused others to step out of his way as he strode defiantly toward the palace entrance.

Hollande Bertolier pressed a button on his desk phone and spoke to a receptionist in the outer office.

"Solange, Monsieur Guilliard should be here momentarily. See him in directly and bring an excellent French brandy for a toast. He doesn't like to be kept waiting."

Hollande tuned to a brief muffle of voices, then heard the click of the silver-tipped walking cane. He knew that Wellesley particularly liked listening to that sound on the marble floors. He rose as his guest entered the sanctum of the Special Events

Coordinator.

"Come in, my friend; I've been expecting you."

"It's my pleasure, Monsieur Bertolier. The adrenaline is beginning to surge as if we are on the brink of charging onto the battlefield. I'm sure I would have enjoyed being the Duke of Wellington and coming face-to-face with the emperor. Nothing that compares to looking a formidable opponent in the eye and seeing fear then ultimate surrender."

Wellesley momentarily drifted to a fantasized vision of himself in command on the battlefield. He was drawn to an ancient painting on the wall of a victorious battle with the French flag raised on the knoll. Standing before it, he gloated as he folded his right arm behind his back. With his left, he tapped the silver stick.

"Yes, indeed, history never loses its thrill, and victory can never lose its luster."

Wellesley lowered himself into an impressive tapestry armchair and reached with familiarity for the cigar box on Bertolier's desk. His host arrived with the cutter and lit the tobacco.

Solange tapped on the door before entering with a silver tray, crystal decanter, and two crystal snifters. She was poised and prim in a formal navy dress suit, her striking black hair pinned in a French roll.

Setting the tray on the sideboard, she slid her hand deftly to the bottom of the tray, then disappeared. At her desk, she discreetly sent a one-word text to an office across Paris.

"Activated!"

Andre Poulin put aside his papers to listen in on the conversation in the sanctuary of Bertolier. Leaning closer, he propped his elbows on his desk and grinned with satisfaction at Solange's efficiency and success.

Hollande Bertolier loaded the glasses and extended a warm toast. "Do you ever listen to the sound of fine brandy being poured, Lawrence? It is something special. Let's make a toast to this occasion, to an extraordinary ball and the downfall of Napoleon."

Wellesley raised his glass with smug satisfaction. "Yes, to victory! A long-deserved, victorious celebration and a king's reward. After all, we owe our future to his love of fame and fortune."

"I wasn't expecting to hear from you until next week, Lawrence. Has there been a change in plans?"

"The manager at the costume boutique is getting edgy. It's time to put a little distance. I believe he's nervous and that makes him unpredictable. How deeply do you have your hooks into Sloane?"

"Percival? Very well. I've known him for years. His costumes are superb and he delivers exceptional service. Our clients return to him yearly; I see no reason to upset the apple cart. We've never had a problem, and he follows instructions to a T. He's a cog in the wheel with excellent instincts. He's never created a problem."

Hollande's protective defense of Sloane caused discomfort to Wellesley. He rose abruptly and strutted to the window to appease his irritation. "Perhaps I was not clear earlier with our outline for the VIP night. Timing and the presence of specific guests leave little room for variance. There will be a wealth of aristocracy, celebrities, and government officials. All of society will be envious of us on that night."

"I assure you we can handle any contingency."

"I have tried to spare you too many details for your own sake, but there will be witnesses of the highest caliber. I will integrate my people among your staff, and they will require clearance to secured areas."

Bertolier looked up inquisitively. "I'll need photo identification for those people. Do you have that with you?"

Wellesley produced an envelope and let it fall on the desk

for impact. Bertolier reached for it and placed it in his drawer without making a review, which irked Wellesley.

"I'll deal with that later."

"See that it gets your priority, Hollande."

"Lawrence, I don't need to remind you that the evening will include many government officials and politicians. The Gala's success will prove financially beneficial to the efforts of this palace and grounds. For months after such an important charitable event, I expect to receive gifts of gratitude and congratulations to earn a favor for my next organized event. I have such opportunities because I wield influence."

"Excellent," said Wellesley, but his curled lip and intonation showed his jealousy. "What is your concern?"

"A petty theft here and there is merely an embarrassment and can go under the carpet. When you alluded to the kidnapping ruse, I was ambivalent. But you assured me it was well-contrived and would not become an issue. Has something changed?"

"If you're worried about Monsieur Coulliere, I assure you he is a willing participant. The planned theatrics will be good for public relations, and you will be paid handsomely for your participation. After this is over, the public's interest will boost admissions and tourist traffic to the Royal Lodge, bringing media coverage without expense. Your audience will be on the edge of their seats with suspense and excitement!"

Hollande sat back to twiddle his thumbs over his chest. He gloated at his superiority while leering at this pathetic man before him. Yet the prize was within his grasp and he could not deny the Duke center stage.

Wellesley's face tightened. "I will require the key to access the Queen's private salon hideaway during the evening. It is essential."

"But that is closed up, and it takes more than a key to open it. I suggest an alternate area for temporary storage, the old guardhouse at the east gate."

"Timing, Monsieur Bertolier! Every minute is accounted for without deviations. Ensure the hideaway I require is accessible. If everything is not according to plan, you will answer to your superiors, the press, and Interpol."

Wellesley stopped and leered until Bertolier became uncomfortable.

"Come back on the eve of the Gala," Hollande said, rising to conclude the meeting. "I'll see you get the key then. Now if you'll excuse me, Wellesley, I must attend another meeting."

Bertolier leaned over his desk. He pressed a button on his phone, and Solange arrived promptly to dismiss his guest. She watched the two men enter the outer hall, then slipped back into the coordinator's sanctuary and removed the brandy tray and cigar stub evidence.

Placing an envelope in a folded Le Monde, she exited to the main floor and dropped it in a canister. Seconds later, the debris was cleared by a custodian in overalls and transported to the Interpol building across Paris.

EIGHTEEN

Rodriguez from Buenos Aires

Bertolier escorted Wellesley to the building exit. But instead of returning to his office, he deviated.

Hiring a private car, Bertolier was delivered to an exquisite boutique hotel near the Arc de Triomphe beside the American Embassy. His pompous demeanor had waned, but he remained confident that he would succeed in his ploy.

Wellesley's boasting of his ease of accessing artifacts enticed Bertolier to check out the demand for Napoleonic swords and buckles. If the Duke could deceive the museum, so could he as King Louis.

Ordering a double whiskey, he plumped himself down on a barstool and waited.

"Monsieur Bertolier?"

"Oui, how was your trip from Buenos Aires?"

"Very well, thank you."

Rodriguez was in his early forties, balding, with a bushy mustache and a stern demeanor. He took the next barstool and grumped to Bertolier.

"I want to get to business, please, as I have scheduled other appointments in Paris. And I made it clear to you earlier that we cannot be seen together."

Bertolier nodded, "Yes, yes, but here are the documents. Please review them, however I cannot permit you to take them. A camera photo will suffice."

"Yes, very well. Are you certain the item has been authenticated?"

Rodriguez remained uncomfortable and agitated while scanning the other patrons.

"Conclusively! The insurance company has declared it to be the original Napoleonic article. The museum has confirmed that."

"You are asking a great amount of money for an item that is relatively unknown on the collector's market, especially in Brazil. If you reduce your price by twenty-five percent, I will agree."

Bertolier was silent as he measured his move. "You've got me against a wall, monsieur. The Gala is coming up in a few days, and I have little time to court another buyer. However, I will agree."

"I will meet you at your office in the palace immediately after midnight during the festivities."

"Agreed. I will arrange for an entry pass for you at the gate." Bertolier sat back in his chair with the sigh of a successful transaction.

Rodriguez retreated without touching his drink. As he exited the hotel, two bodyguards appeared from the curb to escort him.

When Andre received the parcel at his desk, he requested the daily review with the team at Saint Germaine. "I'll reserve the Hemingway table for security," he messaged.

Troubled, he pored over the newspaper articles referenced from the Coulliere's museum cellar, then texted the palace informant, Solange.

"Dispatch a recovery team to Coulliere's office. Disguise them as a carpentry crew to work in the manager's area."

Maxine hiked downhill at a good clip toward the Abbesses Metro station, dodging the shuttle train up and down Montmartre. The street was still sleepy, and the shops shuttered. Every time she walked on the cobblestone streets she felt Parisian, with the sounds, the smells of the patisseries, roasting coffee, and the berets. The threats of being followed or getting too close never deterred her spirit.

She got off the subway at rue Bonaparte and strolled toward Boulevard Saint Germaine, with her sight on the distant, green canopy of Les Deux Magots restaurant.

The morning at the apartment was hurried for Alec and Maxine, as they were preoccupied with their missions.

She stopped across from the restaurant and dialed him.

"Alec, this pace has been crazy."

"It'll be over soon, babe."

"But what is happening to us? This case is all-consuming, and I'm spending as much time with Andre and Dylan as with my husband."

"Whatever's on Andre's plan, let's take tonight for ourselves with a quiet dinner out."

"I knew you'd say the right thing. There's a romantic restaurant at the base of the funicular. I'll make a reservation."

"How about eight o'clock? My phone is buzzing with another call, Max. I'll see you shortly."

He clicked on Dylan's incoming call. "Alec, I've left Les Invalides. But I've picked up a shadow. I can't go directly to our rendezvous. Can you intercept him at the Pont des Arts bridge?"

"Is it Chastain?"

"Likely, the old man wouldn't be able to keep up with my pace."

Andre overheard the banter. "Sloane's tail is inactive; I'll send him your way."

Chastain marched along boldly, congratulating himself on being invisible. He was overconfident tailing Dylan, not suspecting the pair of businessmen who stepped out from the café.

They walked, chatting, shoulder to shoulder with him, then pulled ahead. Blocking the sidewalk, one man turned to make room for Chastain to pass. Kace surged forward to dodge the pair when his elbow was grabbed.

"Mr. Chastain?" the agent asked.

Startled to hear his name, Kace barely felt the pinprick.

The agent radioed to Andre. "Chastain will rest on a park bench for an hour or so. He's become a persistent pest. We'll haul him into the drunk tank."

"I'll back off then, Andre, and meet you at Les Deux Magots," Alec replied.

Dylan arrived at the restaurant out of breath, the last to come. He smirked with satisfaction. "Chastain missed his bus and had to wait a while. It's done. And there's a bonus. The agent recovered an item Kace was clutching, and will drop it at the office."

Andre set aside the menu. "I've ordered wine and open-faced sandwiches with a cheeseboard. From listening to the earphones, we're all on the same page. Let's start with Maxine's tablet photos of the wheelchair occupant."

"The accident report from seven years ago, is here too," she said. "It's useful, Dylan, that you were at the scene as a rookie. The original report has been redacted, but your partner, Dubois' memory was exact about the identity switch."

"I practically got a confession at the museum today," said Dylan. "I was convinced the driver wouldn't survive the scene that night. If the gendarmerie tracked the vehicle to the heist, it would be easy to blame the victim. There's a saying that rings truth here, that dead men don't talk."

"It goes back further than that," said Andre. "Remy, under the guise of Antoine, was being investigated by the museum for embezzlement and the theft of artifacts. The brothers were in cahoots, Remy pressured Antoine to cooperate. Nothing was proven, but the Louvre heist brought fresh attention. The balaclava's DNA will provide insight."

"I'll get those results from forensics today," said Dylan. "But that won't halt the kidnapping and ransom situation at the Royal Lodge. Whichever Coulliere brother we are dealing with will wear the Napoleon costume, and bear the consequences. We don't need to solve the Louvre robbery unless one of the items is the silver sword from the exhibit."

"And the silver belt buckle," said Alec. "With Rawley's clues, we'd be overlooking crucial data if we didn't trace it. Where is it now?"

"Kace doesn't let the buckle out of his sight," said Dylan. "It is the first relic tied to Napoleon from the beginning. We hope it's the item your agent recovered on the park bench."

Andre nodded. "Stop at the Interpol office on your way back, Alec, and inspect the buckle. Match it with past thefts."

"What about Sloane?" asked Dylan.

"I've recruited him," said Alec. "He's scared and ready to help."

"We can use him in the next few days," said Andre. "There was an interesting meeting this morning between Bertolier and Wellesley. I have a disk of their conversation and plans, but it leaves much to the imagination. The only certainty revealed is that Wellesley requires a storage area at the Royal Lodge. Our inside agent will keep an eye on developments."

"If Sloane's confession is correct, we know who Lawrence Wellesley truly is," Maxine said. "An alias, at least, Jacques Guilliard."

"I'll rely on your intuition," said Andre. "As you're our main contact with Guilliard, could you resolve the identity puzzle? Dylan can enlighten you on the newspaper items."

"I can do that," she said. "First, I'll need to talk my way into the prison archives to have search access. The Duke is looking like a career criminal, as well as the kingpin to this whole debacle."

"Be careful, Max," said Alec. "You're always ready to face danger head-on, but be careful not to step on snakes."

"I'll see that you get a protection kit to defend yourself," said Andre. "Nothing more than a bee sting, but it will give you time to get away if necessary."

"Oooh, thank you, Andre, I adore spy toys."

She laughed, but Alec remained concerned. "Be creative, Maxine," said Andre. "I have confidence you'll resolve this."

When the luncheon concluded, Alec stopped at the police station where Kace was detained. "He's going to be hot as a hornet if he wakes up and finds the buckle missing."

Chastain struggled to his feet in a holding cell with some homeless drunks rounded up on the streets. Groggy and with a pounding headache, his natural penchant was to be angry. His hands gripped and rattled the bars as he spewed profanities.

"Guard! Where am I? Let me out of here; there's been a mistake."

The realization that his belt and shoes had been taken away incensed him further.

"You've no right to take my things. I demand my attorney and a phone call." But his words fell on deaf ears.

By two o'clock, Alec arrived at the detention jail and observed the monitor footage of Chastain's outburst. The supervising detective was relieved to see him.

"Monsieur Campbell, we've been expecting you. This man, Chastain, has been a real pain. Your agent said we couldn't release him until you arrived."

"What was brought in with him?"

The detective opened an evidence envelope and dropped the contents on the table.

"Ah, the silver belt buckle."

Alec studied the details, reveling in the thrill of the authenticity. The etched inscription was 'N. de B.', and on the back, '1799, your devoted father C. de B.'" He snapped photos and sent copies to the team.

The supervisor was eager to dispatch the detainee. "I can't continue to hold him without charges. What do you suggest?"

"Tell him he can go; however, his belt buckle will be held as evidence. He should direct his issues to his insurance company." Alec winked at the irony.

Receiving Alec's text and photos, Dylan compared the artifact's specs to a list and photo found in Coulliere's passageway.

He alerted Andre. "We should invite the insurance investigators to make a sweep of the basement."

NINETEEN

Counter Attack

Maxine's phone flashed with a message when they returned to their Montmartre apartment.

"The landlord said several large cartons were delivered from Les Mascarades," Maxine said. "I'm confused as I never returned for my fitting, nor was there a reference to our location."

Alec showed no pleasure at the news. "It's curious. When I met with Sloane, I didn't identify myself as Alec Campbell, but simply as an Interpol agent. I wondered why he didn't ask for credentials. Why would he presume we are associated?"

Maxine turned her bag over and her coat inside out to search for a tracker, then kicked off her shoes.

Alec dialed Andre, with no answer. On his laptop, he accessed his security at Interpol and reviewed the video of his interview with Sloane at the Montpellier Tower.

"It was me, Maxine; I let my guard down and referred to the Duchess de Parma. He made the connection."

"Are we safe? I'm tired of chasing shadows, Alec."

Maxine wrapped her arms around him and planted a passionate kiss. She slinked away, then surprised Alec in her Sézane dress, ready for a romantic stroll up the cobbled hill.

The night was warm, with a gentle breeze and a starry sky. Pedestrians and tourists strolled the winding streets filling the shops and cafés. Artists' easels, musicians, and mimes lined the route as the tram shuttle and funicular shuttled tourists from the lower level.

Max and Alec slowed their pace at Place du Tertre to listen to buskers' accordions and violins, then continued through the crowd to Le Poulbot, wedged between stone buildings in a flower-lined alcove.

Charles, the head waiter, spied the couple lined up with patrons. He caught their eye and waved, then gestured to follow.

"We cannot have our favorite American customers wait on the street when I have just had a cancellation. Follow me."

Abashed at the unexpected attention, they accepted the intimate table midway into the dining room.

"Enjoy our delicacies tonight!' the host gushed and toyed. "The chef's three-course menu presents a superb whitefish, and the hambone with mustard sauce is raved about. It's a delight to see you again."

Charles placed a menu board on the table and returned to his station at the front. Alec reached for Maxine's hand and returned to a long-ago past.

"Darling, I love you a thousand times more today than when I first realized you were my soulmate. Let this be one of our amazing memories in Montmartre."

He kissed her hand without taking his eyes from hers.

"You do know, Alec, that the Duchess de Parma and the Austrian Duke von Neipperg were very much in love. We'll do our characters justice."

"Yes, Sloane's scripts for us are not too demanding."

"Aside from the dinner and dance, there's nothing until precisely eleven when we will be in the Marble Hall within meters of Emperor Napoleon. A diagram shows the players' positions. A location number is on the floor for each person. Napoleon will be by the west door near the balcony."

"And Dylan as the Musketeer—where will he be?"

"The main players are within easy range of one another. I understand the assault will come from the Duke of Wellington or the Count of Monte Cristo. Andre may find more clues when he reviews the meeting tapes with Bertolier."

Alec sipped his wine as he pondered the ramifications. "The palace informant will cue us as developments progress and keep track of the costumes, so there'll be no opportunity for a switch. Otherwise, Sloane can be set up as a ruse with Bertolier, but he's afraid of Wellesley."

Alec nodded to the server. "I'll have the escargot and ham bone. I didn't realize I was so hungry."

"The soup and the duck confit, please," Maxine said. With the waiter gone, she said, "But I'll offer you my dessert, Alec, perhaps the crème brûlée."

The evening was a welcome reprieve for the Campbells, contrasting the conspiracy heating up across town.

Kace Chastain was enraged that he had been refused his belt buckle. Unsuccessfully demanding the arresting agent's name who withheld the buckle, he slammed the door leaving the holding facility.

Incensed, he ran into the closest metro station and headed toward Les Invalides. The logic of the late hour didn't occur to him as the museum would be closed and under guard.

A night security patrol prohibited Chastain from entering the back or front entrance. He only succeeded in triggering alarms, further angering him as he lurked on the perimeter looking for an advantage.

"Monsieur Coulliere is in there, I know it. He'll see me. Tell him that the Count is here."

Instead, the officer apprehended him and radioed for assistance, to contain the offender.

Kace was not to be deterred and struggled to seize the guard's phone before backup was dispatched.

"I have a right to be here. You can't do this--you can't outsmart me."

He tried again with a kick to the groin and a swing at the man's head, and in a panic, he scampered into the darkness with guards on his heels.

Protocol required that the security report be phoned immediately to the museum manager, dispatching an urgent call to the Coulliere residence.

The phone rang in Coulliere's study, and he answered with concern, as that phone would only ring to announce a security problem at the museum.

"Monsieur Coulliere, we had an attempted intruder at 9:08 p.m. at the main entrance. The gendarmerie is securing the perimeter and searching the nearby neighborhood."

"Officer, send me the photo of the culprit. You said he asked for me by name?"

"Sir. I've texted it to you. If you can identify the perpetrator, contact the investigating gendarme at the Marais detachment."

"Thank you, Officer, for your attentiveness. I'll follow up immediately."

Coulliere knew before looking at the photo that it was the hot-headed Chastain. His phone was lit up with angry texts demanding an immediate response.

He turned to his sister-in-law. "Odilette, turn off the porch lights and bolt the doors." In a momentary panic, he contemplated contacting Moreland.

"What is it, Remy?"

He shook his head, ignored her, and scrolled through Kace's messages.

"The belt buckle has been taken," he growled. "It serves you right for taking something you had no right to, Kace. I warned you the night of the heist not to flaunt that; it was a matter of time before someone noticed it belonged to Napoleon and not a scumbag like you."

Odilette came closer, responding to his mumbling. "What was that you said, Remy? You're upsetting Antoine."

She made her way to the window at a noise outside.

"Shh . . . stay back. Take my brother and remain in the den. I'll call an acquaintance to check out the disturbance."

"But I need to pick up the girls from their dance class soon."

"No, do as I say. I'll send a car for Celeste and Claudette. Call the studio to notify them of the change. I promise you, Odilette, everything will be fine."

Coulliere fumbled in his jacket pockets for Moreland's card, then was relieved to hear his voice.

"Agent Moreland, I need assistance at my residence. Chastain is enraged that the gendarmerie seized some of his property. I'm concerned about the safety of my family."

"What did they take?"

"A silver belt buckle."

"Ah, yes. I know many things about that buckle."

Remy Coulliere was silent, and he sunk into a chair.

"Why has Kace directed his anger toward you?" Dylan prodded. "Do you have anything to do with the belt buckle? Rumor suggests a secret concealed treasure map. You wouldn't withhold that from us, would you?"

Coulliere's voice shook. "You saw a photo at my office of the stash taken from the Louvre. The buckle was among those artifacts. Kace took it, and I've never inspected it for anything else."

"I'll need specifics later. I'll check the area around your home and the museum. However, there's no need to respond. Interpol will be in touch but ask them for ID."

After Coulliere ended the call, he turned to another in the room and queried about the treasure map.

"How much do they know?" The soft-spoken voice demanded.

"They're taking stabs in the dark, they won't find anything."

The quiet man rose from his chair and climbed the stairs without speaking.

Within fifteen minutes, Dylan had scoured the La Marais neighborhood for the rogue, then hid behind shrubbery with a vantage of the Coulliere residence.

Kace started to climb a trellis toward an upper balcony. Dylan could see that across the street, a neighbor, a dog trainer, was approaching with his German Shepherd police dog. The click of dog nails on the cement halted, and the trainee's tail went up. Bracing a stance, its ears went back.

Breaking from the owner's control, the dog charged at Chastain. Kace hoisted his leg over the veranda eaves. He froze at the incessant growling as the trainer was close on its heels.

"Stop and yield, and he won't hurt you. If you run or lash out at him, he'll attack!"

Reaching for a pocket knife, Kace tried to defend himself, but the dog grappled with his leg, hauling him down. He was paralyzed in fear, as the dog's jaws locked onto his arm.

Andre was burning the midnight oil at the Interpol building

when a fax arrived from Bordeaux. Roland Ratcliffe's family was determined to defend the professor's honor and insisted on an investigation and autopsy.

The coroner's report declared it was from a bullet to the head, suspected to have come from a driver who had stopped on the bridge to intervene.

"Where was Lawrence Wellesley that night?" Andre mumbled to himself. "It's only a few hours' drive from his townhouse to Bordeaux, and he'd be home again by morning without suspicion."

Oblivious to Chastain's imminent plight and Andre's new Bordeaux revelation, the Duke boarded a train to Lyon to make a purchase.

Intent on rectifying his errors, he looked forward to this confrontation.

TWENTY

Traces Uncovered

Lawrence Wellesley's walking stick clicked across the Lyon station's concrete platform. The noise of trains and boarding announcements echoed overhead, and the smell of diesel fuel was heavy. In his cantankerous mood, he was irritated by the bustling of passengers and porters.

After purchasing the Parisian International newspaper from a newsstand, he took a bench near the exit to the local bus transit.

Scanning the headlines, he stopped on the second page at an item that announced an investigation into the suspicious death of Roland Ratcliffe, a Bordeaux professor. A small mention at the bottom indicated an investigation was underway.

Wellesley sneered with confidence at his alibi for that night. He'd been careful to travel in darkness and not stop at petrol stations or cafés where he could be noticed.

Ten minutes later, a burly, unkept middle-aged fellow with

a ruddy complexion stumbled through the exit door and searched the benches. He wore mechanic's overalls and soiled, steel-toed work boots.

His eyes passed over the Duke and continued to examine other patrons, before settling again on the man with the walking cane. Sitting at the other end of the bench, he lit a stogie and grumbled aloud. Wellesley scrunched his nose at the odor of diesel spilled on the man's boots and the grime on his hands.

"These blasted trains are never on time. Excuse me, monsieur, do you know if the 12:15 came in from Gare du Nord?" Wellesley asked without making eye contact.

The man pulled a soft packet from his pocket and laid it on the bench.

Wellesley grunted and dropped his newspaper over the packet before announcing the dismissal code. "Here you go," he said. "You'll have to hurry to your bus out of town."

The exchange was quick and unnoticed by others, and in seconds both the Duke and the burly man disappeared into the crowd.

Wellesley peered into the packet at the tightly sealed inner pouch on the return train to Paris. He knew it was the poison he ordered through his old contact after he met with Bertolier.

The idea of murder was titillating to the Duke.

"Loose ends!"

The aroma of freshly brewed coffee and homemade biscuits roused Alec from his sleep. He sat up, alerted by the morning sounds of shops opening and the commuter bustle.

"I've awakened, Maxine, and find myself in heaven." He pulled on a tee shirt and strolled into the kitchen. "I hope we have strawberries and cream for those scones."

Max embraced him and lingered in his arms. "I'm surprised

you're hungry after last night's dinner and two desserts. But I enjoy pleasing my man, so I put some white chocolate and dried cranberries in the scones to appease your sweet tooth."

Alec silenced his cell. "My phone is beeping with messages, but coffee and biscuits come first."

She switched it back on. "We can't afford to do that. Someone could need our help."

"You're right." He flipped through his messages. "It was a busy night for Andre and Dylan. We've been summoned for an early meeting."

Maxine batted her baby blues and threw a kiss. "Do we have ten minutes to finish breakfast?"

With a sip of coffee, she packed up. "Okay, I'll bring the rest of the biscuits to the meeting."

At Interpol, Alec flashed their credentials and the pair hurried onto the elevator.

"Ah, Maxine, perfect timing," said Andre. It was a long night, and you're a breath of fresh air." He reached into her morning baking and accepted a latte.

"Good morning, gang!" Dylan said, behind them and hovering over the biscuits.

"I'm sorry we abandoned ship last night," said Alec, "but we've reviewed the night's events."

"So, you know about Chastain," Andre grunted, "that he's gone off the rails. The belt buckle was from the Napoleon collection. It was on the list of items from the Louvre heist and the inscription matches."

"Kace has an intense attachment to the buckle. He has become reckless to get it back. It's like a curse," said Dylan. "He got away last night but will be sporting a few canine bites."

"His rampage burdens me though," said Andre. "He tried but failed to get through on Wellesley's phone, and we lost track around 4 a.m."

"I bet he goes to the detainment center to retrieve the buckle from the duty officer," said Alec.

"They don't have it—we do," Andre replied. "I've sent it for DNA testing and carbon dating."

Maxine sipped her latte as she listened. "Have you had the results on the balaclava's DNA?"

"Yes, this morning before you arrived," said Andre. "The skin DNA belongs to Chastain, and the gray hair is Jacques Guilliard. Proving that they were both together when the mask was discarded. It seems that Rawley Baker may be Kace's undoing after all."

Andre slid the report to Maxine. "Take a look before you check the prison archives. I set the paperwork in motion for you to proceed."

Alec hesitated at the thought of this new danger to his wife. "I'll take you on my way, Max, and make sure you're protected. La Santé Prison isn't far, in Montparnasse."

Maxine's face flushed, surprised he thought she needed an escort. "I'd be perfectly safe, but I'm grateful for the drop-off."

Andre saw the sensitive exchange. "I have an ex-agent in the Justice Department. His name is Gabriel Dupont and he's agreed to help. The archives are off-site from the prison."

"Does Dupont know why Maxine is searching for old records?" said Alec.

"Gabriel has years of experience with Interpol and France's criminal world. I asked if he knew of the Duke or the Louvre window washers, and it twigged a memory. You can count on him to do his homework."

"Where will I see him?" Maxine said.

"Outside the Department at eleven. He'll be there early, waiting for you—he'll find you."

With the baking gone, Andre divvied out the day's assignments. "Dylan, if you could scrutinize the list of museum heist items and trace the buckle if possible—"

"What about the Napoleon sword? Is it authentic?"

"Push Coulliere for documentation, whatever you can get. It's questionable, and the diary too. We've been warned of unusual black-market chatter in this regard. It appears a suspicious person of interest has arrived in Paris."

Alec rubbed his bruised thigh. "I'll keep tabs on Chastain. Although we met on the bridge, he won't expect me to be a tail. He'll no doubt connect with Wellesley to gripe about his side trip yesterday."

"Yes, he was taken off-guard," Andre said. "The man likes to be in control."

"That makes him erratic," said Alec."

"Be cautious and keep your earpiece turned on. I'll focus on security details as a follow-up to Wellesley's meeting yesterday with Bertolier."

At the door, Maxine turned back. "Andre and Dylan, if I don't feed you, you won't have a proper meal at the day's end. I'll pass a seafood shop on my way home. I hope you don't object to a hearty Spanish paella. Shall we say seven?"

Gabriel Dupont waited for Maxine outside the Department of Justice at 11 a.m. He was tall, meticulously groomed, and strikingly handsome for a retired gentleman.

"Bonjour! Andre says you are one of the best. I'm glad to meet you, Monsieur Dupont."

The genial, gray-haired gent smiled warmly. "Andre has a knack for dangling a carrot in front of my nose, and old habits die hard. So here I am, ready to tackle the puzzle about the Duke. It is intriguing. It's long overdue that the law caught up with him. I enjoy a good overture, but the temptation of retirement beckons me back to Paris. How is the rest of your team?"

"We're gearing up for the Masquerade Ball and a duel for Napoleon's sword." Maxine's throat filled with emotion as she spoke. "Gabriel, thank you for helping me with this. Alec and Andre dwell on my safety, and it's hard on my independence."

The retired agent blushed awkwardly at his words; in recovery, he held the door open for her to enter.

An official inside recognized Dupont. "A pleasure to see you again, Gabriel, and I'm pleased to meet you, Maxine. Andre compliments your instinct for details. I've pulled files that might be relevant regarding the name raised. A workroom is booked near the copier. Take as long as you need."

"That gives us a good head start," said Gabriel.

The escort led them as far as the elevator. "Go up to the second. Help yourself with coffee and anything you need. I have afternoon meetings, but my assistant can lend a hand as you need it."

Maxine dug into the files provided in the stack on the table. "Gabriel, what do you know of a career criminal using the alias of Jacques Guilliard, or more recently, Lawrence Wellesley?"

"I hoped that I'd never hear of him again. Years ago, he was a hunted man for theft and murder. He went to prison for fifteen to twenty years when he was finally captured. Guilliard ruled among thieves as the feared leader. Unfortunately, he has garnered life debts and favors that he can call on, as he pleases. He reigned supreme at La Santé, bullying inmates and instilling fear in the guards. He can intimidate anyone, my dear."

"That hasn't changed," Maxine quipped. "But I don't understand why he'd resurface in a public forum to steal the Napoleon sword. He has Coulliere under his thumb, and could just take it from the museum to resolve its repatriation. There must be something else."

"Ah, but he thrives on the thrill. Before he was Jacques Guilliard, he used other names. Once, he had a female accomplice by the name of Myra. They were a bit of a Bonnie and Clyde duo. She died in prison, but he was intent on escape. It's uncanny how he can blend into obscurity and change his appearance. Andre said he was portrayed as an elderly gent using a walking stick."

"I rode on a countryside tour to the palaces and lodges with him, and his tales completely swayed me. Are you suggesting that he's not elderly?"

"I doubt that he's more than forty-five. Whatever deception he requires, he adapts quite well."

Maxine thumbed through mug shots of the prisoner.

Several hours later, Gabriel and Maxine had reconstructed the life of the criminal who called himself the Duke. He first appeared in Paris fifteen years before, fleeing London, where he was wanted for two gruesome murders. He filled his adolescence with mischief and crimes and was sent from institution to foster homes in a constant circle, creating a monster without attachments.

Gabriel elaborated from file notes and police documents, "He escalated from petty theft to kidnapping dogs, then children before he joined the big league. In prison, he met Kace Chastain and they formed a friendship. But it's a tug-of-war relationship.

"Kace was like Guilliard, with a grudge against the world for his social isolation and lack of family connection. Files said he worked up a frenzy if inmates dared to take his possessions and had a fetish like a crow for shiny objects.

"Over lunchroom chats, without consciences, they discussed future crimes and plotted their escape. Once outside, Kace and Wellesley had an underground network of criminals to recruit.

"One of the prisoners suggested that an art gallery or museum would be easy to take if you had an inside person. The Duke pressed for contacts and connected to Remy Coulliere, whose name came up in an embezzlement scheme.

After his escape, he sought out the military museum and the Napoleon exhibit. There's a list here of cellmates that might have overheard the plot. Kace's new obsession developed from the tale of Napoleon's father's sword—as if he were entitled."

Maxine said, "Seven years ago, the *real* Antoine Coulliere would have been head of the museum. Remy was the devious one with the criminal and financial aspirations, taking over Antoine's position. It appears the stronger personality in the twins prevailed."

"I was puzzled, at the time, at the speed and cooperation of the insurance investigation," said Dupont. "Once they paid the claim, the museum was satisfied, and Interpol lost interest."

Maxine's tablet was open at a closeup of faces. "I'm sending you images from my review of Moreland's file at the police department that recognizes their identity switch."

"It would be useful to get the perspective of the first Antoine," said Dupont. "If he's well enough."

"Yes, and to know how Odilette is involved. She hasn't revealed anything about the changeover of Remy or her relationship with the brother-in-law. She seems loyal to the family and her girls. Could she be part of the con?"

TWENTY-ONE

The Invalid Has a Story to Tell

Dylan arrived at the museum director's office, intent on seeing the Ney diaries. The door was ajar with a desk light on, and he heard groaning inside. He pushed it open with his foot, but no one was in sight.

He shouted, "Antoine!"

A crack in the closet door drew his attention. He stepped over file folders that littered the floor. The tapestry over the trapdoor was disheveled as he bent at the sound of moaning underneath. He yanked on the light bulb and gingerly descended the ladder.

Tossed onto a rusty cot was Coulliere, with a gag stuffed over his mouth and hands bound behind his back. Dylan knew it was the work of Chastain.

"How long have you been here like this?"

"Since early this morning, when Kace dragged me from my house. He used chloroform; I can tell from this horrid headache. But I don't remember how I came to be here in the museum."

"What did he want?"

"The man is paranoid and accused me of trying to cut him out with Wellesley. He said he knew the Ney diaries were fake and that the Duke had brought in some gumshoe without his knowledge."

 "So, they *are* fake diaries?" said Dylan.

"The Duke had them created and placed in the museum. It would give credence to my family's right to the sword, and historical groups couldn't claim them. That's what he said."

"When was this?"

"He concocted the story before the Louvre theft."

"What about your brother, the real Antoine?"

"He didn't want to go along with it. But I was convinced it was a sure thing. When the accident incapacitated Antoine, Wellesley demanded I assume his identity at the museum. He can wreak terror if he chooses until he gets his way."

"Who does the sword belong to?"

"From my archiving experience, it is a genuine Napoleon piece with authentic inscriptions representing the Bonaparte family. Every artifact has its own story. I had no reason to distrust the tales of my ancestor Raphael."

"And the buckle?"

"It was originally part of the museum's exhibit, but Kace developed a fetish for it. He brought me here saying I was holding out artifacts from the heist and demanded a bigger share. He's getting more unpredictable every moment and despises Wellesley intensely."

Coulliere rubbed the adhesive tape from his wrists and sat up to pull himself together. Dylan helped him up the ladder and closed the trapdoor.

"Agent Moreland, I'm willing to cooperate if you can guarantee my safety until the Gala. I'll come clean about the Louvre and the deception on the validation of artifacts. I can give you Wellesley and Chastain, but I need you to spare

Odilette and my brother."

Dylan knew Andre was listening through the earpiece, and he turned up the volume to ensure the confession was clear.

"Kace Chastain has threatened to kill me. His greed is what spared me as he wants the silver sword next week. I can outline the plot for the Royal Lodge."

"Enlighten me on why the theft hinges on the Gala," Dylan said.

"Many reasons. Witnesses, substantiation of the theft for insurance, the press, the ego of Wellesley and Bertolier. All of those."

"Are you expendable to the Duke now?"

Coulliere's voice lowered. "The Duke talks of tying up loose ends. In recent weeks, his attitude toward me has been exhausting, and I fear my life is in jeopardy."

"Your claim and willingness to cooperate is the sort of deduction that Interpol can make. But we need irrefutable evidence if you're negotiating. Provide something more convincing."

Coulliere removed a lockbox and key from under his desk and shoved them toward Dylan. He sagged back onto his chair with defeated resignation.

"There's everything you'll need."

Dylan's eyes popped to see written notes, cassette tapes of telephone recordings, gloves, and other items that identified the heist gang.

"There's plenty of DNA there too!"

Waiting for Interpol's instructions to proceed, Dylan toyed with an idea.

"Remy, does your brother remember the heist? Any recollection at all? I want to talk with him."

Coulliere was startled by the suggestion, and Dylan followed the shiftiness in his eyes.

"Oh, my goodness! I avoid being close to him out of guilt

for the accident. Odilette has been a saint and cares for him, and we've been protective these years looking after him. I presumed bringing up the past would be detrimental to his recovery but now and then something isn't right."

"Perhaps not. Who looks after Antoine when Odilette goes to work?"

"Our hired nurse comes on a schedule. She's patient with my brother, and he looks forward to her visits."

"I'd like you to arrange an appointment for one of my people to visit Antoine. She's intuitive, and I assure you she'll be gentle. You can introduce her as a nurse's assistant. We must get a statement from him before we agree to assist you."

Overhearing it, Andre texted Max at the Department of Justice with the proposal to insert her at the Coullieres.

Gabriel and Maxine wrapped up their scrutiny of La Santé's prison archives, extracting contacts and events that would aid in tracking Wellesley's last seven years.

"It's clear he's a man of disguises and deception," said Maxine, "but even after going through files, I still don't know who the man is. The only certainty is that he didn't exist in France until shortly before he went to prison."

"What nationality do you think?"

"I detected a British dialect on the bus."

"Perhaps. He's dangerous, Maxine; be cautious."

"I'm never alone, Gabriel. Andre hears me on this earphone, and we share messages all day, so we know each person's location. They will be at the apartment for a late supper tonight. Would you join us?"

Gabriel didn't have an excuse to decline and agreed to spend the evening in Butte-Montmartre.

"I must hurry to catch the metro to Le Marais; Andre wants me to visit an invalid in the park. I appreciate your insight,

Gabriel. Please come any time before seven."

Maxine mentally prepared her questions for Antoine as she arrived at the promenade park in Le Marais. "Good, the sun is shining, a perfect day for taking an invalid on a stroll through the park!"

She took a bench in a private spot along the creek. Nearby, families of ducks meandered through the bullrushes, and children ran to and fro chasing butterflies and kites.

With a clear view of the Coulliere residence, she watched for the wheelchair to appear on the veranda. A woman, other than Odilette, opened the door. She wore a nurse's uniform with a navy trench coat and a scarf. The occupant sagged into the seat and was tucked securely with blankets.

As the nurse wheeled the chair down the access ramp to the boulevard, Maxine couldn't confirm that it was Antoine. The woman's gaze wandered as she searched the park. When they were close, Maxine neared the trail and waved as if she were hailing a taxi, then extended her hand with a smile.

"Hello, Monsieur Coulliere. Your employer sent me—you can call me Maxine."

The nurse called back. "Oui, I was told you would meet me here. You have questions for monsieur."

She bent to explain Maxine's arrival. "Remy sent Maxine to ask you a few questions."

He nodded. "Yes, my brother said we could talk."

"My name's Heika," the nurse said. "I've attended to Antoine for many years. He is frail in body but quick as a whip in mind."

Antoine's interruption surprised her. "It's a pleasure, Maxine. Don't let my appearance deceive you. I still have all my faculties." He released a gentle giggle and made determined eye contact.

"I appreciate this. My questions are about the night of the Louvre Heist and your accident on the bridge."

"I remember most of it. I was apprehensive when Remy told me what we were supposed to do. They instructed me to wait in the getaway car. It sounds like a Bonnie and Clyde, doesn't it?" Antoine again sputtered out a chortle.

"Heika, were you present in the household on the day or night of the tragedy?"

"Non, he was in the hospital, then in rehabilitation for months before he came home. The house had many renovations and alterations to accommodate his mobility deficiencies."

The withered man raised his finger to attract Maxine's attention.

"I'm right here. You are talking about me as if I have no hearing or faculties. My name is Antoine Coulliere, and it's a pleasure to see two attractive women debating me."

Heika beamed at him, "I hadn't gotten to tell Maxine yet about your charm."

He pointed toward the creek where an entourage of ducks had gathered. "I like to watch the water. It's very soothing, and my thoughts come more easily when I am still and at rest."

"Monsieur Coulliere, you are a wise and thoughtful man," said Maxine. "Life goes by too quickly, but the basics in life provide the most pleasure."

"Yes, I wish I had learned that as a younger man. I am now content to let the world go by without me, and I don't object to Remy assuming my position at the museum or in the household."

Antoine slowly gasped for air. "But when I look in the mirror and see the results of time, it is painful to accept."

Heika removed a portable oxygen mask from her shoulder bag and placed it in Antoine's hands.

"Talk slowly and use this when you need it."

Antoine waved his wrist gently toward the nurse. "Thank you, Heika. Perhaps Maxine and I will chat by the creek for a few minutes, and you could go ahead and get us a cup of tea."

"Certainly. How do you like your tea, Maxine?"

"Clear, just a bit of lemon."

"I wake up every morning like the Groundhog movie—it's the day after the accident, and I'm hooked up to tubes in the hospital. They stand around talking about me, presuming I am unconscious. Yes, my eyes were closed and too heavy to open, but I listened."

Antoine paused to chuckle at the irony. "You know, I've heard it said that hearing is the last of your senses to go. Even those who appear to be dying can still hear you, so you must always be truthful and tell them you love them."

"I don't want to wear you out with questions, Monsieur Coulliere, but the time has come to reveal the whole truth," Maxine said softly, showing compassion in her voice. She reached for the blanket that had started to slip. Antoine's feet were exposed and Maxine saw worn athletic sneakers with signs of recent soil markings.

"Call me Antoine, Maxine; I am eager to unburden myself."

Antoine's eyes followed Maxine's gaze to his shoes and immediately became agitated.

"I must have taken Remy's shoes by mistake. Surely you wouldn't think a man in my condition could sneak out in the early morning hours and go for a jog," he chortled.

"What's a man to do when someone else is wearing his shoes!" Max bumbled her reply, then quickly recovered. "May I record our conversation?"

"Yes, you have my permission." Antoine continued to stare at her intently.

Maxine turned on her phone, aware that Andre was listening too.

"This is Antoine Coulliere speaking. I was the passenger in

the sedan during the getaway from the Louvre robbery. It was the night of the Bastille Day fireworks. I am guilty of participating although unwillingly, and I was a party to the gang of thieves."

"I have researched the other parties," Maxine said, specifically Lawrence Wellesley, who refers to himself as the Duke, and his accomplice, Kace Chastain."

"And Remy?" Antoine asked.

"Presently another detective is at the museum working with Remy, with his voluntary cooperation. We will put the pieces together from his point of view."

Antoine deliberately fumbled for the oxygen mask and took a heavy suction. Maxine wasn't convinced if it was necessary or for theatrics.

"I married Odilette five years before the museum hired me. I had a promising future, and we planned our family. Around the time of the Louvre, Remy reappeared, having had a bad turn of luck.

"He had the misfortune of meeting his old friend Jacques, who pushed him to use his identical appearance to me to access Les Invalides' artifacts."

"How did he pressure him?"

"The Duke held something over Remy's head and he forced him to assume my identity and influence. He gave him an ultimatum with no choice but to cooperate."

Antoine paused and let a gasp of air gurgle in his chest. "I hope Heika comes back soon with that tea."

"Do you remember the actual car accident that night? I've looked at the gendarmerie records and file photos. The rookie officer that attended the scene had concerns about who was driving."

"There were two vehicles. Wellesley drove one with the loot from the theft, and Remy headed toward a pre-determined exchange point. On the bridge, the Duke rammed our bumper from behind and shot out our back window."

"He shot at your car?"

"Yes. Remy lost control, and everything went black for me."

Heika was nearing with a tray of teacups, and Maxine rose to assist her. "Just in time, Heika; Antoine needs a hot sip."

"Antoine, you said you heard visitors talking around you at the hospital. Do you remember anything specific?"

"The Duke was there insisting that Remy assume my identity, and if he disagreed, he would inject something fatal into my intravenous. So, you see, I'm indebted to my brother for saving my life."

Heika was listening. "That awful man that you call the Duke was at the house early this morning. Antoine, you mustn't ever talk to him. He gets your blood pressure up."

Maxine was surprised that the nurse would have known about the Duke. "Have you met him before then?"

"Not in years. The man used to come by the house to harass Monsieur Coulliere, but then there was a huge row, and the madame banned him from ever coming again. I'm not a live-in nurse. I come according to Odilette's work schedule or if they have evening commitments, like next week when monsieur goes to the palace gala."

Maxine noticed a glimmer of delight in Antoine's eyes at the mention of the Royal Lodge Gala night.

"I don't remember a lot," he said, "but those events were like being transported back into a time capsule. If only—"

Heika leaned to adjust the blankets. "Now, Monsieur Coulliere, you've had a long outing, and I can see you're beginning to tire. Please, if you will excuse us, Maxine? We must go now."

"Thank you, Antoine, for a lovely visit. I hope that perhaps we'll meet again soon."

"It's my pleasure."

Antoine waved a shaky hand in the air as they retreated. Maxine waited and watched as the pair ambled toward the house.

"He seems animated enough talking to the nurse!"

TWENTY-TWO

The Rehearsal

Alec tracked Wellesley and Chastain holed up in the Arc de Triomphe townhouse's basement, commiserating over the confiscation of the buckle.

"Stay low for a few days, Kace. It will do you good to sit back and take a long, hard look at the people around you."

The Duke's heart was beating with exhilaration, that he held a deadly dose intended for Coulliere at the gala. But without warning, his mood turned ugly.

"Kace, even at La Santé, you were a hothead, costing me opportunities. The more fuss you make about the buckle, the greater the interest by Interpol."

With raw nerves, Kace aimlessly wandered back and forth in the room, picking up random items from Wellesley's workbench. In the center was the pouch from Lyon.

"What's this?"

Wellesley instinctively reached for his Baretta from inside his pant leg, then calmed himself.

"Put it down, or you'll regret it! You have to learn to mind your own business. You're not a guest here; you're an intruder."

Instead, Kace threw his head back and laughed. "Ah, ha! So, you are manipulating a scam on the side. I know how you work, Larry!"

Wellesley clenched his fists and did his best to step back. He snapped, "One more week."

Kace's eyes were still on the pouch, and his curiosity pushed him to grab it again. The Duke bolted from his chair snatching it from Kace's grasp.

"Don't ever touch this, I warn you, Chastain. You have not seen the extent of my wrath. Go to the fencing studio and practice the Count of Monte Cristo's lunge. I can do nothing for you tonight regarding the buckle, so I ask you to leave."

"Whatever! I'm going to get that buckle back. You wait and see," Kace spewed.

"When you get irrational thoughts, Kace, you make mistakes. Don't think you're not being watched."

Kace called back from the stairs, "The Interpol agent is more concerned with Coulliere to care where I am. I hacked into the detainment center's surveillance and saw a fellow take the evidence envelope. I tailed him one day, and he went to a B&B address in Butte-Montmartre. The one where Rawley tracked him."

"Stay away from Montmartre!" Wellesley barked.

At the top of the steps from the Abbesses Metro station, Maxine chose a side street within sight of the Basilica and stopped to see the seafood shop owner.

"Bonjour, Marina, how are you and your family? I need to study your selections suitable for dinner tonight."

"Hello, Maxine. I've seen you rushing to the train many times. But you haven't stopped. I presume it's a special meal for guests?"

"I had in mind a recipe for Spanish paella. I haven't made one in ages, but I knew you were the person to get me organized. I have four hungry men to feed, so I'll make it generously."

Marina moved quickly about the shelves and the refrigerator for spices, broths, bearded mussels, shrimps, littleneck clams, Roma tomatoes, chicken thighs, prosciutto, and lemons.

"Would you like chorizo sausage or the kielbasa? Do you need saffron and the Arborio rice?"

"I use the sausage combination and the Arborio. It's better to have too much than not enough."

"Yes, men have bottomless stomachs."

Marina packed it quickly in canvas sacks. "We have a chardonnay in the chiller for an accompaniment, and there's a basket of baguettes by the door."

"You made this errand most pleasurable, Marina. I'll come more often; I promise."

Continuing toward Butte-Montmartre, Maxine called out to Alec jogging uphill behind the Basilica tram. "Wait up, babe. A few minutes to ourselves has become rare." She handed off her parcels and slipped her arm into his.

At the apartment, the landlord was sweeping the outer steps. "Bonjour, my friends! It's good to see you in daylight."

Maxine's eyes wandered to a bill posted on the lower door to their loft.

"Ah, yes," the landlord said. "A porter brought large boxes from a costume boutique. I had them taken upstairs for safekeeping."

"That was kind of you. We're invited to the Royal Lodge gala next week, so opening the boxes will be like Christmas morning. We expect the costumes to be elaborate and fun."

"I'll insist on seeing pictures then."

Two wardrobe boxes and a folded garment box with a hat carton for Alec waited at the top landing. Max tore at the seal but stopped. "It's tempting, but I'd better wait and start dinner."

"I'm only imagining what an Austrian Duke would wear, but there's no point opening everything when we're on the brink of our guests."

Maxine trimmed the mussels and started a boiling pot of steaming broth on the stove. After a long day, she always found solace in the kitchen, starting with the New York cooking school years before.

"I asked Gabriel to join us tonight," she said. "He has a wealth of knowledge that inspires Andre."

"I'll set an extra place. We'll need a bigger table if you keep bringing hungry folks."

"Don't pretend you wouldn't have extended the invitation."

"Of course! Now if I pour you a glass of Chardonnay, tell me about your visit with Antoine."

She patted a pull-up chair. "How can I resist? Then I want to hear about your day."

Upon Antoine's confession to Maxine, Andre ordered a forensic team to recover fingerprints and personal items placing Wellesley and Chastain in the museum passageway. He then called the security supervisor to restrict access to the director's office.

The sword's planned move to the Royal Lodge was only days away. It was removed from its case and delivered by armored car to the treasury department.

"Agent Moreland, this deviation in plans will infuriate the Duke," Coulliere bellowed.

"I'm counting on that. Change your access codes and

security keys. You've shared those with your cronies, and I've seen Chastain try to help himself. Also, ditch your cell phones as I have secure substitutes."

"I won't purport myself to be an honorable man, or I wouldn't have ended up in this position. Before I met Wellesley, I incurred a debt, and he presented himself as a solution. I've regretted that decision every day since I first saw his sorry face."

"Nothing we can do for you now will change your past. However, you can improve the future of the people in your life. It's your responsibility. Bad people influenced you, but now you must become a better man."

Coulliere and Moreland exchanged a look that momentarily revealed the depths of their vulnerability. Dylan was shaken to see himself in another man.

When the undercover agent arrived to protect Coulliere, Dylan headed toward the metro.

Gabriel Dupont entered the Interpol offices as the initial forensic information on the silver buckle arrived on Andre's desk.

Forensic results on the silver belt buckle are inconclusive. A historical curator from the Institute of Napoleonic History from the Louvre will attend the Interpol offices to examine it.

The preliminary review has assessed the silver at the high quality of a vintage consistent with Emperor Napoleon's period. Etchings are compatible with others of the same initials; however, the depth of the engraving varies. I would need more supporting documentation to ascertain a guaranteed assessment.

The DNA matches a person with fingerprints on file at La Santé, registered as Kace Chastain. A second DNA hair sample matches another inmate registered as Jacques Guilliard.

A description matching the specimen is on file with the Military Museum, Exhibit No. 119734.

"This is the best we could hope for, Gabriel. It incriminates and ties the two men to both schemes. Since Rawley cannot substantiate the date, time, and location, we needed more."

"If we made the arrest now, it would be a weak case in court."

"We'll see this through and get them both for a lengthy list of convictions. That should keep them in prison for a long time. The evaluation leaves the door open for Coulliere's personal claim."

"The truth will eventually be told—I am sure of it."

In a long, prolific undercover career, Gabriel had been daring and calculating in tracking renowned criminals. For many years, Andre was his partner until Gabriel faced a near-fatal injury and opted for retirement.

Isolating himself in a penthouse apartment near the Louvre, he turned his interests to studying French culture and history.

Andre spoke quietly. "It's good to have you back in the office, Gabe. You were one of the best partners I ever had."

"Don't think for a minute that I'd reconsider my retirement, but working with Maxine reminded me of old times with people you never need to second-guess. You're fortunate, Andre."

"I'm concerned about the Masquerade next week. The Duke is deranged and unpredictable. We believe he plans to eliminate one of the characters. It was important to have you back up my team. I'd put my life on the line for any of those three."

Gabriel patted Andre on the back. "Come, pal. We have a dinner reservation."

Andre instinctively pulled up his collar and lowered his flat cap before scanning the boulevard.

"Old habits die hard, Andre," Gabriel joked. "I used to be paranoid too, but who'd be watching for me now?"

"Guilt by association, my friend."

A shabbily dressed Kace Chastain glanced up from a newsstand across the street. He nodded to himself as he compared a snapshot on his phone of a man he had seen entering the Campbell's apartment several nights before.

He skulked behind Andre and Gabriel to a parking lot. Crouching between vehicles, he watched them enter a small Renault, then steer north toward Montmartre.

Irritated that he'd lost his objective, Chastain strolled to the Interpol building, hoping to get information about Andre from the concierge. Instead, he found he needed security credentials to bypass the front door, and they shooed him away.

He pounded on the glass door until a burly officer and an armed guard surrounded him.

"Move along, monsieur. You must have an appointment to enter; otherwise, we will call for the gendarmerie and charge you with trespassing."

Rejected, he drove to Le Marais to the fencing studio. Bolstered in anticipation of his starring role as the rogue Count, he visualized the silver sword's feel again in his hands. He lunged at the mirror with vigor, admiring his stance, and tossed the saber to his other hand.

At the apartment, Maxine laid her paella platter at the table's center with a tomato basil bocconcini salad and the day's baguettes.

"Thank you all for joining us for a family supper once again," said Alec. "And we're grateful to our new friend, Gabriel, for helping our team on this case. Dig in and help yourself."

"Maxine, the aroma is more than I can bear," said Gabriel. "It's been years since I had a Spanish paella in Barcelona. We, bachelors, use microwave dinners, right Andre?"

"We could get used to this, Maxine," Andre said. "You're not only a cook and detective, but I see your costume arrived, and you're about to become the Duchess de Parma."

"I'll be swimming in crinolines. How will you be costumed, Andre?"

"Ha-ha. I'll attend as a security officer in the folds of the tapestries. Our eventual fate will be in the hands of Dylan, the daring Musketeer."

"I got a call that Kace turned up at the fencing room tonight to practice his moves," said Dylan. "I owe the studio manager a good sum now for his updates."

"What's the man up to?" asked Gabriel.

"Coulliere said Wellesley intends to fill the sword sleeve with a fatal poison," Andre said. "It can paralyze the victim if inflicted on any part of the body, long enough for the person to suffer horrible pain before succumbing fatally. Our agent in Lyon witnessed a poison transaction at the train station, and the buyer matched Wellesley's description."

"Our palace informant has apprised us of the details. At 11 p.m., Bertolier will announce a duel, and the audience will assume it is an entertaining ruse," said Andre. "Once Coulliere relinquishes the sword to Chastain, half-hearted sparring will raise charitable funds from the crowd."

"Should we presume there's an intention to kill Coulliere then and there, in front of a public audience?" said Gabriel.

"During the diversion, the Count of Monte Cristo will escape through the balcony terrace with the sword. The Duke of Wellington will ease into the crowd and discreetly resurface opposite the Ballroom Grove at the Marie-Antoinette garden hideaway."

"How would Kace steal the treasures then?" Gabriel asked.

"We suspect Chastain intends to stash the relics in the royal gazebo to retrieve later. Otherwise, there is no way to walk out of the palace without triggering the alarms."

"It's so much drama simply to obtain more insurance money," Maxine mused. "However, the theatrics make a solid case witnessed by many of the arrest of Chastain and Wellesley, red-handed and publicly humiliated."

Dylan said, "Surely, a masquerade shop would have more than one costume for Napoleon Bonaparte. Alec, can we be certain of Sloane's assurances?"

"I'm convinced he sees us as his only escape."

TWENTY-THREE

Scripted

Over dinner, Maxine and Alec laid out the group's scripts and mapped the route supplied by Percival Sloane. Walking through the scenario's details, they debated and anticipated the timing of events.

"The doors open to guests at eight," Alec said. "Wristbands are assigned, and we'll arrive in stages. Jot this number of a reputable limo service as a backup, but I'll arrange with a Butte-Montmartre gentleman who runs an airport shuttle van. Our landlord said the man would be grateful for the fare. Anyone else to pick up on the way?"

"Dylan, check that Coulliere fully understands his transport," said Andre. "He'll follow the armored vehicle carrying the sword, protected by a security guard. Double-check his times and routing. You'll be with him."

"I'm on top of it," said Dylan. "I'll be at the museum for his pickup. Between the security guy and myself, there's no chance for a switch of the sword."

A mischievous glint in Dylan's eye turned to laughter.

"Imagine if we're seen together en route; we'll look foolish dressed in public as Napoleon and a Musketeer."

"With Coulliere in your constant sight, that leaves Chastain unaccounted for until he arrives at the palace," said Gabriel. "And Lawrence Wellesley, or Jacques Guilliard, if that's his name."

"I'll be at the palace early checking security, and Solange will be on-site all day," Andre said. "She confirmed that the costumes for Wellesley and Chastain were delivered to the Arc de Triomphe townhouse."

"I'll gladly handle an additional task if you need it," said Gabriel.

Andre said, "I have just the job in mind, to shadow the assassin, then join me among the curtains. I'll have a backup plan."

"It's like old times, but I've never been to a costume ball. It's guaranteed to be memorable."

"We'll present ourselves at the entrance of the royal courtyard," said Andre, "then straight to the Marble Hall for introductions."

"Our buffet seating is reserved as guests of Emperor Napoleon," Maxine said. "The tables are large, with ten at ours."

"Is Hollande Bertolier in our group?" asked Andre.

"Yes. Dressed as Louis XVI and accompanied by one of his mistresses. An unnamed senior member from the Napoleonic Society is at our table too."

"And the others? Where are they?"

"Crisscross to us," she said. "Their table shows only initials and codes. Three seats are marked with asterisks for journalists or charitable donors. The others are CMM and D/W, which must be the Count of Monte Cristo and the Duke of Wellington. Oh yes, also the king's court's mistresses with him. The gentlemen at that table will not lack for female attention.”

“An idea hit me,” Gabriel said. “Insert me as a member from the press at the Count’s table. No one would recognize me, but of course, the entire purpose of the Masquerade is not to be recognized.”

“Our inside contact, Solange, could set that in motion. She could manipulate it under Bertolier’s nose.”

“Ah-ha, splendid.”

“Naturally, that will mean a costume and mask,” said Andre. “You wouldn’t be allowed past the entrance without them. They are strict about it. We’ll need Sloane to arrange an appropriate disguise.”

“I’ll call Sloane to accommodate us,” said Maxine. “He’s scared of Wellesley and is cooperating so far.”

Gabriel smirked at being party to the prank. “Go ahead, Andre, enjoy yourself and count me in, costume and all.”

“I’ll make a diagram of the hidden door to the royal apartments the Duke showed me,” said Maxine. “Surely those areas will be closed to the public, but it is a devious option for him to disappear if he chooses to do that.”

“A diagram! I’ll accept any lifelines.”

“How about a daring new challenge?” Maxine teased, lightening the evening with her mischief. “Can anyone dance baroque style? It will be an experience of a lifetime and the opportunity to dance in heels.”

“I can add some fear to that,” added Alec. “The theatrical music is based on Bach and Handel.”

“Fast or slow?” Dylan asked.

“The tempo is quick and staccato, with jumps, twirls, twists, and pirouettes, to the tinny sounds of harpsicords, trumpets, and violas,” said Maxine. “Gentlemen, you’ll be tested to challenge yourselves. Even you can do it, Dylan.”

“Maxine, you can disguise your dance moves with hoops and bustles. But I do look forward to dancing with the

Duchess de Parma."

Alec watched Dylan's eyes, perturbed by the anticipation. "Monsieur Montoya," he said, "won't you be too busy elsewhere, rescuing some damsel from distress?" The tension dissipated into laughter with his quip.

"There's a fifteen-minute dance orientation in the hall," Maxine said.

"Just fifteen? For how many dances?"

"Enough to become familiar. There'll be dancing into the night, with bands, laser lights, fireworks, and musical fountains at the Colonnade Grove. Columnar dances too."

"What's that?" said Alec.

"Couples float from one end of the hall to the other, then return to their partners in counted steps, like the orchestrated movements in the *Amadeus* movie."

"Back to the plan, folks," said Andre. "The fun and entertainment can't take our focus off the attempt on Coulliere's life and the sword's theft. Keep our eyes on our victim inside the royal courts too."

Gabriel studied his pocket watch and attempted to rise from the table. "It's late for an old man. It's refreshing to be in the throes of imminent crime, but I must make my way home."

"I'll fix you a cappuccino first," said Maxine. "It'll warm you up before you go."

"And I'll drop you on my way," said Andre. "There's scum equal to Kace Chastain on the trains at this hour."

When the guests left, Maxine unsealed the wardrobe box.

"A photograph is stapled to the outside, Alec. The dress looks glorious, but I'll never get it into a shuttle van. We could hire an open carriage at a depot near the palace. It's like riding in a pumpkin."

Alec wrapped her in his arms. "As long as I'm your prince charming, I don't care how we get there."

"That suits me. If my costume fits, of course."

"Poor Napoleon lost his first wife, Josephine, too early, then Marie-Thérèse was a convenient introduction and royal replacement. She was acquainted with Marshal Ney before she married."

"I'm convinced the Wellesley connivers fabricated the tales of Marshal Ney's honorary sword to establish a deception," Alec said. "How is the museum's insurance company involved? Will they attend?"

"Your costume store informant would know if a guest will represent them. Security guards will accompany the exhibit."

"Sloane said he overheard Wellesley call a shady gumshoe named Brooks. The fellow runs an unethical detective shop in a slum district, doing anything for a buck. There's more . . . I followed Wellesley last week on the night the professor in Bordeaux was killed. It's more than a coincidence.

"The Engelland & Steele insurance documents might show signs of counterfeit," said Maxine.

"Worth checking out. One by one, Wellesley's accomplices are meeting an inevitable accidental death, so even Brooks' longevity might be limited."

Alec brushed a wayward strand of hair from her face and softly kissed her neck, cheek, and ears. As she closed her eyes, he turned out the lights.

"Enough for tonight."

TWENTY-FOUR

Royal Lodge Preparations

The 8 a.m. sun glistened on the polished sheen of the majestic gold-painted gates of the Royal Lodge. Gardeners and caterers swooned like ants along the walkways setting up tents, tables, stage platforms, stanchions, and portable bars.

Pacing in the luxury of his temporary office overlooking the gardens, Hollande Bertolier gloated with pride at his event's chaos and fluster.

Looking toward the Rue de Rivoli, he envisioned the advancing troops crawling like locusts. At the gate, motorized carts vied to access the promenades with their equipment.

Studying a chart on a conductor's stand by the window, he barked instructions into a walkie-talkie toward the set-up organizer below in the courtyard. Anyone close to Bertolier might think he was becoming unhinged in the belief that he was truly King Louis reigning over the paupers.

His desk phone repeatedly buzzed with calls, further increasing his agitation, and he hollered to the outer reception. "Solange, I asked you to hold all my calls this morning!"

The prim secretary appeared at his door, unbothered by his irritation. "Excusez, Monsieur Bertolier, the caller demands to speak to you. He says he's the Duke and that you will want to talk with him."

"Tell him I'm involved here with preparations. If he wishes, he can meet me here after lunch while I make my inspection," he bellowed.

'Very well, I will advise him."

As she left, he said, "Wellesley is a pompous thorn in my side; I don't know why I bother accommodating him."

Picking up opera glasses, Bertolier focused on the laborers building scaffolded banks of lights high around the perimeter.

As his eyes settled on the private salon it dawned on him that Wellesley would be making another demand for the keyed access to the locked room.

"Solange! Get the head of security. I must make an urgent request."

Lawrence Wellesley was in a foul mood from Bertolier's dismissal. Laid before him on his kitchen table were the Lyon pouch, his silver-tipped walking stick, a timing watch, the Royal Lodge map, and exhibit photos. He picked up and examined pictures of Napoleon's costume and the Count's.

Glowering over his instruments of the Masquerade scheme at the Gala, he allowed his thoughts to envision himself boarding a first-class flight the day after the private sale of the Napoleon sword.

"Finally, I'll enjoy the well-deserved rewards of a life of crime. My accomplices will have earned nothing!"

He dialed through to Coulliere at the museum, but the message box was full. With irritation, he slammed the phone down.

Next, he attempted to ring Kace, who didn't pick up as he

lurked near the Interpol building. Resorting to a voicemail for his accomplice to meet him at the palace, Wellesley set his plans into play.

Kace was still seething at the loss of the belt buckle but realized the futility of accessing the Interpol building. Eventually, his complaint was routed to Andre Poulin's desk.

"Inspector, I believe Interpol has my personal property taken through an illegal search of my person. I demand its return or I will be forced to take drastic action."

"Who am I speaking to?"

"Don't be a fool. You know who I am."

Andre waved for an assistant to begin tracing it.

"If you refer to the Napoleon artifact that was part of the Louvre theft several years ago, it is kept with our evidence for safekeeping. It is unlawful to retain stolen property."

"That was gifted to me in return for services performed. The buckle is mine, and I demand it be returned."

"How do you propose to prove the item belongs to you?"

"You will take it with you to the Royal Lodge tomorrow evening. Instructions will be delivered to you for an exchange. Be assured you will want what I have to offer."

Unfazed by the threat, Andre was curious about what Kace was alluding to as an exchange.

Smug, Kace rang off before Andre could interrogate him further. After retrieving Wellesley's message, he blended into the subway system, oblivious to reality.

The conversation had been cut too short for Andre to trace his location.

"I'm not too concerned," Andre whispered. "Wellesley and Chastain are outnumbered and outsmarted. Unless they have a surprise."

Hacking into the palace monitors and surveillance grid, Kace detected a flurry of activity at the main entrance. Credentials were being examined, and the crush of inspectors made him skittish. Instead, he used the less congested back entrance. His slight build was agile and limber, easily able to climb or be hidden.

The grounds and escape routing were fresh in Kace's memory. The historic secluded hideaway, the private salon, was remote from the main palace, with many options to conceal artifacts.

He watched the cameras aimed at the entry gates and timed their patterns. A caterer's vehicle was unloading wheeled carts, and Kace offered to assist hoping to blend in. But the keen eyes of a crew chief spotted and dissuaded him.

"Stop! You cannot be here. Leave at once or you will be arrested and banned from this site." An alert giving Kace's description flashed coordinates to the security chief, and the message filtered through Andre's informant.

Kace was speechless and backed away to regroup himself. Skulking back down the path, he ducked into a row of shrubbery.

"This is Solange from Monsieur Bertolier's office. Apply suspect code 290 to the intruder before you." She unlocked a room of surveillance monitors and matched her cell photo to Chastain's facial image.

Kace's location was highlighted on the screen, and officers pinpointed his hiding place. An officer clenched his arm.

"Monsieur, it is strictly prohibited without clearance. You have already been warned."

Kace attempted to persuade him appealing for sympathy. "I was purely interested in being helpful. I've applied for a position with your firm, but I'm waiting for my schedule. Work is hard to find."

"Go, now, monsieur!" The officer slipped a tag into Kace's pocket and watched as he withdrew from the entrance.

Undefeated in his mission, Kace fell behind a group of foreign tourists at a bus stop line led by a palace escort.

Following them into the botanical gardens, he kept his eyes on the ground.

"Calling dispatch, a fellow is out of place in my group. He didn't board and looked suspicious. A heads up to avoid a confrontation near the Apollo gardens."

The tag planted by security was easy to trace and pinged on the screen.

Deviating to a path on the right, Kace spied the roofline of the Private Salon in the gardens, partially hidden by a bushy privacy hedge.

Skulking behind foliage, he opened his phone to get details of the escape route planned by Wellesley. His head was down and he was unaware he'd been observed.

Kace mumbled words of Mary Howitt's cautionary poem aloud with irony. While serving in prison, he was placed under psychiatric care, with medication for hallucinations. To hang onto reality, he sang this poem to himself every night to find calm.

"Will you walk into my palace? said a spider to a fly;
'Tis the prettiest little parlor that ever you did spy."

As a guard watched him, he eased onward a hundred yards into a bush, then returned to the trail when the patrol had passed.

Andre's laptop flashed Code 290, and he picked up the Kace tracking. With the urgency to encircle a trap, he called to the group, "Who is closest to the palace to track Kace? He's scheduled to meet the Duke on the grounds to rehearse the debacle. Solange will monitor their location and movements."

"It's Alec, here—I'm near the Montpellier building to meet with Sloane."

"Switch if it's possible," said Andre.

"Maxine, can you take over?" Alec said. "Square up details

with Percival Sloane at the boutique, and press him about the Count's costume. He knows your background, so it shouldn't raise any red flags. I'll go to the royal courts."

"Alec, there's a motorbike rental where you are—you'll get there faster," said Dylan. "Drop it at the turnoff."

Zipping between lanes, and taking pedestrian shortcuts, Alec reached the palace in fifteen minutes. He dropped the bike and ran hard, following Kace's GPS blip on the phone.

The Interpol badge sped up admittance through a security gate, and he sprinted toward the gardens. He screeched to a stop as he spotted a figure ambling the walkway with a silver-tip stick. Wellesley's arrogance and British attire stood out as he waited for Bertolier at the fountain.

"How did The Duke weasel his way past security?"

Through the maze of the gardens, Alec observed the event coordinator's portly shape. Bertolier's voice carried as he called orders to a pair of underlings. Strutting with confidence, he snapped his fingers.

"This could lead somewhere, Andre, but it's a choice," Alec radioed. "I could eavesdrop on Wellesley and Bertolier or follow the blip emerging at the Private Salon."

"Hear out the Duke first."

Getting his bearings, he settled incognito at a garden bench to listen.

"Bonjour, Hollande, it's a fine day for a garden party!"

"Wellesley, I'm swamped—I can only give you a few minutes."

From his vest, Hollande Bertolier produced a giant master key. "This gives you access to the salon. Return it to my secretary before you leave."

"We have urgent agenda details to go over," Wellesley said. "Must I remind you that timing is precise, that my route is to be cleared and accessible without interference?"

"That's perfectly in order, I assure you."

Wellesley's manner changed unexpectedly, and he leered at Hollande. "I must review the plan that Interpol and the Engelland & Steele insurance agent provided to secure the artifacts. I have an accomplice on the inside, so you won't be able to insert decoys. The consequences to you could be devastating should we not succeed."

Bertolier waved away his nearby staff, frightened by the ramifications of Wellesley's threat.

"I will be long gone," Wellesley continued, "and you will be standing in the center of the Marble Hall looking guilty! The guests include notable political and government officials who will expect perfection and not to witness your humiliation."

"I agreed that the Count of Monte Cristo would have access through the balcony at his will, and now you are free to intrude. A sparring area is available at eleven on the ballroom stage, as you requested. I'll introduce the play and make introductions. From there, it is up to your actors. What more do you want?"

"I want your complete attention."

Bertolier huffed with resignation until his thoughts were distracted hearing his name over the walkie-talkie, requiring a decision in the catering kitchen.

"I assure you, Wellesley, we will try to be meticulous. We will carry out your requests precisely, as you say."

Wellesley said nothing and turned his back to seek out Chastain. From his concealed location, Alec zoned in on their conversation.

Wellesley spied Chastain lurking nearby and grabbed him by the scruff of his collar.

"So, where's the buckle now?" said Wellesley.

"I told the Interpol fellow he'd better bring it back tomorrow. I threatened him."

"You idiot! That wasn't part of the plan."

"It is now. If necessary, I'll take the detective lady as a hostage until he gives me back what is mine."

With the stress of Kace's erratic behavior, Wellesley permitted his idiosyncrasies to be exposed. "Kace, our focus is on the sword! Besides, a quick, easy murder to eliminate Coulliere is not the same as adding a kidnapping. Precision to our plan is paramount, do you understand? You can get your buckle back later."

"Then I'll kill her too the same way as Coulliere."

Wellesley briefly contemplated the idea, then scowled, "Did you install the weapons I provided in the guardhouse?"

"Right where you asked them to be—the silencer, cartridges, and chloroform."

Within minutes, an explosive detection patrol's canine unit tracked Kace's route to the private salon weapons cache.

TWENTY-FIVE

The Players Take to the Stage

Coulliere's full Napoleon garb hung in his museum office. But the forensic unit's intrusion overshadowed his anticipation of the gala. They itemized every relic in the basement passage.

In an eleventh-hour review meeting with Coulliere, Dylan reinforced the plan to transport the sword to the Royal Lodge.

"You'll spend the afternoon at the museum," said Dylan. "Then an armored escort is scheduled for six o'clock for you and four guards to travel to the palace. I'll be with you. The silver sword will be sealed in a bulletproof case and handcuffed to two guards.

"When will this be over, Agent Moreland? It's casting an unfavorable cloud over the museum."

"It won't be easy, Monsieur Coulliere. Your cooperation in taking down Chastain and Wellesley will earn consideration; however, you are a guilty accomplice to the Louvre robbery. That bears consequences. We plan to arrest the Duke and his band of thieves, and their confessions will be enlightening."

"What will he do to me at the Royal Lodge?"

"We are prepared for an attempt on your life or even a kidnapping."

"Should I be armed?"

"No. They won't be successful. You'll be under protection every minute."

The words were little consolation to Coulliere.

"Wellesley is unpredictable and resourceful. Bertolier is under his thumb and will do anything to spare his reputation."

Dylan didn't share details about the inside palace informant, or that armed Gabriel Dupont would be beside the Count of Monte Cristo.

"And . . . my brother?"

"Once we have corroborating statements from the night of the heist, hopefully, the real Antoine will be acquitted as being under duress and forced into his role. He has given testimony to our detectives that has proven helpful."

Remy looked relieved for the first time. "That is good. He doesn't deserve to suffer the consequences of my misdeeds."

"If there are no outstanding issues, I must leave now for a meeting," Dylan said.

But Coulliere's demeanor remained suspect, so he waited outside the door. He picked up his private line. "Don't forget the secret place." That was all Dylan heard.

Andre called Alec and Gabriel immediately on hearing Kace's threat to use Maxine as a ransom for the belt buckle.

"Gents, I don't take threats against Maxine lightly. If Chastain even looks in her direction, he is immobilized."

"She'll always be within my reach or sight," Alec assured. "But she may need to accompany Napoleon to the ballroom stage, as the Duchess was his second wife during his exile."

"Are you considering baiting Chastain with the buckle?" Gabriel asked.

"To distract him from the Napoleon confrontation, *you* could wear the buckle as part of your ensemble," said Alec.

"Maxine will meet with Sloane this afternoon," said Andre. "Text her about your costume."

"She sent me a picture and will drop off my duds on her way home," said Gabriel.

"Embellish us. What is it?"

"So apropos that it is Marshal Ney. I could never have imagined such a costume existed. He wore great cloaks and a flamboyant fortress of upright plumes on his two-pointed, bicorne hat."

"Splendid. You'll fit in perfectly."

Andre laughed at the vision. "And, of course, an elaborate battle sword, although the one associated with his infamy is in contention. Fortunately, he stands in Napoleon's good favor. The stage has a full cast for a showdown with the emperor."

"Are we overlooking anyone?" said Gabriel.

"My backup team will be close at hand to intercept surprises. The accomplices will never be out of our sight."

"In the passageways too?"

"Absolutely. And we'll have access behind the Marble Hall thanks to Maxine."

The distinctive red jacket and white pantaloons identifiable to the Duke of Wellington hung in Wellesley's rented townhouse parlor. At his kitchen table, he twirled the pistol chamber of a small-caliber gun, anticipating the evening ahead.

"True to my motto—no loose ends!"

The calculating Jacques Guilliard thrived in the dramatics of enticement and murder, in it for the game. Serving time in La Santé, he had regrettably boasted to Kace of his exploits and dastardly deeds to gain admiration. Relishing in his control over the younger man, he had waited for this opportunity.

"It's far safer to go it as a lone wolf." He spun the chamber again, aimed, and clicked the hammer on a single blank, smiling as he felt success recoil into his palm.

He picked up the Lyon pouch and felt the weight in his hands, then removed an empty cigar cylinder from the bureau drawer and donned surgical gloves. He tapped a portion of the contents into the tube until both hands had equal weight.

The cigar tube fit inconspicuously into the breast pocket of the commander's red jacket, then he slipped the deadly remains of the pouch into the sheath of his right boot.

Maxine unleashed the puff of bustles and crinolines from their carton, with a draped overlay in a wildflower blue, silk brocade, and delicate satin burgundy rosettes. A fashionable box held a bouffant of ringlets encased in a plastic bubble, with a barrage of combs and clips.

A manila envelope pinned to the front listed accessories and instructions to assemble the Duchess de Parma costume.

"This is going to be such fun!" She rubbed her hands together, afraid to touch the elegance, then heard the downstairs door handle.

"Alec, come and see my costume; it is incredible."

"Then I hope mine is equally stunning! An Austrian Duke can't be too shabby."

He froze, looking into Maxine's eyes. He had just come from the meeting with Andre where they discussed Maxine's life at risk despite the audience.

"You're looking at me funny, Alec. What is it?"

Without a word, he held her tight enough to feel her heartbeat.

"Alec Alexander Campbell?"

She rarely used his given name, so he knew it came from her soul.

"We've always known the uncertainties and perils in every predicament we've faced. You are my everything, and I don't relish you in danger tomorrow night."

She brushed her lips over his then pulled back.

"I know what was overheard at the palace," she said. "Kace doesn't scare me, and I'm always on guard. I'll be in the company of the best detectives. Focus on Napoleon and the sword, not on me."

"Again, you'll be at risk."

"Andre gave me a vial of a potent sedative to use if needed. It will be in my silk purse attached to my wrist."

"Regardless, I'll be close."

She kissed him again. "Now, let's look at this conglomeration of silks!"

At the Coulliere residence in Le Marais, Remy was apprehensive about the gala. He found Odilette sitting in the parlor near Antoine, who nestled in his chair by the hearth.

"Odilette, I need a word."

Antoine had torture in his tired eyes. "I know about the Royal Lodge tomorrow, Remy. The Duke has manipulated a trade for artifacts once more, and the outcome could change this family forever."

"We have been through tough times before, Antoine."

"Yes, and I am grateful to you for finding a way to provide for this family during my supposed demise."

Odilette moved to console her husband. "Dearest, there is no need to talk this way, Antoine."

"Please, let me have my say," said Remy. "If Wellesley compromises my position with the museum, I have left a full confession with the family attorney. Odilette, you must take it to Interpol for Antoine's sake."

The feeble brother looked up. "Remy, I am stronger in

spirit than my body would lend you to believe. I remember the Louvre and will tell my truth. I know that Rodriquez has been in contact again! He is a greedy man but should not be too quickly dismissed."

Coulliere was astounded at his brother's comment. "What do you know about that? I have put my confidence in Agent Moreland. I've had no contact with Rodriguez, so he must be up to something with the others. The agent will accompany me tomorrow, and Wellesley will be found to be the criminal that we fear. It will be a difficult recovery, but we must have hope."

"I warn you, Remy, Rodriguez is a black sheep, he's been manipulating Wellesley. I know for a fact."

Antoine stood looking stunned by his brother's comment.

"Remy, I beg you to allow Antoine to rest now," Odilette pleaded.

"Yes, yes, of course." Remy paused, looking at Odilette and his brother, feeling he had overlooked something.

He watched with painful regret as Odilette eased the wheelchair out of the parlor.

TWENTY-SIX

The Sword Exposed

Dylan arrived at Coulliere's office at noon on August 15th, the day of the Gala. Following Andre's instructions, he confirmed the arrangements with the armored transport. Depositing a crated chest in the escorts' care, he was satisfied he could make the exchange. Andre was the only other person that knew what he had done.

Remy was edgy and checked his watch, eager to get on with the sword's removal. He ignored calls from the insurer and Wellesley, as Dylan had cautioned.

"You must hear this recording," Coulliere said.

Dylan listened to a threatening voicemail from Wellesley to Coulliere, warning him to hand over Napoleon's sword according to plan without resistance or face tragic consequences.

"What do I do, Agent Moreland?" Remy pleaded. "My family needs to retain the value of their heritage for financial survival."

Dylan showed no sympathy. "You know that the sword

doesn't belong to your family or even to any descendants of Ney. You relied on Wellesley's cleverness to establish its existence. Do you remember Professor Ratcliffe? He validated the original article, then was suspicious and made inquiries. Fortunately, his notes that have been turned over to authorities in Bordeaux."

Remy paled. "Notes?"

"As a career historian, Radcliffe analyzed the diaries and found they were *not* authentic. He provided evidence to refute the Ney sword. When he began to ask questions, the hornets started stinging."

"I don't know anything about Ratcliffe or his suspicions."

"These facts have not been made public, but Wellesley became aware of his suspicions and eliminated him as a threat. The evidence is in the hands of Interpol."

"What does that have to do with the sword belonging to my family? I have insurance documents that prove I am the owner."

Dylan was harsh in explaining the reality. "Come now, Remy, weigh Wellesley's reputation against your claim. If the sword were authentic, why would the Duke need to use you and your museum? Do you truly believe that you would reap a financial benefit?"

"Then why are you here, and why are we taking part in this ruse? Why don't you just arrest me?"

"We have no interest in destroying you or your family; we want Wellesley and his ring of criminals. This is about the Louvre and the murdered accomplices, not your fake sword."

Coulliere stammered, "At the Royal Lodge tonight, Wellesley will do something dramatic and either kidnap me or kill me. How does this play out?"

"We will see that doesn't happen. You'll wear a wire and never be out of sight. The more incriminating confession you can eke from Wellesley, the more you'll benefit. It will improve your consequences when this is over."

A knock at Coulliere's door halted the exchange.

Dylan said, "It's almost time for the transfer from the museum to the transport, Remy. Then you must transform into Napoleon."

Dylan followed Coulliere into the museum exhibit, with the two transport guards behind. The stanchions surrounding the Napoleon exhibit hall to restrict patrons had been moved to retrieve the artifacts.

On arrival, Coulliere scanned the room for a sighting of either Kace or Wellesley but was relieved. His heart raced to see a man near the door, watching him. He avoided making eye contact lest Dylan take note. But the hesitation was noticed.

Under his breath, he cursed Rodriguez.

"Chastain and Wellesley are under observation," said Dylan. "Don't be concerned about their interference before we get to the palace."

"I never meant for this to happen. I was duped in Wellesley's ploy to deceive, all in the name of greed." Coulliere's gaze went again to check on Rodriguez by the door, but he was gone.

Remy released the casing over the sword exhibit, using security codes and an encrypted key. Dylan videoed the procedure as the great sword was eased into the padded, coffin-style box.

"It's too bad Professor Ratcliffe couldn't have seen this sword here at the museum," said Dylan. "Wellesley did his best to con him to substantiate the Ney diaries and sword."

"My father said we had lineage to Marshal Ney, but it was passed down as folklore."

As the sword rested in the foam bed, Coulliere reached again to touch it with reverence.

"Agent Moreland, if I may point out—these initials on the

sheath are authentic. It is truly a part of history and was commissioned by the Bonapartes. But I won't stand in the way of its return if history is correct."

Dylan picked up his garment bag hanging over an office armchair. "Ready yourself to prepare to go now. I'll join you after I've changed; meet me at the transport truck in ten minutes."

Dylan stood on the outer steps with a mysterious, black cape draping his shoulders. He looked the part of Inigo Montoya, the famed musketeer, with his long, dark locks turned over the nape of his neck, and bearing a costume sword and sheath turned at his waist.

Two women in the group of bystanders gasped at his handsome entrance, and he regretted that the character's flamboyance prevented him from being discreet.

In a quiet tête-à-tête, he took aside the armored security supervisor. "It should fit precisely into the original sheath. You have a signed document of authority to oversee it."

"Yes, sir . . . as you wish."

The guard observed his costume with amusement, and Dylan rolled his eyes with a subtle grin.

"This must remain confidential between yourselves and Interpol. Do not discuss it with anyone, including Monsieur Coulliere."

"Indeed, sir."

Minutes later, Remy strode toward the awaiting troop decked in his regal uniform. He wore a high, white silk swathe bib with period brass buttons, a lacey cravat, and a red sashed collar. His white vest was distinctive, with a sewn sling and his arm tucked appropriately into the sash.

Over his turned-up collar was a heavy cloak, decked with regal epaulets, topped with the emperor's suede black bicorn.

Coulliere assumed an air suitable to his character's role, and Dylan saw the renewed confidence and zeal he would display in his performance. His eyes twinkled with mischief.

"Agent, Moreland, I will don my side sword and saber once we arrive at the palace. I presume this prop sword is simply for appearances. I have a few impressive moves from practicing at the fencing studio, you know."

"Wellesley is unpredictable, so make sure he doesn't get within reach of you. My boss received a report that he made a recent purchase of deadly poison in Lyon."

"Poison? Are you sure?"

"Our agents will surround you, but we will rely on you."

"Where will you be?"

"I'll be close to the Duke if an interception is necessary. Two undercover detectives are at your table; you'll know your dinner companion as your second wife, the Duchess de Parma. Don't let her beauty deceive you into thinking she is not a vixen ready to pounce in the face of danger."

"Impressive. I look forward to meeting her." Coulliere's fear was transforming from fear to excitement.

Dressed in royal apparel, the other masquerading detectives arrived at the palace in the shuttle van driven by their Butte-Montmartre neighbor. Carriages and limousines congested ahead as they vied for positions closer to the entrance to relieve their passengers.

"Merci, our dear friend, anywhere we can disembark will be fine," said Maxine to their driver. "It is part of the gala's experience to mingle with others in their costumes and wait for photographs."

"It doesn't seem right to let a beautiful Duchess have to walk the rest of the way. But if that is what you folks would like, I'm obliged."

Alec helped Maxine out of the van and tipped the driver handsomely. "Merci, mon ami, for kindly assisting us with our costumed burdens."

The driver was buoyed by his compensation. "I'm happy to help a neighbor. I'll be home early and take my wife to dinner. Call me to pick you up."

Alec and Maxine stepped out to the promenade's music and excitement, joining a parade of elegant costumes strolling near the VIP entrance.

A host of hired pages greeted the invitation-only admittances to a musical background of coronets and trumpets echoing beyond the palace walls.

At last, the evening's fantasy was upon Alec and Maxine as they surveyed the crowd, most in masks and the main performers in convincing costumes.

They proceeded to the Baroque dance instruction from the reception, where black-tied tuxedo servers with trays of champagne welcomed guests queuing in groups for demonstrations. The allemande music comprised cellos, violins, flutes, and harps, and began with couples standing back-to-back.

"Mesdames et Messieurs, it is imperative that you count and let your feet follow," the instructor spewed. "The beat is 4/4, 3/4, 3/4, 4/4, first with the allemande and into the triple meter courante. Keep your core structure in symmetry and hold your arms with elegance. We begin now with Allemande by Handel in D minor."

The dance professor had almost no patience as he jumped and hopped with his arms flailing and feet pirouetting to prove the dance's ease. "It is simple, just do as I am doing!" he pleaded.

Maxine could hardly constrain herself at the comical situation and burst into laughter seeing Alec's befuddled face as he realized his turn at the dance instruction was imminent.

"Oh look, Alec, there's King Louis in his haughty glory with the incredible Marie Antoinette. Bertolier looks quite confident, and he's had years of practice. Follow his dance steps, and you'll be fine."

Percival Sloane and an assistant were across the room, making minor costume alterations for patrons. Finishing an adjustment of an ensemble with elaborate, wayward layers of green bustle, he gave Alec a nod as he attended to the Duke's final touchup.

Sloane placed an invisible dusting on the Wellesley's coattail. The result would only be visible under the ultraviolet light during the ballroom's performance.

Alec mumbled, "Sloane has played his hand. Hide and seek will be much easier. Wellesley is a marked man tonight."

Sloane gave Alec a thumbs-up.

"What are you babbling about, Alec?" Maxine asked.

"Everything is in order. Andre says the undercover team is in place. Sloane and Solange will pinpoint the players for us as they arrive. Come with me, my dear, to the Marble Hall.

The hum of chatter welcomed them at the champagne reception. They eased around the room through the crowd of elegant costumes, anticipating the arrival of Napoleon and his adversaries.

"Watch for Coulliere," said Alec. "If you keep your eyes on the sword, I'll follow the Count and the Duke. Check often that your earpiece is working."

"It'll be alright, Alec! When you're nervous, you give me a lot of detailed instructions. Have you noticed?"

"Guilty," he swallowed before stepping back to admire her.

"I rely on my intuition," she said. "For instance, the secret wall opening that Wellesley showed me is now ajar. It appears someone has a plan to use it."

Alec spun around. "That's him now—the Duke has arrived. Why would he explain his remote access route to you on your first meeting?"

"I should have given that more thought. If Wellesley wants to stash his spoils, the passage has hiding places, with alcoves, stone arches, and doors leading to who knows where."

"I have an advantage," said Alec. "I know who hides behind each masque."

"And Kace? What's his game anyway?" said Maxine.

"Andre overheard Kace in the gardens, mumbling, 'Walk into my parlor, said a spider to a fly.' "

"So, it's a trap?"

"Could be. Better resist the temptation to follow anyone there, in case it is. Interpol tracked Wellesley's purchase of poison in Lyon. It's likely here on his person."

With confidence, the Duke of Wellington strode toward the champagne supply. Superiority and arrogance hung over him, and he held his head high, knowing he looked splendid in his battle merits and epaulets. A proper steward wearing white gloves handed him a fluted glass of bubbly.

He patted the pouch tucked in his jacket and stroked the saber sheath. Satisfied, he took his first sip of lavishness.

"He just revealed his play hand," Alec said. "Sometimes people can't stop themselves with gestures that confess."

A static buzz crackled with news in his earpiece. "The armored transport has delivered Dylan and Napoleon to the front gate. The players are all accounted for, other than Chastain. I assumed he'd have arrived with Wellesley."

Maxine scanned the room for the Count of Monte Cristo's costume. "It's complicated with a room of masks everywhere."

Alec continued his scrutiny of the arrivals, expecting to see Dylan with Napoleon. Instead, Gabriel Dupont's voice came from behind him.

"Marshal Ney, your apparition is fresh from the battlefields of Waterloo," Alec said. "I trust I am correct in my assumption behind that mask."

Maxine offered her hand as a Duchess would do. "I'm so glad you could be here." Gabriel kissed her glove.

"The dignity of a great man well justifies the ensemble," she said. "It must be an honor to reunite with Napoleon's treasured sword from Elba."

"My dear Duchess de Parma, you look exquisite," Gabriel countered. "This evening promises to hold many surprises. It'll be such a privilege to meet my dear emperor again."

The five-foot-six Coulliere, wearing the notable Victor's bicorn hat, entered from the outer hall accompanied by an entourage. Dylan Moreland was in the rear, mischievous and mysterious as the vengeful musketeer.

Wellesley, unnerved, watched the arrivals, unaware that Maxine was following his movements. His hand slowly lowered to the sword sheath reinforcing his intent.

"The man has no moral values," Maxine whispered to Dylan. "He practically gloats with anticipation of inflicting his poison."

"It's greater than his greed for the silver sword. It's to win the game and to feed his ego and notoriety."

"I should have seen through his scheme the first day."

TWENTY-SEVEN

The First Act

Excitement rippled through the guests in the garden as twilight descended, gripped by the tempo and crescendo of drums and guitars.

The crowd parted as a troop of silver-winged centaurs strode toward the fountain on luminous stilts, with more on penny farthings, surrounded by a contingent of feathered and ambidextrous gods and goddesses.

A laser show in fuchsia and purple lit up the palace walls, its glow inspiring hallucinations, and a fantasy stage. Parading through were magicians, fireblowers, acrobats, and actors with fiber-optic headdresses glimmering with neon and sequins in the crystal lights.

As stilt walkers passed, guests converged closer, and Alec briefly lost sight of Wellesley and Dupont.

"Maxine, stay with me. Dylan can take care of Remy. We need to worry about Wellesley. I haven't seen his sidekick.

Kace Chastain contrived a plan of his own, unbeknownst to Wellesley. Tired of being under the thumb of a dictator who forced all the decisions, he spent hours plotting his own double-cross.

From their first meeting at La Santé, he secretly loathed Guilliard and now looked forward to the element of revenge.

Kace's lips barely moved as he spoke silently, "So you think the Duke calls all the shots and takes all the glory, and I'll do the dirty work. I've spent years in your shadow, taking the pittance you dole out. Well, that is not happening tonight! I'll take back the silver buckle that I earned and leave a surprise for Interpol. It will be me who has the last laugh!"

Kace sped the motorcycle past the restricted drop-off zone toward the palace's east entrance, where officers directed vehicles to a parking area. Veering to the right, he ignored their ranting and mounted the curb onto the pedestrian area.

He revved his engine and roared toward the Private Salon, where he'd stashed a packet in the underbrush. Tucking the bike behind a security shed, he advanced to the fence, concealing himself as the strobe lights swept overhead.

Dressed as the Count, Kace lurked outside the servant's quarters behind the scullery of the turret, undetected.

In a uniform reminiscent of the Grand French Armée, Andre passed incognito through the security gate with two Interpol men dressed as butlers. He radioed the others when the blip of Sloane's tracker tagged Kace's appearance.

Kace waited outside the Queen's love nest turret beyond the garden's fountains, irritated by the sizeable key bulging in his pocket. He caressed a timer's components, smug that he had the essential tools for his deception.

"The play begins at eleven, so the stroke of midnight should be about right, with enough distraction to complete my task."

He nimbly laid out the explosive contraption, delicately maneuvered the wires, and covered it with moss at the base of the garnet tea roses. Satisfied with his obscurity, he quickly glanced over his shoulder.

Habitualy, his hand went to the absent belt buckle, surging his angst toward Interpol's interference.

"Ah, it wasn't yours to take! You dastardly agent, you have no idea the risks I took to secure that buckle, keeping my secrets for seven years. Except for my departed friend Rawley, no one knows better how that treasure came to be mine. Wellesley and Coulliere wanted the swords, but I was intent on the buckle, symbolic of courage and defiance. Yet here today, I hold the ace."

Kace ruminated over his disdain. "The buckle will reveal to only me the location of the true Napoleon treasure. The map is mine alone."

With evil ranting, he flipped the switch on a portable cassette recorder.

"Will you walk into my palace, said a spider to a fly . . ." He recited the poetic verse with a lilt to its finale.

A security officer followed his actions on the guardhouse monitor and fed the GPS footage to Interpol's commander. "Kace, you're a curse, but a distraction, to be sure!"

Andre routed two agents to the vicinity and informed Gabriel Dupont of the reason for Kace's delay.

"Agent Dupont, Kace Chastain is on the premises! I didn't expect Wellesley and Kace to split up. We'll need an extra pair of eyes as the Royal Lodge doesn't permit cell phones. There must be a plan between Kace and the Duke. Tail Wellesley if he leaves the Marble Hall."

"It appears the Duke is preoccupied with his sword, so I suspect it's not the costume store's prop."

"We have surveillance plants among the guests. Solange is

attending as a housemaid to Marie Antoinette and is placed near King Louis, who is Bertolier."

"I'll find her, Andre," Alec interrupted. "Gabriel, can you please escort Madame de Parma while I seek out Solange? She has inside knowledge of the palace."

"If you don't locate her soon, Sloane will help; he'll know her costume," Andre said.

Solange was dressed as a seductive mistress, a maiden of the King's court. Scanning the crowd of lookalikes, Alec spotted her with Bertolier. He eased through the melee to her and reached for her elbow to steal her away. Bertolier was so enamored with himself, that he barely noticed.

"Solange, I must borrow you for a quick update."

"I've wanted to get a word to your team," said Solange. "In the history of the Kings and Queens, tonight is not the first of many escapades involving kidnapping and poisoning. Unfortunately, I didn't get a chance to enlighten Andre."

"I'm interested in the royal passageway that is presently out of bounds," said Alec. "It seems that the Duke is familiar with it. Could you show me it's intricacies and hiding places?"

"I'm aware of the Duke's curiosity. Come with me. Stand with our backs to the wall, and I will release the opening. Take two steps back when I tell you, Alec."

Solange waited for the music to overpower the room's din, then reached and pressed a special place on the wall. A portion eased back and slid to the side.

"Now, two steps."

Standing in a dim, dank hall, Alec took a few seconds to acclimatize to the darkness.

"Wait until the door closes."

Solange lit a wall torch with a match. "The Duke came here when he visited Monsieur Bertolier a few days ago. I tracked him to an ancient wall sconce. I know for certain as he wears a distinctive aftershave and it lingers in the hallway. This relic serves as a relay point where Madame de Montespan, the mistress of King Louis XIV, left messages for her lovers and had ready access to poison to eliminate her competitors."

Solange proceeded to leverage the sconce turning it halfway to the right. Then, spring-activated, it forced a protrusion of an inconspicuous stone section.

She reached her hand into a cubbyhole. "Here's the poison pouch, at least I presume it is. A few weeks ago, I overheard the Duke asking one of our curators about the palace poisonings and where they found the evidence."

Alec smiled at the thought that Wellesley could accidentally take his own medicine. "Surely, he will be shooting himself in the foot by his deceit."

"Excusez-moi. Monsieur Bertolier will speak momentarily and expects me to be at his beck and call."

Peering over the sea of plumes and feather hats, Gabriel searched for the frilly white bonnet of a maiden. But before he could spot Solange, King Louis' boisterous boom echoed over the speakers.

Striding as if holding court, Hollande Bertolier reveled in the imaginary esteem he felt he had earned. A train of silk cloaks trailed his footsteps, and a path opened up for him to rise to a podium in his majestic posture.

"Mesdames et Messieurs, welcome to the most fantastic Gala tonight, with theatrical surprises, elegant performances, superb cuisine with France's finest wines. We have a spectacular fireworks display to make this a night you will never forget."

As he boasted, Bertolier spied Napoleon in the wings. "I see my opponent Napoleon Bonaparte is in attendance, and you can be assured of a royal challenge. First, however, I hope you will remember me in your hearts for my love of France and its people."

A mixture of applause, boos, and laughter erupted as guests chose between heralding the emperor or loyalty to the monarchy.

"Prepare for a historic demonstration on the stage in the garden ballroom at eleven sharp, where you will observe the prowess of our beloved emperor," said Bertolier.

Coulliere and Dylan were surprised at the unexpected announcement. Their displeasure showed on their faces.

As the orchestra began the dance marches, trays of hors d'oeuvres and champagne revived the festive ambiance, and Napoleon was once more a figment in the array of costumes.

Andre updated the team that he was on his way, pursuing the Count of Monte Cristo.

As tongues loosened from generous liquor consumption, guests quickly became old friends with others at their tables. Even Wellesley's cheeks were flushed behind the mask, and his scowl became a smile; however, his companion, the Count of Monte Cristo, was noticeably absent.

Gabriel Dupont kept his mask in place during character intros, sitting across from the Duke of Wellington. Wellesley paid no heed with his eyes on Coulliere, but he was most eager to get to the theatrical stage to secure the sword.

Alec and Maxine watched the center of attention, Hollande Bertolier from two tables away. As King Louis, he strutted in his brocade vestiture, as he had not yet found his seating.

Maxine had nervous qualms, knowing she'd be Kace Chastain's target if he became irate knowing Interpol had no intention of returning the buckle. However, if she needed to defend herself, a tiny purse containing Andre's vial was secured to her wrist.

"You're safe, Maxine," Alec whispered. "I know you're on edge—that's natural. I won't let Chastain within two feet of you."

"You say the right things. I'm strong, Alec."

"Yesterday, Chastain was monkeying around near the Private Salon. A search found he stashed a pocket recorder with a confession of Wellesley's Louvre plan. Andre copied it and returned the evidence to the location."

The hall suddenly hushed as Kace entered, showing the defiant, flamboyant flair of the Count of Monte Cristo. A costumed Grand Armée Sarjeant was behind with his footmen.

Striding confidently toward Wellesley, Kace whipped his cape around his back, receiving a smattering of cheers to delight him more.

"Bonsoir, mes amis! I see I have missed the entrance, not only of the great Emperor Napoleon, but my esteemed Duke of Wellington."

Chastain snorted with glee at his performance. "I have had many years to plot my return from exile, and I promise you a few intriguing twists during the evening."

Kace grabbed a passing damsel for a twirl on the dance floor and released her to her partner. Then, bowing, he burst into evil laughter and strolled to his table.

Wellesley leaned forward, ready to berate Kace. But his lips trembled, and he remained silent. His eyes burrowed into Chastain's, sensing the brewing mistrust.

The seething exchange entertained an unsuspecting guest nearby, garbed in period elegance resembling one of the royal mistresses. A rich application of powder and rouge obscured the undercover agent discreetly owered her heavy mask.

"So, you are the Count of Monte Cristo . . . a most impressive entrance! Your roguish intrigue enchants me, exuding such confidence."

Dark brown wisps escaped the brunette wigged bouffant

of ringlets, and she offered her hand. "I'm eager to hear of your exploits."

Kace was fully engaged in the new flirtation, but Wellesley grew impatient at this unscripted diversion.

"Monsieur Dantès, if I may remind you, we have a schedule to maintain," the Duke spit out. He rose from his chair. "The buffet has opened now. If you wish to dine, I propose we attend the food tables now."

The damsel accepted her rejection and turned her attention to the next gentleman at the table.

Gabriel Dupont followed suit, a few feet behind, as Wellesley and Chastain approached the dining presentation.

Wellesley's voice rose louder than he realized. "Kace, what's going on? You arrive late, then dare to threaten me publicly. Our plan is precise, and the getaway must be strategic to be successful."

Chastain was calm refusing to defend himself. "Do you have the key to the Queen's salon? I know what I am to do."

He grasped it from Wellesley.

"Perhaps I have landed too much trust in my accomplice," the Duke said. "Truly you are addicted to deception, but we have both invested greatly in this event. We are counting on its success, and our escape depends on that."

Chastain again ignored Wellesley's pleas. "Ah, the seafood table is excellent!" Flippant in his manner, he began filling his plate with salmon, shrimp, lobster rolls, and salads before moving to the prime rib chef's table for a slab.

Dupont edged up near Wellesley's elbow. "The cad has no class," he whispered. "No wonder he was sent to the island for rehabilitation."

Without acknowledging the guest, Wellesley laughed to break the tension. "Indeed! Another session on the racks would straighten him up."

Alec and Maxine were only a few steps behind Napoleon

and the musketeer at the buffet queue.

"I haven't met the emperor, Alec. An introduction would break the ice," Maxine suggested.

"That's appropriate; you were his second wife after the beloved Josephine left him widowed."

"Kace is intent on Andre turning over the stolen property. That makes me a target."

Andre heard her and replied, "Maxine is right. We'll wait for Kace to take the lead. If he dares to touch Maxine, she'll use the vial I gave her. We'll try to leave him at bay until Wellesley makes his move. Then get a clean roundup."

Remaining at Wellesley's elbow, Gabriel nodded at the instruction.

Setting his plate on a serving table, Wellesley fidgeted as he scanned over his shoulder, then glanced at the wall with the passageway to the royal suites.

Alec cautioned the team. "The Duke is making a move. He's walking to the outer foyer of the Marble Hall. I'll follow. Solange gave me an advance tour, and I know exactly where he is going."

"I'll have an agent on your tail," Andre said. "Report on anything out of place."

TWENTY-EIGHT

Center Stage

At ten before eleven, Hollande Bertolier, in King Louis' guise, stepped to the microphone, puffed up with the crowd's revelry and his self-adoration at being master of ceremonies.

"Mesdames et Messieurs, make your way toward the stage in the garden ballroom for a theatrical performance welcoming our esteemed Emperor Napoleon Bonaparte. The spectacle promises to be astonishing and unexpected. Join us for this momentous occasion, one of the highlights of our evening and memory of a lifetime."

A crush of guests pressed toward the promenade leading into the gardens embellished by thousands of sparkling lights. Blue iridescent strobe lights scanned the patrons who were tingling with anticipation.

A dance troupe led, twirling to the music in silver tights and balancing headdresses in neon optics with laser sabers to symbolize a battle charge. Patrons gasped as they became surrounded by the marvelous spectacle unfolding, naïve to the background caper orchestrated by Wellesley.

Andre whispered to the others, "That's our cue to follow the script. You're up, Moreland."

In musketeer attire, Dylan escorted Napoleon, wearing the silver sword Coulliere had agreed to ransom. He was unaware that Dylan had switched to the replica while in the custody of armored guards.

"Humph, I thought solid silver would be heavier than this," Napoleon grunted. Dylan shrugged with no hint of the change.

Stepping behind them in the processional was Hollande Bertolier as King Louis XVI, with Solange following closely.

As Wellesley joined, his eyes were intent on Napoleon's every step.

At a distance was Kace Chastain as Count of Monte Cristo. His focus never left Maxine's exuberant blue duchess costume, as she paced herself next to the emperor. The bemused Austrian Duke kept himself within a single lunge.

Chastain was smug, contemplating the double-cross that would usurp the spoils for himself. Then, slinking behind the entourage, he blended into the crowd as they merged toward the outer gardens' performance forum.

Observing the unfolding conspiracy, Alec leaned in for Andre's help. "Someone has to stay directly with Maxine!"

"We're watching her every minute with undercover agents in the background."

"I'll ensure Kace doesn't get to grandstand without Wellesley present," said Alec. "The Duke is easy enough to watch, as the black dye on his cloak is visible under the strobe lights."

"Solange will take the forefront," said Andre. "The rendezvous in the theater is imminent, and we'll need all hands on deck."

"We're on track," said Alec. "Wellesley has retrieved the poison sachet from his hiding place in the passageway. Thanks to Solange, it's a secure substitute."

"The only one in imminent danger is Wellesley."

"I care little about his health, Andre. I want to see his public humiliation."

"A confession to the Louvre heist would be nice too."

"Kace is unwittingly cooperating with us in that arena," Alec whispered. "He is more intent on the thrill of upstaging Wellesley's debacle than watching his back. I'm off now in pursuit."

Alec kept his sights on the wavering bushes as Kace, thinking he was deft like a chameleon, attempted to blend into obscurity.

Confident he wasn't being followed, he darted quickly, shielded by symmetrical hedges, finally stopping at a giant yew to examine the path ahead. In the darkness, he scaled the trunk for a better vantage high above the pedestrian route.

He'd forgotten who many of the costumes represented, and he didn't take particular notice as the Austrian Duke passed below.

Kace's ruse required precise timing to ensure success. But, he didn't anticipate his watch alarm would deceive him with an unexpected buzz.

Hearing it, Alec slowed but didn't look up, cautious not to reveal his masked face and be recognized. If he lingered, Kace wouldn't show himself, but delay would be critical to his timing.

Just then, a costumed scullery maid bustled along the path.

"Please, sir, move along. This area is out of bounds; it is for catering use. Serving carts will be rolling through any time. There are festivities in the main area that you will enjoy, and you're missing out. The Napoleon challenge is the focal point of the evening and will begin soon."

Alec looked into the eyes of Solange and pointed toward the tree. With a nod, she said, "They need you at center court."

Solange smiled coyly. "My grandmother always said to keep my eye on the mischievous crow that will abscond with the shiny items when others are distracted."

As Alec moved from the yew tree, Kace shinnied down and hurried to his cache to retrieve the tape and pocket recorder.

Across the lawns, a procession led by pompous Louis XVI and Marie-Antoinette marched on with regal pageantry toward their gilded thrones, preparing for the upcoming drama. Guests vied for viewing placement along the walkway behind stanchions and burgundy velvet ropes.

The royals gloated with their luxury and authority over the French peasants, refusing to listen to the people's pleas, of their pain and hunger, their eternal empty plight, and their legacy of poverty.

A mock mob of women and peasant farmers surged through the crowd toward the throne carrying shovels, pitchforks, swords, and wooden muskets. Chanting and swooning, they moved to the central forum.

Surrounding the throne, costumed phantoms symbolizing the mob's oppression and anger swirled red flowing flags representing the blood of Paris.

The rumbling and crooning rose to a spellbinding crescendo, with patriotic drums and groaning, until the royal couple cowered in fear of the aggression. The music culminated in a reverberating thunder and then stopped suddenly.

Louis waved his cloaked arms, offering wagonloads of flour and animals to appease their hunger. Still, the throng denied his empty promises, and the King and Queen were taken away as prisoners, as pink dust of despair was launched into the air.

As the band struck up, the audience began singing in

unison *Le Chant des Partisans*, a patriotic hymn of France that reflected the empire's tyranny during the revolution and later wars. The intention was to inspire rage and a call to arms.

Bertolier spontaneously decided to lead the chorus, invigorated by inciting the angry mob.

> *"Ami, entends-tu le voi noir des corbeaux*
> *Sur nos plaines ?*
> *Ami, entends-tu les cris sourds du pays*
> *Qu'on enchaine ?*
> *Ohé, partisans, ouvriers et paysans*
> *À vos armes,*
> *Tonight, the enemy will know the price of blood*
> *And tears.*
> *Join the sabotage, get off the hills, comrades.*
> *Take the rifles, the guns, and the grenades from*
> *The straws.*
> *Hey, killers, with a bullet or by knife, be bold."*

A page grasped Bertolier by the elbow and escorted him away as the singing faded into the background.

With the thrones vacant, the audience's shouts turned to patriotic war songs and victorious rejoicing, then cheered in anticipation to dramatic music and sound effects. Actors rushed King Louis and Marie Antoinette and forced them from the stage.

An official narrator stepped forward. "Mesdames et Messieurs, King Louis XVI, and Marie Antoinette have been evicted from the palace and imprisoned for three years, and the revolution continues to be fraught with uprisings.

"The bugles, battle cries, and pounding of hooves you hear present the rush of troops banding across Europe. Lawlessness pervades France until the victor led by the new Emperor Napoleon will arrive to restore order."

Under Gabriel Dupont's watch, Wellesley craned his neck in search of Kace. The Duke kept his hand close to the saber sheath at his side, but instead of confidence, his face showed concern that precision was in jeopardy. The theatrical chaos of the play was an unexpected distraction.

"Where is the blasted Kace? His cue was the arrival of Coulliere. Incredulous to be sloppy after so many months of planning."

Unseen by the crowd, the actor portraying the emperor exited the garden stage and was replaced by Coulliere in authentic Napoleon garb. His mannerisms were superb, and he relished in the knowledge that the regaled Napoleon sword was at his side.

The crowd hushed again, waiting for the emperor to speak as if he would genuinely deliver them from their tyranny.

Coulliere rose higher in his boots and transformed into a taller stalwart emperor. His back was straight, and his chest puffed out to accept victory.

As the spellbound audience held on to every word, he paused to study their faces, and for a proud, fleeting moment, he wondered what Raphael Coulliere would think of him now.

Kace worked his way through the crowd into Wellesley's line of vision and gave a consenting nod. However, the Duke was not the object of his antics; it was the Duchess de Parma. He realized he had a distance to overcome as a surge of hooped skirts and cloaks obstructed his pathway.

When the bugles stopped, Wellesley's voice rang out. "My dear emperor, how did you earn your battle wounds?"

Coulliere was perplexed as he'd never received a script. He slipped his limp arm into the military sash and stepped forward, knowing Andre Poulin was behind as a bodyguard.

"Dear Duke of Wellington," Coulliere said, "You led your troops well during the Prussian Allied advance. But you see, it is I who succeeded in arriving in Paris to resume my authority.

I'll restore this great country to its people to give them the patronage and prosperity they deserve."

Wellesley replied, "Since you have addressed property undeserved, Emperor Bonaparte, I see you carry the sword of the denied King Charles. You have taken it from its rightful place in Ajaccio, the birthplace of your father and brothers. I dare to challenge you to see that my own father's initials are borne on the sheath as the silversmith and craftsman. Draw your sword and return it as I demand in front of these good people."

"Preposterous!" Napoleon said.

Wellesley stepped forward and drew the sword he had tipped with poison, unaware that Solange had replaced the contents with graphite powder. He let his rage unfold in spewing words and lunged forward with the lance before him, and his balance arm staggered behind.

"Draw! Defend your honor, such as it is!"

"You look a fool, dear Duke. However, I will no longer address you as the Duke of Wellington but as the criminal you genuinely are.

The crowd hushed in shock.

"You, Lawrence Wellesley, or Jacques Guilliard are none other than a thief that stole from the Napoleon exhibit at the Louvre years ago. You're a common criminal dressed to deceive us as a historic war hero."

As the audience gasped, Wellesley paled and stumbled backward, almost losing his balance.

"Absurd!" he shouted " Foolish words can only incriminate you."

Kace thoroughly enjoyed the exchange and stepped up immediately, knowing he would add embers to the raging fire.

"Patrons and honored guests, let me clarify what is happening before you. You can see that I am dressed as the Count of Monte Cristo, who was wrongly imprisoned for merely delivering Napoleon's correspondence and was condemned as a treasonist. I have come to avenge him and right the wrongs. I have here—"

Kace waved a handheld tape recorder in the air at the buzzing crowd.

"I have with me a confession . . . and the identity of the evasive Louvre robbers of seven years ago, myself included."

Gasps and chatter rose from the onlookers. Security personnel looked from one to another waiting for any cues to action.

Kace's eyes darted to a surge of officers pushing through.

"I implore you to stay back if you do not wish to injure your guests. This display of props is deceiving you."

Kace turned to face Coulliere. "Emperor Napoleon, I will relieve you of your silver sword, and your life will be spared."

Overlooking the stunned audience, he laughed and mocked, "It is only right that the avenger leaves with the spoils."

Andre whispered a stand-down order to the gendarmerie's commander until he would give the signal.

Kace seized the saber from Wellesley's right hand in a swift jerk. Holding it in the air, he waved it in Coulliere's face.

"The poison tip of this sword will extinguish you in seconds, so suggest to the gendarme that they ease back."

Dylan Moreland pounced between Kace and Maxine, ready to make his play.

"Ah, Monsieur Moreland, or shall I address you as the famed Musketeer Montoya? You prepare to take me by surprise," Kace declared. "You will have to avenge your captors another time. I'll be taking over here."

Maxine judged the staging distance and backed out of range, knowing the syringe was accessible in her bag.

"Don't take another step, my dear Duchess Marie Louise," Kace snapped. His tone pierced the air hoping to intimidate her. "There's a price for your freedom."

Coulliere was baffled by the goings-on. "Take the sword. I'll throw it to the floor. And leave her alone."

The emperor moved to toss the sword in apparent surrender as Andre Poulin and his aide closed in.

Kace shouted, "Nobody moves!" Everyone froze, and Kace nodded to Coulliere.

"Proceed!" he demanded. "The sword, please."

When the saber settled on the floor, Kace kicked it aside, keeping his focus on Coulliere.

Watching patiently, Wellesley saw his best chance. Stooping to retrieve the prize, he wobbled on his high shoes, and before he regained his balance, Bertolier instructed a young page boy to secure the sword.

"Non, non, Monsieur Wellesley, I said *nobody* moves and that includes you."

Kace was savoring the confused look on his conspirator's face, and in the distraction, he didn't notice the sword had disappeared.

TWENTY-NINE

The Spoils to the Victor

The astonished crowd hushed as Chastain pulled the cassette from his pocket and raised the recorder over his head. "First, ladies and gentlemen, I insist you listen to this tape."

He gestured and called to the balcony's audio technician. "Gentlemen controlling the sound, set the speakers so everyone can hear me, inside and outside the palace."

The spell-bound audience didn't budge, and as static died down from the adjustments, Kace scanned the audience with a villainous stare.

"After you have listened, you will stay exactly where you are and not move an inch."

Puffed up in confidence by his instant celebrity, he boasted at securing their undivided attention.

"The emperor will secure the Napoleon sword in my sheath," Kace said, "and Inspector Poulin will turn over to me my silver belt buckle, my property, in return for the safety of Napoleon's beloved spouse, the Duchess de Parma. The police will then escort me to the palace gate and send me safely on my way."

The audience gasped and hushed again to hear Andre Poulin's response, standing beside him. "Monsieur Chastain, I did not believe you to be sincere when you demanded that I bring the silver belt buckle; the suggestion seemed ludicrous. I'm afraid it's not on the premises.

"Furthermore, the sword is the Bonaparte family's property, and I cannot transfer stolen goods. You may feel entitled as the buckle has been in your possession these last seven years; however, the fact remains that it's a stolen historical artifact belonging to the Louvre."

A few feet away, Wellesley was wavering from side to side, angry and preparing to make a move until Dylan gripped his shoulder. "Hold steady! There's nothing to be gained by interrupting a good historical movie!"

Wellesley froze, surprised to see the Interpol agent. "You! You should mind your own business."

"This *is* my business."

Dylan poked his back like a pointed gun.

"You won't get far tonight, Duke, as we have a marked sign on your back. You'll be seen anywhere in Paris in your failed escape. La Santé Prison is preparing your room as we speak."

Wellesley struggled to peer over his shoulder, searching for a visible target.

"It's not for you to see, Monsieur Wellesley; it is for the authorities who monitor your movements. Furthermore, your deceit intending to poison your counterpart has been intercepted. You have been outsmarted!"

Kace clicked the recorder's ON button and raised the volume.

"The first voice you'll hear is my dear Duke here, representing the Duke of Wellington . . . but in reality, he is the common thief known as Jacques Guilliard." Alec knew

Wellesley's voice as it boomed from the recording:

"Antoine, we have five minutes. I need to know which of the swords was the one intended for King Charles. Chastain, you take whatever you must have—

"The rest of you just grab from the Napoleon jewels and exhibits that are most valuable. Kace! Don't bother with the buckle; we must go. I have a dealer in South America willing to take it all. Grab the scaffolding and secure the bins!"

Next, they heard the real Antonie Coulliere.

"Wellesley, you won't get away with this!"

"I didn't ask for your moral opinion," Wellesley snapped back. "Fill the duffels with as much as you can grab."

The crashing sounds of breaking glass and splintering wood echoed over the speakers, as the thieves exited out the window. Guests covered their ears at the volume, then at a bang as the scaffolding jolted under their weight.

Voices filtered through the noise as they escaped. "Kace, what's in your hand?"

"A measly silver buckle. You won't miss it in your tally."

"There's Antoine at the boulevard," said Remy. "Good man—he's started up the getaway car."

"Easy! Don't rush the ropes, or the scaffolding will collapse."

Napoleon-costumed Remy was jolted that the Louvre burglary was recorded, and his shoulders cringed with embarrassment and shame.

As Kace basked in the bombshell of his presentation, Maxine opened the silk sack and prepared the syringe, careful not to alert him. Holding it in the back of her hand, she squeezed closer. Alec and Andre created an opening on the stage for her hooped skirts to surge forward.

Feigning a collapse, she lunged, grabbing at Kace's arm on

the pretense she would fall.

He roared in delight at the irony. "Come into my parlor!"

As his arms supported her, she jabbed directly into his neck veins. His eyes bulged with rage, realizing he had fallen prey to her deception as the color drained from his face. Maxine's eyes locked onto Chastain's for a second, and she could see his evil heart. He gave her a look as he was sinking, a defiant surrender then a smirk. Finally, his knees gave way underneath him, and Andre knelt to seize the fallen man.

Max whispered to Kace. "You aren't the spider, you're the fly!"

Wellesley's instinct was to get to Kace and finish him off, but Dylan and Gabriel firmly laid hands of restraint on him.

The audience was delighted that the villains were captured, and cheers filled the festive air that their beloved Napoleon had been saved.

Hollande Bertolier watched from the wings and swooped onto center stage to take a bow. He held out his hand for the Duchess de Parma to join him in receiving accolades, then gave a weakened gesture toward Coulliere.

As if on cue, the orchestra started up, 'La Marseillaise', the French Revolution's patriotic ballad.

Bertolier's voice crackled off-key over the show.

> Allons enfants de la patrie,
> Le jour de gloire est arrivé
> Contre nous de la tyrannie
> L'étendard sanglant est levé
> Entendez-vous dans les campagnes,
> Mugir ces féroces soldats?
> Ils viennent jusque dans nos bras
> Egorger nos fils, nos compagnes!

Guests sang the refrain and verses with bolstered pride, and as their patriotism and celebration grew, dancing broke out throughout the gardens. Then, with champagne flowing, the party went on until dawn.

With the culprits under guard, Wellesley glared at Maxine.

"How did you know about me?"

"You slipped and called me by my first name here on that day," she said. "Then, your story about Myra didn't hold up. I'll confess that I fell for your impassioned tale and I'm sorry you are not that person."

A glimmer of sadness crossed his face before he flared back with his challenge.

"That's not enough for an accusation!"

"There were the videos at your exchange in Lyon. Then you lurked outside the hospital. Oh, and at the toll bridge in Bordeaux. Why do you tap that blasted walking stick; it gives you away every time. Shall I go on, Jacques? Who are you really, before this all began?"

"I was born to thrive from a challenge," he bragged. "I attract weak people to trust me and observe things about other's boring lives. I manipulate circumstances when I choose, and you will not change that."

"Was it worthwhile?"

"I found that no one cared. Insurance companies keep hiking their premiums and return it all to the criminals. That's the way it works, it's not personal for anyone."

Poulin frowned. "Why murder an innocent kid and a promising professor? And explain your plot to kill Monsieur Coulliere."

Wellesley displayed the first signs of apprehension in his voice. "I hate loose ends, Captain. But, that's the profession. It mirrors yours, wrapping up a case, rounding up loose fragments, and putting them where they belong. Surely you understand that premise?"

Remy Coulliere was cuffed to be escorted away for his involvement but turned back to Wellesley. "Why did you ram us on the bridge, Jacques? It was deliberate. Did you intend to murder both of us? Then tonight, with the poison?"

Jacques laughed. "It was a luscious temptation. I already told your Captain that you and your brother were nothing but risks to me. You've heard the saying that loose lips sink ships."

Remy lurched toward the Duke, his hands reaching as if to strangle the rogue.

"You are the devil, Wellesley. You can rot in jail."

Two gendarme officers held Remy Coulliere's arms and led him away with his head low in defeat. The pair were locked in separate wagons for transport to the jail.

Wellesley, escorted by Dupont, was rigid and defiant, blaming everything on Chastain. As the van drove away, he banged on the closed window. "It wasn't my voice on the tape!" he shouted. "I'm being framed, I knew nothing of this atrocity!"

"Andre, I do feel sorry for the family," Dylan said. "They didn't conspire to participate; it just happened that Antoine was in charge of the museum, coinciding with the Louvre heist plans."

"It's not so cut and dry, Dylan. Remy got himself into gambling debt, and that didn't come about by his being innocent. He chose to deal in the dark world of predatory lending and get involved with ruthless people. He was in the wrong place at the right time, and records will show he received financial compensation for his part. Everyone has a choice between right and wrong."

"And he remained quiet all this time and played along," said Alec.

"I want to chat with the real Antoine to get more background," said Maxine. "He was cooperative, and I believe he loves his brother. There is something unique in the bond of twins, but also uncanny. I'm not sure when one was good and the other evil, that there wasn't any collaboration."

"Before you do that, look at Moreland's statement as a rookie on the day of the accident," Andre said. "Bring him up to speed; his insight might unravel details."

Gabriel took her hand. "I'll escort you, Maxine. I've missed the atmosphere of the old precinct."

Andre broke the festivities with an urgent team alert. "Dylan! Join me right away. The Napoleon sword has disappeared during the melee. Guards momentarily lost sight of it, and now it can't be found."

"I confess that I didn't leave that to chance. The armored truck has the authentic sword in its secured cargo. The one you say is missing is merely a souvenir of interest, although there is always a fool somewhere who will try to pawn it on the black market."

"I'm relieved, Dylan. But, before I leave, I'll find our host, Bertolier. I believe he knows more than he volunteered. Where is he?"

Solange said, "During the Duke's audio show, he kicked aside the sword as Chastain played his recording. He then disappeared through the hallway to his office upstairs. Monsieur Poulin, follow me. I'll take you to it."

She led Andre into the passage and up a staircase. They stopped at the back entrance of Bertolier's office hearing loud voices inside.

"Monsieur Rodriguez, I assure you this *is* the authentic sword," Bertolier stammered. "I wired its photos from the museum exhibit and sent you copies of authentication by the insurer. I went to great pains to acquire this; we discussed its value and agreed on a price."

The Brazilian examined the sheath with a jeweler's prism and raised his head. "We did agree, Monsieur Bertolier."

"Then it's done!"

"However, this is not the same sword. It is *not* solid silver. It is a shoddy reproduction." He raised his voice in anger. "How dare you deliberately bring me here under pretenses to extract a ransom. I am not a petty dealer! I have a reputation to uphold."

"There has been an embarrassing mistake. Give me twenty-four hours, and I assure you I'll recover the authentic sword. They must have inserted a prop in the play."

Solange inserted her key and swung the door open, intending to startle the occupants. Poulin watched through the open door.

Bertolier was aghast. "I beg your pardon, Solange. What are you doing here?"

"It seems that you and your deception are exposed, Monsieur Bertolier. I was disappointed that you have become a party to a crime against our government."

"You're mistaken, I assure you, Solange!"

"Silence! You achieved an honorable position here at the palace and have taken advantage of that. Therefore, you must accept my immediate resignation."

Bertolier stared with his mouth open. Slowly the impact dawned on him that he'd been set up.

It was almost midnight when Kace was escorted out of the palace still intoxicated by Maxine's injection. Staggering, he babbled incoherently to Dylan, unraveling the details of the fateful day.

"I've been poisoned, but you cannot thwart me. I will get the last laugh, Monsieur Moreland. You will find out precisely at the stroke of midnight."

He tapped his watch. "Any time," he said.

Suddenly, an explosive bang echoed followed by a thud

from beyond the gardens, and a cloud of dust rose over the private salon through the window.

In seconds, sirens and fire trucks poured into the stone lane of the Royal Lodge as guests pushed toward the exits.

"Chastain was loitering there this afternoon," said Solange. "He wouldn't know me, but I was there too as the scullery maid."

"The disturbance blemishes the festivities," said Andre, "but I doubt the blast caused much damage. We took precautions to protect any artifacts."

The audience was thrilled by the surprise drama that had unfolded. By the time the crowd had thinned, the sunrise breakfast was served. The orange and pink inferno rising over Paris was awe-inspiring. The final stage of the evening left everyone satisfied that they had partaken in a historic pageantry ruse.

Hollande Bertolier was flustered with the unplanned excitement. However, he focused on his promise to deliver the silver sword to Rodriguez. The warning to him was stern and precise.

"I must find that sword!"

Rodriguez was irritated but anxious to get to a telephone. Stepping into the hall, he waited for someone to answer in La Marais.

"Antoine!"

THIRTY

Unraveling the Crime

Dylan Moreland arranged a meeting the next morning inviting Maxine and Gabriel to join him at the station house. His manner was businesslike as he laid out photocopies of pages of the accident report that maimed Antione Coulliere.

"Bonjour, Maxine and Gabriel, this is Detective Dubois who was a rookie with me on the day of the Louvre heist seven years ago," said Dylan. "We will try to recreate the moment of the crash with you. Since we last spoke, I studied the case many times. It was one of my earliest investigations and made an impression on me."

"Excellent process, indeed," said Gabriel. "We are all humbled to take risks if we can save even one person and bring criminals to justice. It's often the little forgotten things where the best clues can be found."

"I have an observation," said Maxine. "Could the accident have been deliberate? Can you tell from the on-scene photos if someone rammed the Coulliere brothers' vehicle?"

"That's not in the report. But I noticed at the time that

there were no skid marks."

"What about the car behind?"

"It didn't attempt to halt or slow down, and its engine was running and revved up. Then the driver got out and came to look into the Coulliere's car."

"When you arrived at the scene, had either of the brothers been removed from the vehicle?"

"No. The passenger was unconscious and was making soft sounds," said Dubois. "The driver was excited and animated, even though he was bleeding about the head."

"Was the driver's condition serious?" Gabriel asked.

"No, he didn't appear severely injured and refused immediate medical attention. However, we had to restrain him as he wanted to attack the other driver, still looking into the vehicle. He was outraged and took the situation personally."

"How did you determine which brother was which?"

"The one driving made the identifications. As you know, we were both rookies and not accustomed to looking for criminal intent in a car accident," Dylan said.

"Ah, I thought as much," Gabriel said.

Maxine persisted. "The ones in the second vehicle—did you speak with them, Detective?"

"That driver was somewhat older, had gray hair, and had the tongue of a serpent. He yelled at us to get out of his way, then burned rubber backing up and spun out of there. Suddenly we had a hit-and-run case too."

"Did they find him?"

"The gendarmes took off to chase him, but I'm unaware of subsequent action as I remained at the scene. He wouldn't have gotten too far as his rad was split and steaming."

Gabriel jotted down the two vehicles' descriptions and noted the damage to Wellesley's car from the photos.

"We might be able to track the damaged vehicle to a service mechanic or a tow service within a few kilometers of the bridge. The law requires documentation for any bodywork done on a vehicle that appears to be from a collision. Was that an angle that was followed?"

Dylan Moreland was about to say more but hesitated. Intuitive, Maxine waited, making the silence uncomfortable.

"Something else is burdening you, Detective Moreland."

"It's purely off the record. Officers are cautioned not to get emotionally involved in cases, but I was a rookie and I felt bad for the passenger. Then, finally, the man opened his eyes, mumbling as if he needed to say something.

"I went to the hospital that night for a follow-up on his condition. He recognized me from the scene. He sighed as if I were a priest and he wanted to confess."

"What did he disclose?" asked Gabriel.

"Let me get my words in order, or it won't make sense. Monsieur said that his brother should retrieve the box from the passage—the secret place. 'It is our birthright,' he said."

"How odd that he would say something like that when his life was in the balance," Maxine said.

"It seemed to be very important that he relay that message. I really couldn't make much sense of it."

Leaving Moreland, Gabriel and Maxine relayed the conversation to Poulin.

"If you can spare us, Andre, we'll check garages and mechanics for any record or recollection of the accident."

"Fine, then we'll tally up our evidence as soon as possible." But something else burdened Andre, and he radioed back.

"Dylan, as you are the only one who has been in the museum passageway, does this make sense? The brothers' relationship seems to be at the crux of the Louvre theft."

Moreland pondered, taking himself on a visual walkthrough of the trap door, the ladder, the storage room, and the alcoves, all appearing undisturbed for many years.

"Forensics have been through everything," said Dylan.

"Go back and examine it again."

"I doubt we missed anything, but I'll go again. A secret place, you say?"

"Let me know before I visit Odilette and Antoine," Maxine said. "The old man is still sharp. Perhaps I can help put the puzzle together."

"I'll go now and stop at the insurance agency."

With caution, Odilette answered the knock at the front door in Le Marais. It struck Maxine that she had never really looked at the woman. She was younger than the first impression, and her eyes flashed with suspicion or defense.

Although she forced a smile, it was obvious that she was not pleased to see them. Taken aback by Maxine, she looked perturbed.

"You could have told me you were a detective when you came to see me. You didn't have to sneak around behind my back. Is it your doing that caused Remy to sit in a jail cell?"

"My sincerest apologies, madame. You see, Remy hired us to protect his family, and I was doing the groundwork to know about routine activities and locations. I was checking on everyone's well-being. However, I love history, and the book about the Duke of Wellington was fascinating."

Odilette seemed appeased but turned her angst toward the man beside Maxine. Then, as if she caught a glimpse of herself in a mirror, she adjusted her hair and smoothed her dress, tossing an apron onto the handrail.

"Pardon my manners, Madame Coulliere. May I present Gabriel Dupont, my esteemed colleague, who will help us build a case against the Louvre heist's other partners?"

Dupont offered his hand, and Odilette gingerly accepted it. "We are inclined to believe that both brothers were unwillingly coerced into participating," Gabriel said. "We'd like to remove the shadow hanging over your family's reputation."

Odilette widened the door and let her shoulders relax.

"Come in then. I'll put a kettle on. It is a very long story, but it will be truthful."

Maxine's eyes scanned the room for any sign of Antoine or his wheelchair or oxygen apparatus and saw nothing, not even a shawl. But there again, were the athletic sneakers she had seen Antoine wear at the park.

"I see your searching eyes," Olidette snapped. "He's not here at the moment. Make yourself comfortable; I'll be right back."

Maxine was struck by the words 'not here' as she surmised to herself. "Where else could an invalid be, unless the planned appearances are for other reasons?"

Gabriel paced the room with his hands behind his back in contemplation. Perusing the parlor bookshelf, he noted shelf after shelf dedicated to French battles and Napoleonic history. Finally, his eyes froze at an obscure book in the top right corner.

As Odilette returned with a tray of a teapot and cups, she glanced disapprovingly at Gabriel, who continued focusing on the bookshelves above.

"They are nothing more than history books, monsieur. Now tell me, what is it that you want to know?"

"Where is Monsieur Antoine today?"

"He's resting. He doesn't know that Remy has been arrested, and I'm unsure how he will deal with the news."

"I can appreciate you are concerned. However, as detectives, I assure you that we are thorough, and if we can find any evidence to exonerate Antoine and Remy, you would not want to hinder that."

Odilette's impatience showed in a roll of her eyes, and boredom rose in her voice. "Go ahead and ask what you must."

"We have come from the gendarmerie office," Maxine said. "The officers that wrote the accident report provided facts previously uninvestigated. This information is, of course, off the record, but I believe you should know."

"What did they say?"

"Both Detective Moreland and Detective Dubois were rookie officers and took a personal concern about your husband's condition. Detective Moreland recalls visiting the hospital as a follow-up. Antoine spoke a few significant words to him."

"How can you assume that?"

"Because Antoine relaxed, and it took a burden from his shoulders. Do you know a secret hiding place where the brothers would stash a secret?"

Odilette wrung her hands with uncertainty before her eyes instinctively returned to the bookshelf.

Relieving herself of guilt, she said to Gabriel. "You were right, that is it—the book."

Gabriel smiled and reached toward the upper corner. "May I, madame?"

"Yes. Bring that one down, *The Secret Place*. I haven't touched it in years."

The dusty cloth binding was fragile and well-aged, and Gabriel gently eased it from its moorings to a flattened newspaper that Odilette laid on the bureau.

"I know what kind of book this is," he said. "I believe it is a hollowed-out treasure box. Many libraries had at least one of these in past times. It appears to be very old."

"That is correct," Odilette sighed.

Opening the lid, they were astonished at the two items—a tiny map once held within the silver belt buckle showing the Napoleon treasure location and an aged diary written by Raphael Coulliere, the footman of Marshal Ney.

"Oh, my gosh!" Maxine gasped.

"It is extremely fragile, madame," said Gabriel. "With your permission, we'll have it examined by a professional to take proper care so it does not become damaged."

"What does this mean to you?" Odilette asked.

"It adds enormous credibility to the Napoleon exhibit and the story that Remy told to Interpol of Raphael Coulliere. But why has it been kept here away from the museum?"

"Antoine was very protective of it and said that one day, it would be their birthright. He feared that some people with access to the museum were thieves and conspirators waiting for opportunities to replace original artifacts with counterfeits."

"He was quite right to make that assumption, madame," Gabriel said.

Odilette deftly swept her hand over the book as if she were reminiscing, but Maxine saw what she did. When Gabriel carefully swaddled the book in newsprint, the miniature, folded map was absent.

Maxine looked back at Odilette and knew the truth.

THIRTY-ONE

True Confessions

Interrogations of Wellesley and Chastain were going nowhere, each blaming the other. They knew how to buck the system and demand delays, while they dutifully continued to dismiss court-appointed attorneys.

Based on DNA evidence, Jacques Guilliard was fingerprinted and booked as the Louvre heist's ringleader. But ironically, it was Rawley's evidence that cinched the connection.

Guilliard boasted of his notoriety as news splashed onto the front pages of prestigious broadsheets and tabloid papers across Europe. His career of mischief fired up the press and journalists, and moviemakers were hounding the prison authorities for the pairs' stories.

Reports elevated Guilliard to the hero status of William Tester and James Burgess who orchestrated the Great Train Robbery, with stolen bullion taken from England to France across the Channel.

Interpol denied outsider access as the Louvre investigation

grew and tried to quash the illusion of romantic characters being heralded as heroes.

Rather than be charged as an accomplice, the Lyon affiliate willingly added evidence of Wellesley acquiring the poison intended for Coulliere. The toll bridge video and the weapon's match incriminated him in Ratcliffe's murder in Bordeaux, followed by a slew of attempted murder charges threatening the Coulliere brothers and others on the Duke's hit list.

Maxine's injection had wracked Kace Chastain's head with pain, but he shook it off, with glory waiting to lift his ego. He boasted of his success in exposing Wellesley and the theatrics of his bomb at the private salon. He became an icon of his theories and an unwitting representation of loose lips.

"I would like to have seen the confusion myself," he boasted to his cellmate. "The Count of Monte Cristo deserved better recognition than a costume and a cloak. But I'll be out of here before they can blink as I have sources and skills they have never noticed."

In the cell's darkness, Kace took off his shoe and twisted the heel, removing a minuscule pick.

The drunken burglar in the upper bunk listened to the bragging and pleaded, "If you can get sprung, I can go with you. I'll watch your back."

The colleague's esteem secured Kace's confidence to rant on. "When I'm out of here, a treasure will be waiting for me, There's a map hidden in the silver belt, *my* silver belt."

"A treasure map! Just give me a small cut—I don't want much, but I can't return to La Santé."

Kace's eyes lit up on acquiring a devotee who would do as he was told. "Have you heard of the treasure of the Count of Monte Cristo?"

"Impossible! You know of it?" the prisoner asked.

"Do you know who I am?" Kace pressed with eagerness. "If you knew, you'd be very cautious and mind your tongue about things I tell you."

"I've seen that look in a man's eye before, and I recognize it as the soul of a murderer. But, be assured, sir, my lips are sealed."

Guards listening from the interior room found humor in the comedic scheme afoot.

A senior one expounded, "The poor kid. It seems he has no family, at least none that care. Discarded people fill our prisons, many feeling they have no value in life other than to commit crimes to get worthy attention."

"Sad," said an older guard.

"It was his choosing! He didn't leave a choice for his landlord or his sidekick on the bridge."

"He won't see the light of day until he's a very old man if he lives long enough to serve his sentence."

From the hour the culprits were arrested, Andre was deluged with inquiries from the museum's insurers, journalists, and anyone associated with the Louvre robbery, clamoring for details and reports of recovered artifacts.

The insurance company quickly filed a suit against the Military Museum to reclaim payouts. The silver belt buckle held in Interpol's evidence was among them. As certificates purported the sword to be authentic, suits didn't proceed against the Coulliere family.

The family asked for privacy and patience considering the debilitated state of Antoine. Although they had private discussions about *The Secret Place* and its contents, they expected absolution and the return of their rightful property.

The museum's directors were unprepared to accept the imposter's diary as authentic. Instead, they preferred to wait for an official validation of the rediscovered journal of Raphael Coulliere.

"There is no need for a public presentation of the discovery," Andre explained to Gabriel. "Exposing the switch would shed a discouraging light on the archives administration of any museum."

"I studied the diary's contents at the Interpol office," said Gabriel. "The contents were enthralling, with specifics about Ney and Napoleon that only a person with first-hand experiences could recount."

"We have a few more questions for the Coulliere family. It's best to discuss it separately with feeble Antoine and Remy."

"I can help with it," Gabriel said. "We'll get a grip on their interpretations of events and the symbolism to their family."

"We mustn't overstep Maxine," Andre said. "She has invested in a relationship with Antoine, and he has put his faith in her."

"And Odilette should not be overlooked."

"No, she's been the caregiver for the family all these years and is wise and clever. Women notice little details that men overlook."

Gabriel smiled at Andre's meaning. "Of course, Maxine should be the one to have the tête-à-tête with the brothers."

"I expect they never mentioned the book to Wellesley or Chastain, or it wouldn't still be on the shelf," said Andre. "Gabe, you've talked in the past about a treasure map. We assumed tales of its existence were myths and legends."

"A time will come when Chastain realizes the map is no longer in the silver buckle," said Gabriel.

"His future hangs on his hopes of the buried palace treasure even if his incarceration postpones it."

"When we could access the palace blueprints, I checked for such a burial place but couldn't find it," said Gabriel. "And

Odilette doesn't know we saw her remove the map."

Andre opened a tablet photo. "Here's a surveillance image and data of the Brazilian buyer in Bertolier's office. It matches him as the insurance fellow by the name of Rodriguez. Gabriel, could you drop the file in Montmartre for Alec to track? He's exceptional at this sort of thing."

Andre gathered his thoughts in his brisk walk to meet with the Louvre curator.

Dylan flagged a taxi to La Santé Prison to continue questioning Wellesley and Chastain. Presented with the sign-in log, he was startled that the name directly above his own was Hollande Bertolier.

"Bertolier has committed his involvement by his signature here!" Dylan muttered. "Why would he need to talk to Wellesley so early this morning? They must have barely finished dismantling the party decorations. It took him by surprise there had been a prop switch. He must be motivated by greed to locate the authentic sword for the dealer, despite Andre's encounter with Rodriguez in Bertolier's office."

Dylan waited in a questioning room to deal with the Duke first.

Wellesley had regained his superiority air and scoffed at the sight of Moreland. "Well, if it isn't the suave Interpol agent! I didn't expect a courtesy call so soon."

"How do I address you, Monsieur . . . is it Wellesley or Guilliard? I see your reservation here is in the name of Jacques Guilliard, formerly of La Santé. It seems you have racked up some frequent stay rewards!"

"I've impressed many with my career," he boasted. "Have you not noticed that?"

"I'll give you credit for masterminding the Louvre heist, using the scaffolding as window cleaners in broad daylight. No one had done that before. It was quick and efficient, I agree."

Wellesley reveled in the compliment.

"The most satisfying deceptions are under the noses of those least expecting a sting," he replied. "First, they don't suspect it; then they're too humiliated to interfere. The insurers were the ones to certify the artifacts but were too embarrassed to rescind them."

"You may have overlooked Rawley Baker," said Dylan. "Did you know of his university degree, that he studied law and found you and your group as interesting subjects? In addition, you should also know that he secured DNA evidence from the Louvre putting you at the scene."

Wellesley paled at the news but didn't respond.

"Also, Remy Coulliere was clever by recording your conversations when you blackmailed him into cooperating in your scheme. And we can't forget Chastain's tape played last night, exposing you in your own words."

Dylan paused before laying on the topper. "I believe you forgot you have too many loose ends! It seems you are losing your precision."

"Give it your best shot, detective, but it's all concocted and circumstantial. Chastain isn't a credible witness and the Coullieres profited and assumed guilt, with opportunity and motive."

"Is that your defense?"

Wellesley scowled. "It doesn't matter what you do to me. I'll be back in a few months, sharper the next time."

"That's if you are only looking at incarceration for conspiracy to rob the museum, blackmail, assault of a federal officer, and buying illegal drugs."

"Insignificant!" Wellesley shrugged.

"Those don't add up to life, but you forget Professor Ratcliffe when your loose-end efforts went off course. The coroner has declared Ratcliffe's death a homicide."

"You can't pin that on me."

"Wrong," said Dylan. "Sources put you on the Bordeaux bridge and surveillance photos."

"There's no evidence."

"The bullets match your revolver recovered in the passageway at the palace last night. And did you forget that Bertolier is a first-hand witness?"

"He's a pompous buffoon and knows nothing," Wellesley stammered, realizing that another complication had opened.

"I won't elaborate on the details. But Bertolier outsmarted you with a backup plan. He had a buyer for the silver sword who was waiting upstairs in his office."

"A buyer? Preposterous!"

Enraged, Wellesley was on his feet. "Guard, take me back to my suite," he hollered. "Order me room service!"

Minutes later, Chastain shuffled into the interview room in ankle chains and handcuffs. When he saw Dylan, his eyes widened, and the veins on his neck bulged.

"Kace, I hope you slept well last night. Unfortunately, you missed the fireworks in the garden. Too bad you had to leave early."

"Moreland, don't waste your time cajoling me! But you can thank me for the fireworks at the private salon. It was a little extra theater."

"Don't flatter yourself, Kace; it was merely a thud. You miswired the firecrackers you laid. Would you care to see yourself on video? You are not nearly as clever as you think."

Chastain jumped to his feet to lunge at Dylan but was restrained by a guard.

"Our agents and security monitors followed you throughout your escapades in recent days. A canine sweep for explosives is customary before an event such as this. It was merely a replay for us when you were ready to perform."

"Why are you here then?"

"I like to pour salt on the wounds of criminals. However, if you have anything significant to confess, we'll consider leniency if it is corroborated."

"Leniency! What is that?" asked Chastain. "You know very well that the Duke orchestrated the Louvre robbery and the fiasco last night. I'm merely an accomplice, and others like me will face you again tomorrow."

"Regarding your obsession with Napoleonic artifacts, you should understand that the silver buckle will be returned to its rightful owner, the museum. Unfortunately, the treasure map has gone awry, and we are currently hunting for it."

Dylan watched Kace's pained reaction to the pretense that the map was missing.

"Your planning for the Gala was showy and not too bad, Kace, but you overlooked one of the witnesses. One who saw and heard everything, yet you never even glanced at him. Those little things come back to bite you. Don't leave a trace of yourself behind when you dispose of a threat, like DNA under the fingernails—Rawley and Severini!"

Chastain's face was perplexed as he rose. "I'm done here for now."

He focused on the words, 'the map has gone awry' and didn't hear Dylan leave.

"How did they know? Who took it?"

THIRTY-TWO

Raphael Testifies

Remy Coulliere hired a private attorney to represent him in the museum fraud perpetrated by Jacques Guilliard as he was named a co-conspirator and robbery participant.

But he was stunned to hear that Odilette and his brother had given up the hidden diary. He rehashed through his memories.

"I didn't think Antoine would remember that in his ailing state. I never told anyone about *The Secret Place*, so how did they find it? Great-grandfather said never to let it go, that it was our birthright. The diary is our proof."

Odilette was the first call Remy made when he arrived at the station for arrest, and she was urgently concerned about how it would affect Antoine's health.

"Remy, this is terrible," she shouted. "You promised us we would be spared any humiliation."

"This will be rectified, Odilette. I was a victim of a career criminal, Jacques Guilliard, and when the facts are presented, they will dismiss my charges. Everything I did was to spare the Coulliere name."

"It looks humiliating, Remy, for you to be in jail. Give me your lawyer's contact, and I'll arrange a bail bond. You must be at home to watch out for Antoine's interests. There are people at the door all the time asking questions."

"That will help, Odilette. I assure you I will face the truth, and Antoine will not be implicated. Don't send the girls to school today or let them watch the news; I'll talk with them as soon as I get home."

"Remy?" Odilette hesitated, fearful of the answer to her next question.

"What is it? Don't withhold from me; I can't defend Antoine if you don't give me the truth."

Her voice quivered. "Do you remember that nice event man who organizes the Gala? He called here this morning, sounding upset."

"Hollande Bertolier? What did he want?"

"He was concerned about the theatrics last night and said you left with his sword. That wasn't the plan, Remy. You told us that everything was secured by those Interpol people and the sword would never be at risk. What is he talking about?"

"Call my attorney and make arrangements. I will be home as soon as possible and make the necessary calls. In the meantime, don't talk to anyone."

"I'll admit, Remy, that this frightens me."

Odilette hung up and stood by the window for a few minutes, allowing a smirk of satisfaction, then bounded up the stairs to Antoine's room. He was sitting by the balcony window smoking his pipe.

"It's all set, Antoine! Confirm with the Brazilian."

Hollande Bertolier was livid that he'd been unsuccessful in tracking down the authentic sword. The page boy who rescued the sword from Kace during the ruse guaranteed it was the artifact he'd offered to Rodriguez. But the excessive champagne at the party skewed his recall of the page's name and face.

"I was assured it came directly from the museum by armored transport," he said out loud. "I was at the museum when the guards came to remove it."

Bertolier's early morning jail visit to Wellesley only brought more questions than answers. Barrelling into the museum's visitor's desk, he was unaware of his beleaguered condition. Surveillance camera footage confirmed that.

The Duke admitted that he thought the weight of the silver seemed off, but he was convinced that Interpol wouldn't risk the lives of Remy or Maxine over the sword.

As he left, Bertolier mumbled, "Rodriguez has come from Brazil, on my good word. The black market is just that for a reason, threatening and dangerous. I was a fool to get involved for a small profit."

Returning to the palace office, he attempted to ring Solange. With no answer, it dawned on him that she'd resigned, and he was on his own.

Rerouting his phone calls, he thoughtlessly dialed the military museum. "It is urgent that I speak with Monsieur Coulliere. Has he returned yet?"

"I'll put you through to the officer in charge."

Stunned that someone had temporarily assumed Coulliere's role left him flabbergasted, but he waited for a voice.

"Hello, can I help you?"

Click.

"That was the musketeer agent," he surmised.

He hurried to the museum entrance gate to check the log for the armored truck service that brought the artifacts to the palace. Calling directly, he asked the dispatcher for the ID of the guards assigned.

"I'm sorry, we cannot give that information for security reasons. Did you want to leave a message?"

"This is a matter of paramount importance. I'm calling from Engelland & Steele, the museum's insurer, and I must track the authentic sword taken from Monsieur Coulliere. I need an immediate answer to avoid the press heckling you for information."

"Leave your name and number, and I'll talk to the supervisor. Someone will call you back."

The dispatcher received no reply.

Bertolier still had the imitation sword in his office. He removed it from the office safe and inspected it once again.

"It's an impeccable duplicate! I can't see the flaws that Rodriguez pointed out."

Demanding packing material from the service staff, he secured the sword in a crate with a plan to go to the museum and make the exchange.

Using the palace's shuttle, he departed for Les Invalides, having little thought of tackling the problem once he arrived.

Without sleeping for worry, he didn't adequately remove the King Louis make-up and wasn't aware he was a curious sight, with his cheeks still flushed with circles of rouge and remnants of lipstick.

Arriving at the museum, Bertolier was surprised that the Napoleon Exhibit was closed. Stanchions restricted tourists from entering the east wing with the emperor's artifacts. But he was persistent and managed to slip into the east wing, believing he was undetected.

A security alert flashed in the manager's office, catching Andre's attention and interrupting his meeting with Dylan and the insurer. Together they watched Bertolier's image, attempting to find his way unobscured.

"Oh, I see," Andre said, laughing at the spectacle. "I do believe the King has arrived!"

"It seems he wants to bring something back for a refund!" Dylan said. "I'll find him." He opened the double doors, to become visible to Bertolier.

Coincidentally, the armored truck arrived outside to return the crate Dylan had secured with them for safekeeping.

"Ah, the Coulliere sword has been returned," Dylan called, letting his voice rise to the ears of the approaching Bertolier, who hadn't noticed the guards.

"I'd left the sword at the palace," Bertolier exclaimed, turning quickly to Dylan. "I've come to ensure that it is returned to its proper place."

"Bonjour, Monsieur Bertolier. It was a wonderful evening. And your timing this morning is perfect."

Dylan stepped aside to reveal that Andre Poulin and Pietro Rodriguez were watching with him.

"Let me introduce you to a special guest at the Royal Lodge last night," Andre said. "I present Monsieur Pietro Rodriguez of Engelland & Steele Insurance Group. He just told us of a fascinating experience he's had here in Paris."

"I don't understand."

Bertolier's eyes went to Rodriguez, then Andre, and back to Dylan. The red flush in his neck rose into his cheeks and led to sweat on his brow.

A brief flashback struck Dylan—it was the sword's removal on the day of the Gala.

When I took pictures, I saw a funny look on Coulliere's face. I had my phone but someone remarkably like Rodriguez was by the door.

"How did you know the authentic sword was to be delivered just now?" asked Dylan.

"I've gone out of my way to return it," Bertolier blathered, groping for words on his feet. "As Monsieur Wellesley protested the sword that he carried wasn't the proper weight, I assumed you had made a clever switch. "

Rodriguez smiled in disbelief at the spontaneous concoction. He glared at Bertolier, and the buffoon wondered if it was an intended gesture to play along.

In his fluster, Bertolier was at a loss for words to explain himself. He had not fully absorbed that the ruse was for his benefit and entertained the idea that Rodriguez was up to a scheme to cut him out of his payoff.

Andre gestured toward the foyer. "Ah, here is Monsieur Coulliere now and my American cohorts Alec and Maxine who helped me through the adventure. Everyone, join me in the manager's office."

On the way, Rodriguez whispered to Bertolier for a private aside. "Hollande, my dear friend, we must conclude our arrangement privately. It would be much too embarrassing in front of these fine people."

Before Andre could start the meeting, Remy Coulliere grunted for attention. "Enough of this bantering. I can give you the truth. Months before the Louvre heist, Wellesley came to me, with a silver sword he'd obtained on the black market. He claimed it was Napoleonic, and I didn't know the difference to decide. It was my brother that knew that sort of thing."

"How did Wellesley find you?" Alec asked.

"He had come to the museum many times," Remy said, "always trying to make a connection with me. He said he'd paid off my gambling debt, and I was now indebted to him. He proposed the scheme to rob the Louvre."

"What about the sword?"

"Wellesley sent the black-market sword to a silversmith to have it altered. It was genuine silver sterling, but there is no reason to conclude it was the coronation sword as claimed."

"How did you scheme under your brother's nose without him becoming suspicious?" Maxine asked.

"Antoine was dedicated to the museum and the very history of France. He brought me on to help him, but instead, I helped myself. The Louvre requested the loan of the Napoleon silver belt buckle for an exhibit, and Antoine agreed. The buckle is authentic and has been in the Coulliere family for many generations."

Rodriguez stopped writing notes to interject. "The insurance company agrees that the silver belt buckle is authentic. The portion paid to the military museum for its loss will be reclaimed, and the artifact will be returned to its owner."

"Antoine will be gratified to know of its return," Remy said. He carefully opened the journals. "We also venture that you will find that these Raphael Coulliere records are original and validate his existence on Elba."

Rodriguez leaned close to review the documents, eager for a personal assessment.

"These are incredible! I would agree that they are of the correct historical vintage. My preliminary assessment is that it was written in the hand of Raphael Coulliere, as I have examined his writing before."

Rodriguez's gaze never left Coulliere or Bertolier.

"What makes you so certain, Monsieur?" Dylan asked.

As the conversation paused, Bertolier took the opportunity to make his departure. He leaned with a half-bow of gratitude. "If you'll excuse me, Gentlemen, I am needed back at the palace."

Rodriguez looked at him with disdain. "You were quite willing to part with the genuine artifact last night when you offered me the fake. You contacted me; I didn't pursue you."

"That's not exactly true. I was curious about who is looking for stolen goods, and I saw your online ad seeking artifacts from the Napoleon era. My interests are in protecting the palace and its historical relics, and I was taking precautions to root out potential absconding."

Maxine leered at the pair, perplexed by their stand-off. "Monsieur Rodriguez, were you employed by Engelland & Steele at the time of the Louvre heist? Did you participate in the investigation?"

"I specialized in evaluations, certainly not investigations of robberies. So why are you questioning me? It is Bertolier who is deceiving you."

Alec whispered to Andre, "Are you buying the story?"

Andre Poulin turned to Dylan in a low voice. "Would you review today's jailhouse visitor records for Wellesley and Chastain?"

Dylan left discreetly to call the prison, then Sloane.

"Remy, have you met Monsieur Rodriguez before today?" asked Alec.

Rodriguez scowled at the affront. Troubled by the events, Maxine focused on Bertolier's face for a reaction, whether relief or satisfied guilt.

"Monsieur Rodriguez, there's an admission clearly in the voice of Lawrence Wellesley," Bertolier said. "It's recorded by his accomplice, Kace Chastain. He claims to have arranged with a South American buyer for goods taken from the Louvre. What would you know about that?"

"Of course, everyone in the insurance and artifact arena is aware of the Louvre heist," said Rodriguez. "At the time, it was astounding that anyone could orchestrate such a con in daylight. But, if you ask me if I was involved, certainly not."

"Monsieur Rodriguez, do you have any objection to our rechecking your travel itinerary?" said Andre. "We'll go back for the last seven years? It could remove a cloud over your head."

"I am embarrassed by this line of questioning. Please do

whatever investigations you believe are necessary to exonerate me. Engelland & Steele have employed me for twelve years. I have family in Brazil, but I have only visited twice for the Christmas holidays."

Remy studied the insurance agent and pondered over the many faces that made inquiries during his tenure. "Monsieur Poulin, when you asked if I remember meeting Rodriguez, I can't think of an occasion before today."

Remy's eyes burrowed into the Brazilian's stare. Rodriguez looked panic-stricken.

THIRTY-THREE

Restoration

"Engelland & Steele investigators had been to the museum on numerous occasions. However, I do not recall meeting this man before," Remy Coulliere concluded.

Maxine was still observing Bertolier and remained puzzled by his costumed appearance.

"Monsieur Bertolier, would you kindly turn around for us?"

Bertolier had doffed the King's coat but was still in the silk ruffled shirt he wore when Poulin and Solange found him during the counterfeit transaction.

"Dylan, do you still have the ultraviolet pocket light from the palace?" Maxine asked.

"Yes, I do." Stepping behind Bertolier, he waved the light over his shirt. The purple illumination confirmed he had been with Wellesley at the gala the night before. As he was about to scan Rodriguez, he stopped to receive an incoming call from the prison.

That was enough for Andre.

"Monsieur Bertolier, I'm afraid you are under arrest,

complicit in a scheme to defraud the military museum. With a warrant, we'll examine your financial records; if we find a further connection to Wellesley and the sale of any artifacts, you will pay further in the courts."

Bertolier's defensive demeanor suddenly erupted. "This is ludicrous! I have friends in high places, and you won't make this stick. You can't defame my reputation and expect no consequences, even if you are Interpol."

Poulin nodded to a pair of agents waiting aside. They approached Bertolier and led him away, ranting.

One whispered, "Please, Monsieur, for your dignity, be quiet!"

With Bertolier removed, Rodriguez turned to Remy Coulliere and Andre Poulin.

"I'll officially conclude for my company that the diary does prove the right of such a sword to the Coulliere family. However, I cannot say that the sword in this exhibit case is the same artifact. Since it was not stolen, it belongs to the lender. That is you, Monsieur Coulliere. Also, the original diary will be returned once examined."

"I wish I could offer good news, Remy," Andre said, "but the tape and evidence regarding the Louvre heist implicate you as an accomplice. Find a good attorney to protest that you were blackmailed and coerced against your will, and possibly you will only serve minimal time."

Remy was a defeated man, but finding he had hope, his pride slowly revived.

"I've temporarily resigned here at the museum until I sort out my situation. Odilette and Antoine have forgiven me for my part and offered their support. I've learned about Antoine's injuries to rehabilitate him to a better quality of life. We've had talks, and I'm ashamed that I felt his spirit was gone because he appeared weakened. He has proven to me that I was wrong, and his faculties are still quite sharp."

"Will he ever become strong enough to work?" asked Maxine. "I noticed he can walk."

Remy was stunned by her remark. "What do you mean!"

"Well, I'm sure you've noticed his shoes are somewhat worn and soiled. I just assumed that he was getting recent exercise."

"He has expressed interest in returning to the museum in a diminished capacity but I had no idea he was mobile."

Maxine hoped to divert the discussion. "We were privileged to attend the Royal Lodge event. We're glad that, in the end, you can restore your family heritage."

"Merci, Maxine, for your kindness in understanding Antoine's sensitivities. He enjoys history buffs and says he hopes for your future visits." Remy laughed at the irony. "Odilette is also grateful that you persisted in finding the truth."

The expression on Maxine's face was perplexing. *I'm curious that Odilette would now want to be friends. Her reason is cause for concern.*

Outside, she radioed the other detectives. "With the museum agenda resolved, I've planned a Montmartre wrap-up dinner. Can it be tonight? We will be returning home to New York next week."

"Tonight?" Dylan asked.

"Why not?" Andre said. "We've accounted for everyone. A celebration is in order before we go our ways again. Tonight, we won't need to look over our shoulders."

Andre and Gabriel were in, but Dylan hesitated until Alec pushed. "Come on; we can't have a send-off without you, Cousin."

"Something is bothering me," said Dylan. "But, yes, I'll be there."

"It'll be your favorite Lamb Pops à la Rosemary and garlic with a root vegetable mash and fresh white asparagus," urged

Maxine.

His eyes twinkled, admiring her intuition.

At seven o'clock, Andre and Gabriel mounted the dark steps together at Montmartre, with armloads of flowers, baguettes, and bottles of burgundy.

Maxine's voice echoed from the top. "Come in; you know your way around. Help yourself to cocktails."

An hour later, she was concerned. "Alec, where is Dylan? He's never tardy, especially for dinner."

Within seconds, the lower door opened with a knock.

"Dylan, we've been waiting for you!"

"Mmm . . . I haven't smelled a fragrance so good since I was here last," Gabriel teased as the platters were passed.

Alec knew from Dylan's brow that a problem still lingered. "Come on, pal, what's troubling you about the case?"

"Instincts said something was off today at the museum. Earlier in the case, I went to Engelland & Steele to view the authentication certificates. While I was there, I met Rodriguez. The man we saw today was not him. Then when I was with Remy collecting the sword for the Royal Lodge, a man was watching from the doorway—I'm certain it was Rodriguez. But Remy denied having met him before."

"Are you sure?" said Andre.

"I called Engelland & Steele this afternoon to ask about him. Unfortunately, Monsieur Rodriguez died of a heart attack two weeks ago."

"Are you saying the man today is an imposter?" said Gabriel.

"Remy Coulliere did hesitate when asked if they had met before," Alec said.

"Who has the diary then?" Maxine asked.

"We entrusted it to the insurance company for evaluation. However, they haven't received it."

"It will be up to the insurance company to investigate if

it's internal fraud," said Andre. "I'll include suggestions in my report, but for now, it's hands-off for us."

"There's another detail that doesn't add up," said Maxine. "When Gabriel and I were in Le Marais, Odilette hid the treasure map from us."

"At this point, it is only a historical document," Andre stated. "So, it doesn't incriminate anyone of a crime."

"But she was devious and could have volunteered it to be authenticated."

"Regrettably, this hour's late for me," Gabriel said. "I think I'll bow out for now, Andre. I thank you all for this wonderful experience. It was a pleasure, Alec and Maxine, to get to know you, perhaps I'll see you in America one day."

"And it's time to return to our lives," said Alec. "We'll see our children and return to family life."

Andre Poulin looked at his disintegrating troop with concern.

Engelland & Steele had sorted insurance logistics, and prosecuting authorities were leveling charges for Wellesley and Chastain and negotiating leniency for Remy. Coulliere was out on bail pending sentencing for probation.

The Coulliere household in Le Marais organized a routine to benefit the two brothers and hired a therapist to assist Antoine in his recovery. Remy became nocturnal, obsessing about the military museum.

But Antoine's secret outings in his athletic sneakers were more visible than the wheelchair.

Days later, over breakfast, Remy saw a glint in Antoine's eye that had been absent for seven years.

"Something on your mind, Antoine?"

His face lit up, bold, and he no longer appeared feeble. "Odilette did as I asked, holding back the treasure map. I've made some foreign connections on the internet that are intrigued by the map's mysteries."

Antoine's manner changed suddenly, erupting into a devious laugh.

"I used a disguised alias, of course. I've had plenty of free time to plan this scheme, better than the last."

"What are you thinking, Antoine?"

"It won't be hard to fool them one more time. I encountered a Brazilian artifact collector at the museum a week ago, and he made me a proposition thinking I was you, Remy. He uses the alias of Rodriguez, a fairly common Spanish name." His eyes twinkled in anticipation. "The man is convinced we pulled the wool over the detectives' eyes. He is paving the way for access to the palace's basement foundation, the treasure's location."

Odilette sidled over to stand beside her husband's wheelchair.

"I'll be sending the girls back to their mother in Normandy. We can't take chances with them any longer."

Antoine rose from his wheelchair, wandered to the parlor bar, and poured three drinks.

"To Napoleon's fortune!"

Dylan decided to go home through Marais. Although the case was concluded from Andre's perspective, something needled him. He remembered the deception in Coulliere's eyes on their last meeting.

Standing in front of the Coulliere residence, he noted the parlor lights still glowed and the front door light was still lit. An unoccupied wheelchair was parked on the veranda.

"Someone is not yet home and why would they leave the chair here?" Dylan mused.

There were shadows in the parlor moving about and talking in low voices. He waited closer to the porch window, but at a sound behind, he turned and looked back at the street.

The shadow of a man limped toward him. Dylan assumed he had not yet been seen and froze in the darkness.

The footsteps were very near now.

"Monsieur, you should not be here!" a familiar voice echoed close to him.

He could now see into Antoine's gray eyes. They didn't look feeble at all, but dangerous.

"Why did you pick me to bring into this debacle?" Dylan asked.

"I needed some amusement in my wheelchair. You don't remember me, do you? You were always thorough in your validation and I relied on that." The voice was calm yet threatening. "We have no further use for you now."

The front door opened. Odilette stepped out. "Thank you for your help, Monsieur Moreland. And your friends too have been helpful."

Dylan knew she was toying with him, but he desperately feared for Maxine's safety. His last thoughts were of his friends as he said goodnight. At a slight click of a stiletto, he fell to the ground. It wasn't Wellesley this time, but Antoine Coulliere.

Antoine and Odilette heaved Dylan's limp body into the wheelchair, across to the park and the riverbank.

Incapacitated by the chloroform, Dylan's eyes stayed open and he stared at his attacker. In his last moments of consciousness, he hoped the earpiece might reach Andre.

Antoine and Odilette returned to their residence satisfied that loose ends had been resolved. From the front door, he strutted to the parlor bar. "Time to celebrate, Odilette."

In the near distance, a rush of sirens headed toward La Marais.

THE END

About the Author

Shirley Burton is a Canadian author in fiction genres, including suspense thrillers in the Thomas York Series, old-fashioned whodunit capers in Inspector Furnace Mysteries, and nostalgic, family-oriented Christmas stories. Journey on her historical fiction from France in the 1500s, and let your imagination take you on the inspiring fantasy adventure *Boy from Saint-Malo*.

Shirley's residence is in Niagara-on-the Lake, Ontario, and Calgary, Alberta.

"I've been privileged to explore the locations of my books, walking the characters' neighborhoods and streets. Research has taken me to Istanbul, France, Italy, Greece, London, Amsterdam, Brazil, California, New York, and Quebec.

"Join me in my 600-page historical fiction, *Homage: Chronicles of a Habitant*, that portrays ten generations of a typical family migrating from France to the New World, paralleling real-world events over 500 years.

"There comes a time in life to take the leap into writing. It's that time for me."

Shirley Burton

OTHER BOOKS BY SHIRLEY BURTON

UNDER THE ASHES

Book One of The Thomas York Series. Debut suspense thriller set in upstate New York. It begins at an electrifying pace with a high-speed chase that leaves the protagonist barely alive, his unknown passenger dead, and his mysterious passengers on the lam. Daniel Boisvert recovers from his injuries but remembers nothing before the moment when a train slammed into his automobile. However, he soon begins to suspect that the name he's been using may not be his own.

THE FRIZON

Book Two of The Thomas York Series begins with a plot to steal great artworks from museums is afoot. This trio of rogues accumulates stolen works until a mysterious shadow recruits the assistance of our series protagonists, Thomas and Rachel, to infiltrate a forgery scheme in Paris that is wreaking havoc on the art world. A fast-moving action thriller in the charming art community at Montmartre, Paris.

ROGUE COURIER

Book Three of The Thomas York Series. A client with suspicious motives recruits Thomas and Rachel in Paris to find her spouse, a courier gone missing. The trail of clues leads to London and Amsterdam to a ring of diamond thieves. Filled with deception and murderous intent, the courier turns the tables, and a double-twist seals the couple's fate.

SECRET CACHE

Book Four of The Thomas York Series. A young man vacationing in Brazil is kidnapped and conned into participating in a bank robbery. Years later, one of the captured thieves set on revenge seeks the cash booty taken, leading him to a California vineyard with a connection. Thomas and Rachel race from Paris to Napa Valley to assist in a murder investigation of her Uncle Zach.

THE PARIS NETWORK

Book Five of The Thomas York Series. The attractive young protagonists, Thomas and Rachel, are back in Paris. After the Bataclan terrorist attack, an encounter at the Sacré-Coeur Basilica in Montmartre sets them on the track of a terrorist plot to collapse the catacomb system in Paris with a sophisticated drone scheme. A former Interpol agent comes to their aid when Rachel's life is at risk. A contemporary story of terror and suspense.

MASQUERADE: STEALING NAPOLEON'S TREASURES

A Paris-based undercover team unravels a scheme by museum criminals previously involved in an old robbery of Napoleon's treasures at the Louvre. An American couple receives an invitation to a palace's costumed gala to join the French detectives in their plan to stop a potential ransom heist of valuable Napoleon artifacts. The criminals have internal conflicts and hidden future motives.

RED JACKAL

A thriller in Istanbul and on a Mediterranean cruise. Finn receives a letter from an Afghanistan war comrade, enticing him with an insurance reward to retrieve an Ottoman artifact stolen from a Sultan's tomb. He infiltrates a smuggling ring to flush out the criminals and kingpin. Mistrust with double agents and Interpol keeps him on the run with Nicole Colbert, and he'd do anything to save her.

SENTINEL IN THE MOORS

A warm, comical vengeance in a charming setting. A museum archivist, Gabe Farrow, takes a sabbatical at a seaside village, Staithes, in England's North Yorkshire Moors. He stumbles upon a plot to steal a valuable hoard of Viking treasures buried in the moors, abandoned after the Battle of Hastings. As he befriends the colorful townsfolk, his landlady and a bright young fatherless lad assist him in exposing the plot, testing the entire village's loyalty.

HOMAGE: CHRONICLES OF A HABITANT

The ten-generation historical fiction begins in France in the 1500s, written as a light series of chronological stories. A 500-year journey based on a family's lives, tragedies, and immigration to North America. Experience typical life as the early migrants travel from France to settle in Quebec, with generational conflicts and cultural clashes in the new land. Share the joys and experiences of the immigrants to Canada, paralleled with researched historical events.

A CLOCKMAKER'S CHRISTMAS

A nostalgic Christmas story for all ages. A mother of two small children travels from Manhattan to Heidelberg to resolve an estate. In the magical setting of the Castle and the Christmas markets, she is tempted into a whirlwind romance. With matchmaking charm, a clockmaker bestows unique gifts on the couple. A warm and sentimental story with an old-fashioned Christmas.

CHRISTMAS TREASURE BOX

A charming Christmas romance. Polly Perkins operates the family antique shop in a small town after her parents' tragic death. In the days leading to Christmas, she finds old family diaries from her grandmother, unveiling a lost love she had held from others in her life. Polly meets a man who whisks her into a subtle romance. A distant relative makes a surprising claim on the family's resources, and Polly pursues a resolution to lead to a memorable Christmas Day.

A WENCESLAS CHRISTMAS

A Christmas story of love and charity in the French Alps near Chamonix at a centuries-old luxury hotel. Chef Marceau's niece catches the eye of the young sous-chef, sparking a romance at the hotel. Following an avalanche and isolation of a family in the mountains, a spirit of charity grows throughout the hotel, inspired by tales of the ancient king, Good King Wenceslas. Together, the employees and guests carry the Wenceslas spirit of joy into the village.

MYSTERY AT GREY STOKES

An Inspector Furnace Mystery, an old-fashioned whodunit. In a charming English country manor at the height of Christmas festivities, guests arrive for a splendid feast. The characters' intriguing cast includes the butler, housekeeper, the Berwick family members, and social guests. Introducing Inspector Furnace and his helper Detective Prentice, called by the manor to untangle the web of deception and solve the case.

SWINDLE: MYSTERY AT SEA

An Inspector Furnace Mystery, another old-fashioned whodunit. The Inspector and his bride Martha set out on a honeymoon sailing on the luxurious Queen Elizabeth to New York. When a body is discovered in the cargo hold, Inspector Furnace takes charge, and a host of passengers and onboard celebrities become suspects and amateur detectives. Everyone is a suspect at the nightly Captain's Table dinner to analyze clues and reveal the culprit.

BOY FROM SAINT-MALO

A fantasy adventure. An orphaned boy in explorer Jacques Cartier's hometown dreams of being a mariner. Young Gaeten enters a magical world of visionaries and inventors that guide him on his life's adventure. Sailing to the new world in the crow's nest on Cartier's ship begins an unbounded future. This story's theme can inspire all ages to live with a belief in oneself and without barriers.

DON'T OPEN THE DOOR

A thought-provoking suspense thriller that moves quickly from the first pages to the conclusion. The romantic tension between Tess and her husband turns into a vacuum as she follows his advice for a shopping day in Manhattan, then disappears. The mystery deepens as she finds herself in the shopping district, but two years have passed without her knowledge. Detective Mitchell uncovers the past lives of Tess, Deane, and others in and out of their circle, exposing a criminal connection that threatens Tess to the end.

EPITAPH OF AN IMPOSTER

A suspense mystery with an imposter, a blackmailer, and unscrupulous members of the House of Lords. The astute collector of rare books in London comes upon an incriminating set of valuable post-war family journals of stuffy Lord Tannahill, with secrets of past crimes and of an imposter who crept into the Tannahill family. The bookseller conspires with an employee to expose a blackmail plot, as the drama intertwines past and present generations linked to an old English manor.

Visit us at

shirleyburtonbooks.com

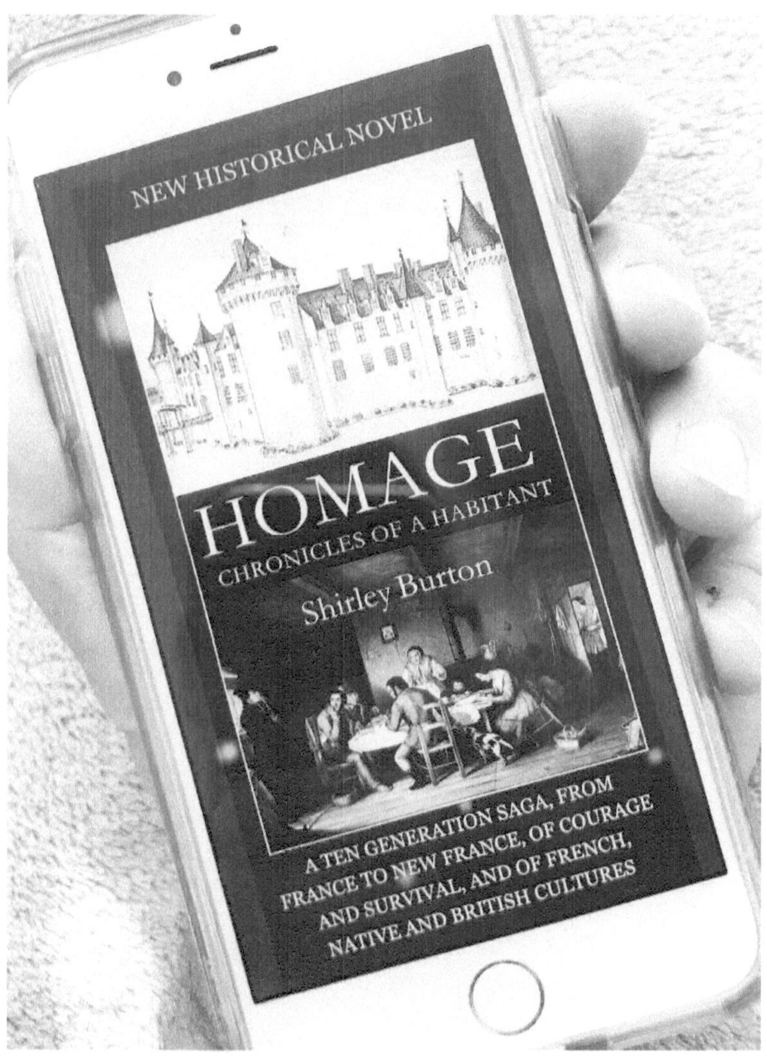